# tranquility

Micah,
This is a
fine beginning!

Christo Conklin

# ENDORSEMENTS

*Tranquility* is a refreshing take on the fantasy genre. Filled with magic, prophecies, and plenty of mythical beings, Conklin weaves an intriguing, imaginative tale that grabs you and doesn't let you go until the last page. With a rich cast of characters, vivid world building, and a story you'll be talking about long after you finish reading, *Tranquility* leaves readers both satisfied and yearning for the next adventure in the series.

—**Kathryn Lee Martin**, author, the *Snow Spark Saga*

With brilliant world building and unforgettable characters, *Tranquility* will leave readers wanting more.

—**Jennifer Salvato Doktorsk**i, author, *August & Everything After*

Conklin constructs the world of *Tranquility* into a living, breathing realm filled with secrets, creatures, lores, and meticulous beliefs. Her tale paints a vivid picture of an oppressive society, where diversity is stifled and criticism is squelched, but an undercurrent of hope lives through it all. It's a smart, eye-opening read. By the end, you'll be longing for more.

— **Sonia Poynter**, author, *The Last Stored*

# tranquility

## CHRISTA CONKLIN

PUBLISHING THE POSITIVE

ELK LAKE PUBLISHING, INC.
Plymouth, Massachusetts

Cover and Interior Design: Jessica Schmeidler, Derinda Babcock

Editor(s): Cristel Phelps, Deb Haggerty

Author Represented by Golden Wheat Literary

PUBLISHED BY: Elk Lake Publishing, Inc., 35 Dogwood Dr., Plymouth, MA 02360, 2019

---

Library Cataloging Data

Names: Conklin, Christa (Christa Conklin)

*Tranquility* / Christa Conklin

262 p. 23cm × 15cm (9in × 6 in.)

Description: She must prove there's more to life than peace and more to death than dying.

Identifiers: ISBN-13: 978-1-948888-66-0 (trade) | 978-1-948888-67-7 (POD) | 978-1-948888-68-4 (e-book.)

Key Words: Young Adult, speculative fiction, fantasy, unity, magic, shape-shifting, coming of age

LCCN: 2018958443 Fiction

# DEDICATION

To my father, who fed me fantasy books from the early days of my life until the end of his, and Marisa, my nieceling, who proves family is deeper than blood and longer than mortality.

Part of the proceeds from this book goes to the Marisa Tufaro Foundation.

# ACKNOWLEDGMENTS

A story begins with the writer but blooms in each reader. Thank YOU for giving this story life.

Much cultivation takes place between the author's nurturing of the seed and the reader being drawn to the blossom. I am forever grateful for the following folks—

Family comes first, and mine has been encouraging, patient, and supportive—Joe, my husband, my beta reader, my champion, and the reason this book is a book and not just a manuscript in a drawer. Thank you for being consistently confident in me, especially when I was not. My mom, for fiercely believing in my abilities and being her grandchildren's playmate, allowing me to sneak away and write. My children, Ethan and Alexandra, who have supported and loved me on the long bumpy road to publication and never complained about the lousy dinners during deep edits. I love you all so much.

My fabulous agent, Jessica Schmeidler, whose passion for my story transformed manuscript into novel. I needed a team to make my debut the best it could be and having an experienced, talented agent at the top of the lineup made all the difference.

Oh, the editing! Thank you to L'Editrice Sarah Cloots who chiseled my story into a novel, allowing me to collect the remaining marble for the sequel. Her keen book sense gave shape to my words and was key to my securing literary representation and a publishing home. Lisa Rouh, friend and copy editor extraordinaire. The grammar police are real, and she is the eagle-eyed chief. Speaking of chief, the acquisition of this book by Editor in Chief Deb Haggerty was the realization of a longtime dream. Deb's

# tranquility

editorial guidance along with that of my incredible editor Cristel Phelps carried the manuscript to novel level. I am thankful for everyone at Elk Lake Publishing Inc. who used their talent and passion for books to get my story to its readers.

I am grateful to those who read my manuscript, especially the early versions. Jennifer Salvato Doktorski, for suffering through that first draft, responding with encouragement and wisdom, and being a friend and mentor throughout this journey. Emily Caccia, my first young adult reader, for recording her emotions and reactions in the margins as she read. What an encouragement to know my words were expressing what I intended. My friends who read early drafts and provided invaluable feedback: Robert Attanasio, Brian Farrell, Amy Hardy, Cyndi and Greg Tufaro.

The Philadelphia Zoo for having a Zoo School program when my son was very young. This homeschooling, writing mama had two hours a week to scribble surrounded by fascinating animals and supportive staff who cheered me on in my endeavor. The messengers in the last chapter of this book are inspired by a pair of Southern Ground Hornbills who still reside at the zoo today.

Finally, the mountains, lakes, trees, creatures, and fragrant breezes of the Northwoods. I thank God for creating these inspirational lands, especially the Adirondack Mountains which inspired setting and characters for this book. By his grace I have been blessed with abundant time in these forests and on the ponds they embrace. The intimate encounters I have had with Adirondack loons stirred a love and respect for them I hope I shared well in these pages. To learn more about these enchanting birds, visit the Adirondack Center for Loon Conservation, adkloon.org.

# PART ONE

# PROLOGUE

Phovul awoke and renewed the struggle against his restraints. Chains engulfed every inch of his body. They crisscrossed his eyes and covered his ears. He'd forgotten if he was in a room of stone, tile, or earth. Chains were all he knew.

"Soon, servant, soon you will move," said a muffled voice, "by obedience to my command."

Phovul jerked his head toward the voice. Masses of mangy locks had entwined with the bonds around his head, and he groaned in pain as the hair was ripped from his scalp.

"Your desperation entices me," said the voice, now clear but grating and coming from the opposite direction. "I have removed the chains from your ears. Your work will soon begin anew. If you resist me, I will reinforce your bondage. If you are with me, show me as much and I will free your eyes."

Phovul peered through the minuscule spaces between the layers of metal, but as always, couldn't see the speaker. He attempted a grunt of agreement but produced a mere squeak. His intention was understood, and his eyes were unbound. Without the chains, the room appeared checkered with light. Days would pass before he could see his surroundings without the negative vision of those accursed links.

"Realm folk claim every mortal sneeze to be the prophetic fulfillment of one of their little rhymes. Fools! The time has come to reveal my power governs Unemond. You will go amongst the One People to gather followers. I want mortals who are tasting power and desiring more. I want those the Realm believes to be marked by prophecy. No need to gather me an army. A specialized battalion will suffice."

Phovul gave a long blink of understanding, and at last, his arms were no longer secured to his sides. He was too weak to lift them, as they were still draped in metal rings. In a display of his master's power—not possibly an act of pity—the heavy chains encircling the length of each arm fell away.

"You stumbled through your youthful attempts to serve me and have now fulfilled your penance. Your work with the Great Council was not fruitless. Our sabotage took root and has crept throughout the One People. Words of the Realm are now foreign. The days of mortal and immortal solidarity have faded and moved from history to fiction. The One People have never even heard my name, but my intention has become embedded in their days and nights as they embrace their precious *Tranquility*."

The remainder of Phovul's chains rattled as he shuddered at a cold caress of his arm. A laugh like a hyena's filled the chamber.

His master tugged hard at Phovul's beard and whispered close to his ear, "Now is your chance to serve me. Do not fail. Youth is no longer an excuse."

The chains continued to shake as Phovul trembled with fear and revulsion. The insane laughter echoed once more, and then Phovul heard his master lick his lips and swallow the taste of opportunity.

"You, Phovul, will be my link to the One People until I may greet them in my full glory."

Phovul reached toward the voice. Cold claws supported his trembling arms.

"If you renew your oath to serve me and to gather those I name, I will remove your remaining bonds."

Released from the chilling grasp, Phovul fell to the floor. He pushed himself forward until he was prostrate at his master's feet.

"Your willingness is rewarded."

Phovul rejoiced silently as bulky metal shed from him like a snake's skin. What remained was a layer of fine chain mail. He tried to rise but was too weak. A rat scampered past him. Phovul caught the rodent's tail and mustered all his strength to break its neck. His now bare hands bled from the creature's angry bites and scratches. Vermin had been his cell mates throughout his captivity, but until this moment, his abundant restraints had kept them from touching him. In the early years, he was thankful for this aspect of his confinement. As time wore on, the varmints appeared less threatening and more like a meal out of reach. Phovul was pleased to discover his breakfast was a pregnant female. The tiny blind wrigglers made an adequate side dish.

"Your determination pleases me. Soon you will have the strength I need. Do my bidding and you will be rewarded. Desire, ignorance, uncertainty—use these as your foothold. Feed your stomach, and I will provide you with the strength your punishment stole away. When you are of sound body, I will return to unleash you upon the One People."

Phovul heard a loud snap, and he was alone. He never did see the speaker. He never had. His master spoke of his imprisonment as a thing of the past. Although he could have moved about if he had the strength, he was still covered in chains, albeit lighter ones. He would regain his strength, do his work, and reap his reward. Then he planned to shed his shackles. Permanently.

# CHAPTER ONE

Iridescence trickled down the stone wall, hit a jagged edge, and cascaded into his cupped hand. The tiny puddle of sparkling colors reflected in the one circle of glass that remained in the gold wire frame he carefully returned to his nose. In the damp darkness of the deep corridor, he swirled the liquified spectacle lens, reveling in the beauty and power he wore every day—hidden in plain sight.

He rolled up his sleeve and dipped his fingertip into the shimmering fluid, pressing a glowing droplet deep into a large stone in the wall. As he removed his finger, a tendril of fog wisped through the newly formed diminutive tunnel, lit from behind by gray light shining in the blackness. A haunting wail sounded from the other side of the wall. He placed his ear against the hole, smiled, and closed his eyes.

While listening to the mournful answering calls, he considered how the lens, when secured before his eye, improved his mortal vision. Now in this form, the same lens provided a way for him to hear his distant, immortal home.

The ring of a bell echoed from the far end of the long hall. He sighed and reversed what he had begun. The tiny tunnel disappeared, and the liquid transformed to solid. He removed the reformed glass disk, secured the lens in his spectacles and placed them on his nose. If only he had stayed on task, he would have entered—not just heard—the Realm. No one would have noticed his absence. He quickly gathered his robes and strode back up the hall to serve those who rang again for his assistance.

Atop the high, distant stone wall, the lamplighter was dousing the flames that lit the Village of Dale throughout the night.

Drethene walked past a small barn and heard young voices chanting:

# Tranquility

Crouglan is our Leader,
His nose is bent all wrong,
It sits above his feeder,
That always talks too long.


Drethene elbowed her best friend, Trem, and whispered, "Ha! Did you hear that?"

"Yes, yes, I did," Trem sighed, his face buried in *Tranquility* as he strode along beside her. "You should be proud. You created a rhyme certain to ensure your legacy of disrespect and immaturity."

The lantern Drethene carried was disturbed by her sudden movement and rocked like a pendulum from its well-oiled handle. She steadied and lifted the lamp back in place to light her friend's book. "Oh, Trem, they're just children having fun, and so were we when I came up with the ditty."

"I wasn't having fun. That chant always made me uncomfortable."

"It's the closest they will ever get to singing. Be happy for them."

Trem slammed his book shut.

"Just one more thing our leaders will have to undo to keep the Peace."

Drethene handed him the lantern.

"You're too young to be such an old man, Trem."

Their parents were walking well ahead of them. A choir of cleared throats interrupted the teenagers' bickering. Trem's father gestured for the two friends to follow—in silence.

The sun hadn't yet risen, but the sky was brightening. Drethene's father looked at her mother, smiled, and nodded. He was proud their families reached the village before sunrise on Gathering days.

Trem extinguished the lantern.

They entered the Village of Dale, home of the Academy. The road narrowed, lined on both sides by small stone houses, leading to the center of town where the Academy loomed over all other village dwellings and shops. Although an homage to *Tranquility*, Drethene liked the scholarly ambiance of the training ground for leaders.

As the road became more crowded, Drethene honored her parents by looking down to hide the red rings around her pupils. The sight of them could disrupt the Peace.

She continued scanning the ground as they walked until she saw an elderly man kneeling beside his wife. The woman was lying on the side of the road trying to recover from what must have been a fainting spell or sudden bout of weakness.

Their parents avoided the couple and continued on as did everyone else who passed on foot, horseback, or cart.

Drethene veered toward them as the man removed a corked, glass medicine bottle from his wife's satchel, shook the vial, and hung his head.

Trem grabbed Drethene's arm. He was a walking index of *Tranquility* and recited, "'Tend to your own family always and immediate neighbors in times of emergency, and we shall all have care. Uphold the wisdom of *Tranquility*, and we shall all have peace.'"

Neither of the two were Drethene's relatives nor her neighbors. However, she believed there was purposeful ambiguity in *Tranquility's* words for situations such as this.

She pulled away from Trem and dropped to her knees beside the husband. "The apothecary is just a few blocks away." She pointed to the bottle. "I can have this filled in moments."

The shocked couple stared at her. The woman's eyes softened, and she said, "Dear girl, your heart is big, and your years are few. Go on to the Hall. Enjoy the Gathering. Study *Tranquility*, and you'll see how best to keep the Peace."

"Keeping the Peace isn't always enough. If I help, no one is hurt," Drethene said as Trem lifted her to her feet. "This isn't right!"

"Keep the Peace," said the woman. "Keep the Peace."

The woman closed her eyes, and her husband cradled her in his arms.

Now standing, Drethene pushed Trem away and faced him.

"Trem, he can't carry her to Doll's. We can say we're getting medicine for your sister."

"We can't." Trem inclined his head toward the dark gaze of a nearby Watchman.

Drethene turned in a slow circle and counted four more in their identical long brown cloaks and low-brimmed hats. The Watchmen's eyes, though unseen, never appeared to have difficulty spotting the slightest transgression against *Tranquility*. Drethene lowered her eyes but stood her ground.

"We must go," Trem said. "If we disobey *Tranquility*, the Watchmen will escort us somewhere other than the Hall. They'll watch until she recovers. If she doesn't, they'll know what to do."

"And what'll they do, Trem?"

"'Questioning the motives of those who study and enforce the doctrines of *Tranquility* is an act of suspicion and leads to a breakdown in the Trust.'"

"Don't recite Defining Actions to me. Those words didn't come from the Great Council. They don't even attempt to create peace. They control. They weaken. They—"

The guardians of *Tranquility* commenced their approach, and Drethene fought to stay put as Trem used all his strength to force her away from the couple, leaving her words scattered in the dust.

Drethene regained her feet and forced Trem to face what passed behind them.

"See, more are coming to help," he said.

"No. They're circling like vultures." She turned in defeat. All four parents were staring at her. Drethene gave a small nod acknowledging what they all knew—Trem had once again saved her from herself.

They walked on, eventually lining up to enter the Hall. A strong hand engulfed Drethene's shoulder.

"Trem, you go ahead," her father said. "Drethene, I want to speak with you."

She followed her father around the corner and past silent shops housed in squat stone buildings. She wanted to run, to start the day over, to start her *life* over.

He stopped halfway down the block, and seemingly satisfied by the seclusion of the street, turned to look at her.

"I know your ma normally talks to you when you make imperfect choices," he said in a forced, uncharacteristically gentle manner, "but can't we walk from the farm to the Gathering without you drawing the Watchmen from their posts?"

"I'm sorry, Pa."

"You need to apologize to Trem. All that boy wants to do is live his life according to *Tranquility*." She wished she could join the flock of pigeons taking flight as her father's attempted tenderness crescendoed into his familiar tone of frustration. "You challenge, and maybe even threaten, his abilities, daughter. You're his neighbor, he'll always tend to you in times of emergency. Please stop testing him."

"I'm not testing—"

Her father raised his palm, and she went silent.

"Please think before you act," he said. "Or speak," he added. "Even better, talk to your ma before you do or say anything."

"Okay, Pa."

He stared at her for an uncomfortable moment, turned back toward the Hall, and signaled her to follow.

She trailed behind her father, dragging her hand along the limestone walls lining the cobblestone streets. He joined her mother in the queue pressed against the immensity of the Hall. Drethene continued along the line until she found Trem. She stared up at his profile with pleading eyes, her chin nearly on his shoulder.

The cap on Trem's head hid his distinctive shock of blond curls. With his blue eyes trained upon *Tranquility*, their unusual color was tempered by his devotion even when noticed. Trem had managed to blend in with the crowd despite his abnormalities. For Drethene, every attempted deception had proved futile.

Trem took a step closer to the stone wall. "Just get in line," he said without glancing up from his reading.

She smiled, sidling into line next to him. They stood close, still and silent.

The great doors groaned open, and the One People began filing into the Hall.

As Drethene ascended the steps, a young boy came up behind her and intentionally stepped on the edge of her skirt.

She lost her footing, but catching herself, smacked her hands on the slate.

Her loved ones made clear their frustration with her, yet she was expected to silently endure the antics of children and judgement of adults. She wanted to make cat claws and hiss at the giggling troublemaker as he jogged up the steps, but all she did was make eye contact with him. He yelped, stumbled, and scrambled on all fours to escape to the safety of the Hall. Trem's arm, tense with annoyance, came under Drethene's, putting an end to her chuckle.

"You're almost eighteen. How do you manage to grow more immature the older you get?" Trem half-dragged her up the steps as he spoke.

No one appreciated the self-restraint she exercised every day. It would never be enough.

In the bottleneck of the impressively tall, narrow Arch of Remembrance, Drethene kept her hands folded in front of her, determined not to bring attention to herself or to bother Trem. She looked up at the figures of the ancient Great Council carved in relief and lining the underside of the Arch. The stonework showed war-torn military leaders and royalty engaged in passionate debate. Framing the scene were scrolls embossed with minuscule passages from *Tranquility*.

The chiseled faces had always fascinated Drethene. They appeared more authentic to her than the deliberately blended countenances of the One People. The stone was true, each image purposely unique, while the One People were the resulting composite of generations of forced matchmaking, specifically arranged to breed out physical differences.

Voices interrupted her thoughts. Small and distant but much clearer than last time. "Think more. Listen less. Read more. Study less."

The same phrases repeated over and over again by unseen lips. She nodded her head to the endless rhyme.

"Are the statues talking to you again?" Trem teased.

"Friezes!" Drethene said, much too loudly. "They're friezes!"

Another familiar arm, strong with indignation, embraced her back and scooped her forward.

"You're freezing?" Drethene's mother said, loud enough to benefit those around them. "I thought you looked pale this morning. Poor dear, you have a chill. Here, this will keep you warm until we get home."

"Ma, I didn't say I was freezing. I was about to, once again, explain to Trem the difference between—"

Drethene was cut off by the uncomfortable tightening of her mother's arm as she simultaneously wrapped a heavy, wool shawl around her shoulders.

"I know very well what you were doing," her mother whispered, pretending to kiss Drethene's temple to check for fever.

Then she whisked Drethene into the Hall.

"Wait right here. Don't move," her mother said as she deposited Drethene on a bench.

Only a mother could protect and punish at the same time. The shawl smelled musty, and the sweat began to trickle down Drethene's back.

"Nice try, Drethene," her father said when he saw her on the bench. "Up front with the rest of the youth."

"But, Pa! Ma told me—"

"Not this time. Move up front ... *now*."

She stood up and moved slowly to the front of the Hall, trying not to add to the sweat tickling her back. Once again, she was in trouble with both her parents. Overhearing a conversation a few benches ahead of her, she stopped and pretended to adjust her boots.

"I've always said," whispered a woman to her husband, "children should follow *Tranquility's* codes just like the rest of us. That girl must be coming of age soon. See, pulling them back from outside the rules is tougher than teaching them right from the beginning."

"Aw, now," her husband said. "Children can find themselves in the Honor Room as quickly as any adult if they do serious harm. You and I were young once. The Gatherings are long. Give the young ones time to play with their wisdom before they forget they ever had some."

"You sound like a blasphemer, husband. Have you been hypnotized by looking in that girl's eyes?"

"Hush now, wife. Who's blaspheming now? She's a member of the One People. She's the same as you and me."

Drethene walked past them, verbally beaten into silence. She was supposed to do two things—hide her differences and bring no notice to those she couldn't cover in fabric. She was terrible at both.

She easily located Trem's cap in the sea of brown-haired heads. She continued to the front of the Hall and sat down next to him.

"Sorry, Dreffy," Trem said. "I took things too far."

When they were small, he couldn't pronounce her name. He didn't use the nickname much these days but timed it well when he did.

"You?" she said. "You were spot on earlier. I'm worse now than when I used to swipe *Tranquility* from you and make you figure out which hay bale I hid it under."

"I'll never forget the week I spent without *Tranquility* because of your fabulous 'Mastery of Concealment.'"

Drethene had forgotten she'd coined a magical talent to disguise her inability to find the book. She'd hidden *Tranquility* from Trem and had done such a fine job even *she* took seven days to remember where the book was stashed. That was eight years ago, and he still couldn't laugh about her trick. Trem stared at nothing, his mind probably replaying the horror of that week. Drethene slowly reached for the very same copy of *Tranquility* from years ago, now on his lap.

"Really?" he said, snatching up the book, incredulity flooding those blue eyes.

She smiled sheepishly, folded her hands, and sank onto the bench. She turned to stare at the window. A single droplet was gently sliding down the outside of the stained glass. Alone. Bringing attention to itself.

Drethene watched as the bead of water caught the golden sunlight and illuminated the image of a man in battered armor, trumpeting a horn. The drop added drama, sliding down the crimson glass of his bloodied body. Drethene sighed. She could hear the trumpet call, smell the dirt turned up by horse hooves, feel the weight of the arm—

A painful pinch on her arm woke her from her reverie.

"Ow! Why did you do that?" she whispered at Trem.

The drone of the leader's voice continued uninterrupted. Drethene hadn't even realized the Gathering had begun.

Trem's eyes shifted as far as they could from left to right, checking the faces of those seated around them. "Hush, Drethene." His whisper had always been quieter than hers. "If you keep this up, that visit to the Honor Room you joke about might actually happen."

Drethene rolled her eyes and began to search her satchel.

Trem turned a page of *Tranquility*, dipped his quill in ink and wrote on the parchment spread on the bench between them. The scratching of the pen seemed endless. He stopped only to dip his quill in the ink jar. Every time, Drethene hoped he'd finally discovered an idea not worth recording.

The scratching began again, sending a shudder down her spine. She was about to close her eyes when Trem elbowed her. An eager smile on his face, he pointed to the last line of his handiwork. *Herb garden. Easy care. Great abundance. Myriad benefits.*

"Myriad?" she said.

"It means—"

"I know the definition," she said, shaking her head and returning to *War with a Purpose*, the library book she'd pulled from her satchel.

Now was Trem's turn to roll his eyes.

Drethene heeded the instruction from the Great Arch. She read much and listened little and must have done so for a couple of hours. She was startled when "Keep the Peace!" thundered through the Hall, chanted by four hundred voices.

Having brought the Gathering to a close, the leader approached the center aisle while everyone watched in silence. As he proceeded, each row's congregants bowed their heads and shuffled their feet so their backs were never toward him. Soon, everyone was facing the back of the Hall, yet gazing at the ground.

The leader stood in the center of the Arch of Remembrance.

He turned to face his bowing people and raised his arms. In the profound quiet, the rustle of his robes was a clear indication of his gesture. The four hundred heads rose up as one and belched forth another "Keep the Peace!" The members standing in the back rows filed into the aisle and made their way toward him.

The youth sat in the front of the Hall and would, therefore, exit last.

Drethene read another chapter of her contraband book as they edged their way toward the aisle.

Trem elbowed her again and gestured toward the leader, all the while giving her the *how-badly-do-you-want-to-see-the-inside-of-the-Honor-Room?* look.

Drethene was accustomed to Trem's weekly anxiety and remained steadfast in her lack of concern. There were fifty people between them and the leader. She finished her chapter and returned the book to her satchel.

"Grand Leader," Trem said when they reached the archway, "Drethene and I shall plant an herb garden to benefit the creatures, create remedies for our people's maladies, and aid in preserving food for the cold months."

Trem held out his Gathering-inspired plans with a flourish fit for a groveling courtier at the feet of his king.

Drethene desperately wanted to roll her eyes, but she fought the desire, hoping Trem's enthusiasm might keep Crouglan's attention away from her.

"... chamomile to calm nerves, mint to settle stomachs, garlic to fight infection," Trem's monologue continued.

Drethene stood still and silent. She hoped the leader's internal herb garden discussion clock would gong during Trem's recitation. As he listened to Trem pontificate about planting times and seed germination, she saw the leader's lips form a straight line. This might have been his equivalent of a slight grin. She studied Leader Crouglan—a small man, miniaturized further by the immensity of the Hall. He was of middle years with little hair, a crooked nose, and small close-set eyes. Although rarely seen, his smile never moved above his cheeks.

She looked longingly at the busy street just beyond the Arch. She was drawn to the hum of conversation between Academy students punctuated by the polyrhythm of their feet rushing to class and the trotting horse hooves delivering leaders from across the Land of the One People.

"And you, Drethene, have agreed to these well-laid plans?" Crouglan's voice woke Drethene from her thoughts this time.

She managed to meet his solid gaze with a calm expression. Sweat poured down her back. Maybe groveling was worth a try after all.

"I'm fortunate to have Trem as a friend. He can take your teaching and create a plan even I can help with."

Crouglan's unchanged expression and steadfast silence clearly indicated he had no intention of letting her slide this time.

"Dear Leader, Trem and I discuss ideas daily, and he surpasses me in knowing how to make them real. I trust him, his methods, and his values. By participating in his project, not only will I help our people, but I'll be made a better person."

Either Crouglan was pleased with having made her squirm or his internal clock finally gonged. Whatever the reason, Drethene was thankful to see the palms of the leader's hands presented to them, signaling they were dismissed from the Hall, but not before Crouglan's frown returned to his lips.

Hints of autumn were in the fragrance of the cool air, bidding farewell to the steamy heat greeting them after summer Gatherings, carrying the unfortunate scent of every village compost pile. Today's pleasant weather and sweet smell improved Drethene's mood a good deal.

They began their walk home a few paces behind their parents in compliance with *Tranquility*. As they passed students, Drethene admired the rainbow of Academy robes, each color indicating the number of years the scholar had attended. The general population wore a natural, earthy shade blending with their skin. The brilliant robes of the students attracted attention and set them apart as the respected future teachers and enforcers of *Tranquility*.

"Leader Crouglan called them 'well-laid plans,' didn't he?" Trem asked.

Drethene was surprised when Trem broke the traditional post-Gathering silence, but once he finished his question, she understood. Trem seemed to perspire liquid desire as he worked to impress Leader Crouglan, who was not only the leader of the largest village in the land of the One People, but also the Headmaster of the Academy. Crouglan could handpick any young man he thought worthy of an Academy education.

"Yes, Trem, I believe Crouglan's very impressed with you."

Her words were sincere, and she awaited Trem's satisfaction. However, he'd stopped to look past students walking through a doorway in the side of one of the smaller buildings. Typically locked, the door now lay wide open, inviting Trem to feed his longing to know the Academy intimately. He stood gaping at the doorway, his head jerking from side to side as he tried to see beyond those milling in and out. In a rare instance of role reversal, Drethene tapped Trem on his shoulder and pointed down the road, indicating the great distance growing between them and their parents. He gasped and reeled himself into an awkward trot—not quite a Peace-disrupting run but not truly a walk, either. With a bit more grace, she caught up to him and their parents.

As Drethene passed open kitchen windows of village dwellings, she tried to list what would be laid on each table based on the aromas wafting from the hearths.

"Potatoes and gravy," she said after a while.

"What?" Trem whispered.

"I knew I'd seen that old couple before. We just passed their home. They were going to have potatoes and gravy for supper."

She expected Trem's silence. He neither liked playing "What's for Supper" nor appreciated its clever name.

However, as soon as they passed through the gate, he said, "They may still have their supper, Drethene. Don't assume the worst."

She looked at him, but he pretended not to notice. She kept watching his face, hoping he'd finally slip up and somehow reveal he did not believe his own words of comfort.

He remained resolute. He'd be a good, stubborn father someday.

Their families' farms were an hour's walk from the village wall. Once outside the gate, before the cobblestones changed to dirt, their fathers discussed what crops they'd plant to complement one another, and their mothers talked about what they'd share to not duplicate efforts. Drethene's mother was a wonderful weaver, while Trem's baked the heartiest breads. *Tranquility* stated, "Peaceful living begins with your next-door neighbor," and these two families, descended from generations of upright members of the One People, lived by the book.

As they walked, Drethene buried her nose in a history book—her reliable comfort. Thankfully, her dear Uncle Drithon allowed her to borrow Academy library books. The only way she could avoid thoughts of the older couple's fate was to flood her mind with words just as she might swoosh a gulp of apple cider around her mouth to wash away the taste of a bad nut. She shut her eyes. So much better.

Drethene relaxed as the distance between her and the village grew. Sweet pine fragrance wafted across the meadow skirting the road, beckoning her to the trees.

"Hey, Trem."

"Yes?"

"Is it time?"

Trem closed his book, and they were off running into the grasses heading toward the woods.

Trem's mother shouted at them about being useful and gathering berries while in the forest. Trem's swift gait removed the cap from his head, revealing almost white drifts of hair. Drethene followed. He'd need a bigger lead to reach the edge of the pond before she did.

Once amongst the trees, Drethene exhaled an impish laugh as she effortlessly leapt over rocks and roots. Her scarf was swept from her head as she closed in on Trem—an easy target, his hair shining in the sparkling light piercing the canopy of dappled leaves. She looked over her shoulder as she passed Trem, catching a glimpse of her own glimmering black hair uncoiling into a long flowing wave.

They arrived almost simultaneously at the edge of Hushed Pond and sat down against an ancient willow tree to catch their breath. Across the water, rolling hills began their ascent into the Rosewater Mountains. The One People thought the name lovely, but Drethene knew from her history books they were named for their blood-tinted waterfalls when battles were waged there long ago.

Drethene rested her feet on a trunk-sized root reaching into the pond. She stared at the shimmering water. Having her long, silken hair free to flow down her back felt wonderful.

Trem was staring at her, or through her, lost in thought.

"You're starting to annoy me," she said.

He slipped off his perch, his hand landing in a muddy puddle collected in one of the hollows between the roots of the tree. Drethene smiled. Trem walked to the pond to wash, then returned to sit next to her.

"Sorry," Trem said. "Your eyes stand out so much more when you're not wearing that scarf. I guess there's a legitimate reason our parents hide what they can about us. Even I get caught staring." She knew that even after a lifetime of friendship, the red rings surrounding the pupils of her hazel eyes still unsettled him.

"I wish my eyes were all that stood out." Drethene pouted. "I'm pale as milk. I hate being draped in all this fabric. My feet would dance if they could wear sandals instead of boots."

Trem winced. She knew the mention of any forbidden diversion scalded him like boiling water.

"Don't forget, you're not the only one forced to hide." Trem ran his fingers through his hair. "Imagine how much better life would be if we were ordinary."

"Different, I think, but not better. The rest of the One People may not need to hide, but they have no more freedom than we do."

A shadow passed over her face.

"Oh, to have lived during the warring times." She almost sang the words. "One might fall by the sword but needn't worry about rotting in a hole dug by one's parents as protection from the very rules they think are perfect."

She spoke like one of her forbidden books, and her words left Trem speechless.

"You know the upper walkways of the Hall from which our behavior is observed for accordance with *Tranquility*?" she asked.

"Yes."

Drethene kept the long sentences coming, which paralyzed his defense of the Peace-keeping necessity of such watchfulness.

"Well, the one in the front was built where an organ used to be. The back walkway was a choir loft. Now all we hear are footsteps and the scratches of quills on paper. Did you know the ink wells were originally candle holders? Imagine the warm dancing light of hundreds of candles serenaded by song. Now, *that* could bring me peace."

Trem kept a fitful silence.

"And women were in leadership roles as much as men," Drethene added.

"Oh, here we go." Trem walked to a patch of rootless, flat ground and turned to Drethene. "Now I know you're looking for a fight. Just last week I heard you say—"

Trem prepared himself for his Drethene imitation. He had taken her bait. She always acted like she was insulted by his exaggerated flamboyancy and high-pitched voice, but his impersonation of her was just the medicine she needed to cure her blues.

"Why would I ever want to be a leader?" Trem squeaked, batting his eyelashes. "My creativity would be squelched, and my passions extinguished."

He dramatically placed the back of his hand on his forehead before he continued.

"I know there is purpose to my uniqueness but becoming the One People's first female leader is not it."

He added an undefinable accent that sent Drethene's head into her hands, hiding her smile and avoiding Trem's pursed expression. He knew how to break her.

"If I am not meant for something grand," Trem continued, "then we may as well reinstate the Trint."

"I knew I would regret telling you that!" Drethene said, lifting her head and revealing the smile she'd been hiding.

Trem put his hands on his hips, cocked his head, and continued his act, "Do you know what that is, Trem?"

"Please don't!" Drethene covered her grin with her hands.

"It's my own term for the intentional international intermarriage forced upon our ancestors. Trint. Get it? Three words. All starting with 'int'." Trem cocked his head the other way.

"Okay, okay," Drethene said. "You've proven I can be obnoxious. Please stop."

"It still happens you know," Trem whispered, leaning closer to her, still using his Drethene voice. "There are those who live in the Far Reaches of

Unemond, beyond our shores, who have yet to become members of the One People. The Last to Follow still endure the Trint."

Trem's air-quoting of the last word succeeded. Drethene let her laughter sing out.

She looked at her friend. His face was beaming with his success.

"Shall we swim?" she asked.

"Absolutely."

Trem dived in. As he emerged, he heard, "You're so predictable!" A well-aimed splash filled his mouth. He spat, wiped the water from his eyes, but saw only a ripple in the water. True, he typically swam the same distance from the shore before needing air. Drethene could disappear beneath the water, and five minutes might elapse before he'd notice her swimming, barely discernible, in the middle of the pond. His only opportunity to find her was when she faced him. Otherwise, her midnight hair provided excellent camouflage.

He searched for what seemed an eternity, then decided to get back to his own swimming. As he slowly submerged himself, he felt something cold on his shoulder. He turned to meet the bulging eyes and gaping mouth of an unhappy bass, struggling for freedom. He lost his footing and knocked into Drethene, causing her to lose her grip on the fish. All three went below the surface. The friends reemerged. The fish made a final appearance to smack the water with its tail before disappearing. Drethene initially looked annoyed, but then they both laughed, his friend emitting one of her less than ladylike chortles, letting Trem know all was well.

Once they were dressed, the sun was almost behind the mountains, and the pond reflected the pinks and purples of the sky. The quickly cooling air urged them on as they gathered berries to appease their parents and placed them in Drethene's satchel. They retrieved her scarf and his cap for good measure. Their walk home was quiet and pleasant, interrupted only by the familiar, mournful cry from across Hushed Pond.

# CHAPTER TWO

"Drethene, my dear nieceling, I was hoping you were coming today!"

Uncle Drithon knocked a pile of scrolls on the floor with the sleeve of his white-trimmed, brown robe as he rounded the corner of his desk to greet Drethene.

His kiss on her forehead made her smile, and she threw her arms around his neck. He pulled away, righted his spectacles, and patted her cheeks.

He smiled and said, "I hear yesterday was full of old sick people, prankster kids, and cranky parents."

"I'm coming of age soon. Will my parents always report my troubles to my boss before I get to work?"

"As long as you're employed by your favorite uncle, probably."

Then his eyes brightened, and he lifted a finger in the air, grazing a tuft of his uncombed silver hair. "Ah, there's a reason for my being exceptionally excited to see you."

He almost knocked her over as he turned and slipped on spilled ink, performing a graceless pirouette. He set the ink jar upright and returned to his desk, leaving a trail of diminishing black footprints.

A bird startled Drethene, sailing not far above her head, then darting up through the cavernous heights of the library. The ceiling was embossed with images of books, scrolls, pens, and ink jars dancing amidst oversized likenesses of the Great Council. The members were shown well-armed and sporting plate armor, symbolizing their strength and the ultimate defeat of their enemy—war. They were depicted swirling in a vortex. Those approaching the center were distorted as if they were being pulled into the core, a golden replica of *Tranquility*.

"That little guy has been visiting my library on a regular basis," Drithon said. "He must be a flyaway pet. He's sweet, but he's making a mess of my top-shelf books. Now, what did I do with it?"

# tranquility

As Uncle Drithon continued his search, a group of new Academy students paraded through the library on their welcome tour. The guide had the visitors and their families form a circle directly under the decorated ceiling as he described the images. Inspired by the colorful mosaic beneath their feet, the younger siblings of the novice Academy scholars created a leaping game. When they began hurdling the golden sphere embedded in the floor directly beneath the sculpted *Tranquility* overhead, Drethene held back her laughter.

"No, no, no," said the tour guide in his shaky, nasal voice. "Please refrain from doing that. This isn't a toy. This is the image of the Peace."

Drethene watched as mothers restrained their youngest children while the guide described the design of the floor.

"Please notice the seven elongated teardrop shapes emerging from the central sphere. Each different color represents one of the seven ancient lands. You can see how they create a sort of, um, bendy pinwheel."

Some of the young children giggled and were shushed by their mothers, who held them tight.

"Well," continued the guide, "this illustrates how the seven ancient lands were united. They escaped the filth and bewilderment of the war surrounding them," he swung his arms wide to refer to the plain, gray stone flooring of the rest of the room, "and centered on *Tranquility*."

He made eggbeater motions over the colorful pinwheel and gestured grandly toward the golden orb in the middle. He held his "ta-da!" pose until his guests felt forced to nod with increasing enthusiasm. He was finally convinced that although the central object was not in the shape of a book, they understood the symbolism.

He folded his hands in front of him and continued, "The citizens of these lands became the first generation of the Pun Weeple. Um, I mean, the One People."

All of the young children—and some of the older ones—giggled this time.

Drethene hoped this was merely a case of first tour jitters.

Her interpretation of the floor mosaic was the seven ancient lands were being thrown from *Tranquility*. Tangled and confused, they became one colorless lot. Her personal perception was exactly the reason the only art in the Land of the One People resided at the Academy and within village

Halls. All art had been created by those born before the first generation of the One People. Their techniques died with them.

The tour guide and his guests were all pointing and looking in different directions. Drethene suspected the newcomers were now trying to help him locate a particular section of the library.

Drethene smiled. Her mother's voice filled her thoughts. *Just once in a while, sweetheart, try to find something good to share with me about Tranquility. Please, for me?*

Well, this could potentially appease her ma. Even though this poor kid was a terrible tour guide, no one would say anything negative. Following his next evaluation, he would likely be appointed a new job without reprimand. This would continue until he found his niche. His permanent job might be brutally mundane but would still contribute to the One People. He would never complain, of course, and would be saved from disgrace. Both complaint and humiliation disrupt the Peace.

*Okay, Ma, we have agreeable dinner conversation, and our topic is* Tranquility.

"Drethene, I found the book!" Uncle Drithon held up a thick volume bound in leather.

"Jack rabbit! Is this the *History and Prophecies of the Realm?*"

"Oh, no, dear girl. I've only just begun my search. Even I can only inhale so much dust in one day. What I stumbled upon is the *Sacred Writ.*" Drithon motioned her to come closer, placing his finger to his lips, suggesting she speak more quietly.

Drethene's eyes widened, and she extended her arms to accept the text she had heard about only from her uncle.

Uncle Drithon tucked the book behind his back.

She lowered her arms, staring at him in disappointed shock.

"Allow me to speak before you lose yourself in these pages, my nieceling."

Drethene attempted patience. Her uncle smiled but was not willing to yield without first providing direction.

"I believe you need to read these words more than anyone else in this village," Uncle Drithon whispered as he drew the book from behind his back, "and maybe even in this land or all of Unemond."

Drethene's impatience melted into curiosity.

"You're different, a difficult thing to be amongst the One People. I hope this book will help you see being a unique person is a good and purposeful thing. My greatest desire is for any resentment you feel to transform into hope and love for those who have wronged you."

The significance of the gift was awesome, even though, as often was the case, Drethene didn't fully understand her uncle's intention. She reached toward the book as she let out a nervously quavering, yet resounding laugh.

"Please take the book, my nieceling, and quiet that racket of yours. The *Sacred Writ* is not on record as existing in my collection. This book shouldn't be missed. Nonetheless, bring the tome with you whenever you come here. Now, follow me."

Drethene hugged both the book and her uncle and followed him to a private staircase. He unlocked the gate, revealing steps heading down. Weeks had passed since she'd walked through this low-ceilinged, narrow entrance into the cold, stone-enclosed hall.

Uncle Drithon lit a lamp. Drethene remembered torches used to light their way. She'd once suggested not leaving fire unattended in a building full of books. She was happy to see Drithon now chose to carry his light source with him.

They passed five doors before reaching the study. Drethene often wondered why her uncle had chosen one of the furthermost rooms as his own. He'd said the other rooms remained vacant. She imagined when given the choice of a study space, he was lost in thought as he passed the first five rooms, remembered his task at the sixth door, and thereby made his choice.

Once inside, Uncle Drithon lifted the lamp to her face and said, "You're remarkable, child. Too often you're gray and melancholy, and yet now you've not even opened the *Sacred Writ* and those radiant eyes are shining bright."

Drethene rolled those eyes. He was being mushy, but she really didn't mind. "If only my father felt that way about my eyes. He never notices their emotion, only their difference from everyone else's. He works hard at hiding them, not admiring them."

Uncle Drithon cupped her face firmly in his free hand. "My brother loves everything about you, nieceling, never doubt that."

"He doesn't show it."

Her uncle gave her chin a quick squeeze, opened the lantern, and held a candle to the flame. "He works hard at leading his family on a safe, contented walk through life."

"He thinks nothing of joy. I wonder what he'd think of all the books you help me find. Imagine what he'd say about this." She held out the copy of the *Sacred Writ*.

Drithon smiled at her persistence in the growing golden light of the candles he lighted.

"Don't underestimate what your father knows. You're pulling no wool over his eyes. He knows who I am. We may be very different, but we're family. He chose to send you here—to me. He might've done so in silence, but certainly not in ignorance."

"You should spend more time with him."

"I've spent enough. It's not my place to lead him on a different path. That task belongs to someone else."

"Well, they've got their work cut out for them."

Drithon looked at his niece as she examined the book in her hands. He smiled, knowing she wouldn't notice his expression.

Further discussion of his brother would be nothing but a whirlpool leading into the funnel of Drethene's assumptions. She needed less talk and more experience.

"Searching for the *Writ* forced me to organize what I'd set aside for you to do," Drithon said. "Let's find you a comfortable place in my sitting room."

They proceeded farther into the room. The ceiling rose to a significant height, providing relief from both the near head-bumping pitch of the hall and the study's otherwise modest dimensions.

Drithon pointed to the hearth, "As you see, the fire is hot, and the tea is brewing. Would you like a cup?"

"No more torches in the hall but a blazing fire in here. Interesting."

"I can suffer carrying a lantern. Waiting for tea is another story."

"How can I say 'no' to a cup of tea waiting for me? Will you join me?"

"For a few moments. And *you're* joining *me*, dear girl."

Drithon filled two cups. He kept almost as many varieties of tea as he did books. Stored in a myriad of canisters of all sizes and shapes—earthenware, glass, metal—some labeled and others not—he knew their medicinal properties and the gastronomic qualities he appreciated in each. He handed Drethene her tea and read her quizzical look as she sipped.

"Amler root," he said. "It'll provide calm for sitting and reading and also the mental focus needed for absorbing multitudinous pages of written word."

Drithon sipped his tea and smiled at Drethene's little laugh. Big words and long sentences always amused her. He watched her tuck her legs underneath her body and nestle into the chair with her book, keeping her tea within arm's length. She tenderly turned the first delicate page and devoted herself to her task.

Expecting a response was futile. Drithon decided against parting words. He quietly rose from his chair and walked toward the door, wincing at the clink of his cup and saucer as he placed both on a small table. He left the room, closed the door, and continued farther down the hall, in darkness.

Eventually, the floor sloped downward, and the passageway turned. He felt along the stone wall until he found a small indentation. He removed his spectacles, popped the left lens out of the frame and inserted the glass into the depression in the stone. The lens glowed an iridescent blue. Overcome by this brilliance, the lens melted into liquid light and spilled forth into Drithon's cupped hands. He tossed the blue radiance onto the wall in front of him and smoothed it in a circular motion. The substance rotated with his movement and grew into a diaphanous opening of shimmering light. Drithon slowly approached, basking in the cool glow. He easily slipped through the entryway and turned around. The portal looked identical from this side. He felt along the surrounding stone wall and found another indentation. He removed the right lens from his glasses frame and fit it into place in the wall. The shimmering light disappeared, and the wall was whole again. He placed the wire frame in his pocket.

Drithon turned to face another long stone hallway. Although there were still no lanterns or torches, the stones shimmered, reflecting an unseen light. He easily found his way, rounding a bend and quickening his pace until he caught the sound of dripping water. He also heard the familiar thump of tapestries flapping against the walls in the breeze of his rapid gait.

He wished he had time to enjoy the woven images of feasts, bustling markets, and creatures never seen by the One People or imagined by their children. He hoped the stories entwined in these threads might once again become reality in Unemond.

He soon stood in front of a door hiding the source of the rhythmically falling droplets. He reached into his pocket and removed the frame for his glasses. He folded the wire in half and in half again into the form of a key he inserted and turned in the keyhole below the knob.

Hearing a click, he pushed the key forward into the door. He grabbed the doorknob with both hands, twisted gently, and the door suddenly swung inward. He tumbled into a waiting boat, causing a small wave of water to splash onto the floor of the hall behind him. The door slammed shut. The key fell into his waiting palm, and he placed it in his pocket. The door disappeared into the large trunk of a tree on an otherwise barren island. His boat slipped forward into the still waters reflecting the twilight sky. Eventually, he ran aground on a grassy shore.

Not far from the water's edge, a magnificent creature was seated in a huge nest of fragrant flowers and glistening treasures. Her neatly folded wings were covered in black plumage speckled with white. Her belly and chest were covered in neat, shimmering white down. Above, the delicate shoulders of a mortal-sized fairy emerged. Her long arms ended in elegant hands clasped gently before her. Her elongated neck was covered in black feathers decorated with thin, white vertical stripes. More pure black feathers ruffled up like a high-necked collar just below her jaw. Her wide red eyes were set in a porcelain face. Her short, tousled hair was as black as the feathers beneath her chin. Her ears, nose, and mouth were small, and her expression stern.

"My lady, you promised a new meeting place for each visit, and you don't disappoint." Drithon bowed low, almost toppling himself out of the boat.

"Son of the Realm, how you are burdened as your mortal body ages," said the Lady.

Her trilling voice held a hint of amusement, but her eyes showed pity. Her tone reflected the same as she added, "Wrapping immortality in a mortal vessel is a noble hardship."

Drithon managed to disembark without losing himself or his boat in the water. He pulled the boat farther aground and settled himself on the marshy grass. In the distance, he heard the familiar sounds of tambourines and drums, singing and laughter. He could smell the fires burning and could almost taste the sweet bread and spiced wine. Closing his eyes, he smiled and breathed in the cool evening air. But when he opened his eyes, the smile left his face.

# tranquility

"The people of Unemond live their entire lives with this hardship," Drithon said. "They work to maintain a quiet life. Meanwhile their souls thirst and starve. They've forgotten immortality abides within their mortal bodies. I'm glad I chose to join them in mortality for this short time. I hope mortals come to know they can choose their eternity."

The Lady nodded, spread her wings displaying their white undersides, and resettled herself.

Drithon made himself comfortable as well. Pains and sorrows were expected side effects of mortality. He'd voiced his concern for the mortal condition. Now to discuss the progress being made to cure it.

"So, our little chick is discovering the truth as we speak," the Lady said. "You have nurtured her well."

Drithon couldn't hide his doubt.

"Giving her the *Sacred Writ* was my greatest joy and duty," he said. "She's hungered for wisdom and needs to know there is loving purpose in her being burdened with individuality in the midst of the One People. Yet, she's still so young. I fear handing her the *History and Prophecies of the Realm* will frighten her."

The Lady stretched herself to her full height, extended her wings, and threw her arms back. She shone with intensity when she looked down on Drithon. Her voice lost its trill and became a haunting wail.

"Drethene will embrace the words unhindered by the intentions of men. The significance of the past and what has been foretold will be her power."

The Lady settled herself again, as echoes of her voice were heard from across the pond. Her feathered brethren responded, as only loons can, and their wails calmed her. "Your time with her is not yet ending. Drethene must learn *Tranquility* was accepted by exhausted people desperate for the end of war, while the *Sacred Writ* was embraced by those able to receive truth and accomplish the work inspired by this knowledge."

Drithon had always understood his charge, but a firm reminder helped relight pathways dimmed by emotion. The Lady reached behind her and handed him a metal box.

"You are a guide to Drethene, as I am to you. You know we have an enemy who works to raise a legion in Unemond. Please, do not allow your mortal love to blind you to the fact you no longer abide in the safety of the Realm. Keep your head."

Drithon placed the gift in the boat, took the Lady's hands in his, and touched his forehead to each elegant set of fingers. She extended her wings with an impressive whoosh and embraced him. Her wings remained rounded toward Drithon, so he released her hands and took hold of her wingtips. He touched his forehead to these as well. The Lady folded her wings and hands. They exchanged bows, and Drithon boarded the boat, gliding back across the pond.

Out of the mist appeared the tiny island supporting its one large tree. Once on land, he removed the key from his pocket, found the hole in the bark, and unlocked the door. The door handle fully emerged, he stepped over the threshold and heard the distant, mournful wail urging him to return to the Realm. The beckoning pulled more strongly after each visit. He shut the door and sighed.

The clink of metal landing next to him reminded him he had good reason to not heed the call. Drethene needed him still. He retrieved and unfolded the key, recreating the spectacle frame he placed on his nose.

Drithon began his return walk past the tapestries. The sourceless light allowed him to find the familiar place in the wall. He rubbed his hand along the stones until he found and removed his eyeglass lens. The shimmering passageway appeared, and he entered the hall leading back to the library.

He turned to watch the luminescent blue doorway begin swirling. In moments, the brilliant color was caught up in a miniature hurricane. The tail end touched where his first lens had been, stopped and reversed direction, as if the ghost of the lens were reeling in the blue cloud. The glowing glass was taking shape. The remainder of the tiny storm now looked more like a fiddlehead. The curved tail was forced straight, snapping and whipping in defiance until disappearing with a pop. The lens now clear, Drithon removed it from the solidified wall.

He followed the curve of the hall and walked up the incline, passing the room in which Drethene read. The next door led to a room less comfortable but still offering a fireplace and tea.

He sat down, opened the metal box, and smiled broadly at the dried leaves, flower petals, berries, and fruit rinds. He'd not had tea of the Realm since his time in Unemond began. The Lady had kept this gift for the moment he showed need of such a simple joy.

# tranquility

Drithon closed the box and brewed instead the identical herbs he'd prepared for Drethene. When he searched for peace, he'd drink the tea from the metal box. For now, he needed great focus.

He took a book from a drawer in a small bureau and began his own studies, seeking wisdom from the words he knew so well. He was to lead Drethene in understanding them, so he'd examine the text with her in mind. He knew his niece better than did most of her family and friends. He prepared to read the words of those who understood her even more deeply—*The Prophets of the Realm.*

# CHAPTER THREE

The words of the *Sacred Writ* rushed into the theater of Drethene's thoughts, shaking hands with her suppositions and filling every empty seat. Access to the Academy's history books had always thrilled her. Stories of war were exciting, not because of battles and bloodshed, but because of the passion and loyalty with which the warriors defended their beliefs. After reading the *Sacred Writ*, she could imagine herself proclaiming and defending instead of hiding and speculating. Indeed, there was more to be done in the world than simply coexisting without argument.

That evening, she reread the last phrases of the *Sacred Writ*.

*Love will triumph,*
*Hope will surround,*
*Peace will infiltrate,*
*Joy will abound.*

Not realizing she spoke aloud, Drethene said, "Jack rabbit! Why'd anyone shove this treasure aside for *Tranquility*?"

"The choice was not theirs, Drethene. By the time the *Sacred Writ* was compiled, the One People were already living under *Tranquility*."

Drethene hadn't expected anyone to answer, but she was glad the voice was a familiar one. Withdrawing her attention from the book, Drethene noticed her half-drunk cup of tea, her cramped fingers, and the loving but serious stare of her uncle.

"A good while after the Great Council," he continued, "copies were brought to Unemond from the Realm. The folk bringing them were welcomed and their gifts received. Sadly, the books like this one were destroyed or hidden away."

Drithon held out what appeared to be a duplicate of what Drethene had just read.

"Here, take this one to share in private with someone you trust. Present the book not as something forbidden, but as a long-lost gift."

Drethene accepted the tome.

"So, Uncle, you just happened to stumble across two copies of the *Sacred Writ?*"

Drithon patted her cheeks and began tidying the room.

"Interesting how these things happen." Drithon rinsed her teacup with boiling water from the kettle. "I hope to come across your next reading assignment as easily."

Drethene never ceased inquiring, but she also didn't question her uncle's answers. She enjoyed and respected his mysterious side.

"I certainly hope the next book is a tutorial on what to do with all I now know."

She massaged her fingers, trying to get them to straighten.

"And what do you now know?" Drithon asked.

"I know I can win my next argument with Trem."

Drithon looked at her over glasses fogged from the steaming kettle. His silence begged a more astute response.

Hesitating, Drethene looked at her hands and said, "I know I'm not crazy for thinking there is purpose behind my peculiarities. Beyond that, honestly, I didn't understand some of what I read."

Drithon laughed loudly, pulled up a chair, and sat in front of Drethene. He placed his hands on his knees and looked her in the eye.

"Honesty is a great strength, Drethene, an important aspect of the teachings of both *Tranquility* and the *Sacred Writ*. Be honest with yourself, and your learning will increase a thousand-fold. Be honest with others, and they'll help you learn the rest."

He patted her knees and returned to preparing another pot of tea.

"Reading the *History and Prophecies of the Realm* will answer many of your questions. But not tonight."

Drithon breathed the steam of the steeping tea. He reached out his hand, which Drethene accepted and held tightly, to steady herself and reestablish balance on her stiff legs as she stood for the first time since sitting down to read.

"For now, you need to get home. It's late, and one thing we don't want to do is draw attention to what you're learning. Not yet."

Drithon dried her teacup and placed it on a shelf.

"Uncle Drithon, even though I don't understand all I've read, I feel happy. Like when I was small, and I'd wander off only to discover myself laughing from the sheer delight of feeling free."

"My nieceling, don't forget these emotions, but keep them private. This passion is foreign to our leaders. Daydreaming during Gatherings is one thing. Renouncing *Tranquility* is quite another."

Drithon placed Drethene's satchel over her shoulder.

"Are you really sending me home now, when you know I have so many questions?"

"The best way to truly understand is to share the knowledge you're given. Choose those who'll listen, even if you're stumbling through your first attempt, and then let them read for themselves."

Drithon draped Drethene's cloak over her shoulders. "We'll have much time to talk about this—very soon."

He gently lifted Drethene's jaw and smiled. "This is a fine beginning, my nieceling."

Although she was frustrated with the burden of unanswered questions, she knew he was protecting her by rushing her out the door.

Her need to overdress finally helped her. She easily hid her book-laden satchel beneath her cloak. Drithon led her through the passageway and up the stairs. He unlocked the gate, and she walked through the library to begin her journey home.

Generally, few students of the Academy paid attention to Drethene unless they needed help navigating the library. There was one scholar, however, who was always looking to talk. She doubted he was particularly drawn to her. Rather, he'd simply exhausted his fellow classmates. Chamlon was different, he had Drethene's empathy. This evening, she really could have done without him.

"Drethene, I looked for you earlier." Chamlon's limping trot made his voice shake as he came up behind her.

Upon hearing her name, with the "n" emphatically pronounced, almost creating a third syllable, Drethene hung her head, then turned with as friendly an expression as she could muster.

"Chamlon, I lost track of time, and now I'm hurrying home."

She patted his arm apologetically and began a steady stride toward the outer corridor, her sweet escape.

Undaunted, Chamlon met her pace. "I'll walk with you as I'm filled with enthusiasm near to bursting, and I have another hour before curfew."

Chamlon was not tall, but he had the hunched shoulders of someone who wished he were smaller. He walked with his head lowered, most likely a side effect of pushing his natural gait to keep up with those who were attempting to escape him.

He was one of the smartest people Drethene knew, though he never boasted of his intelligence. One of his less-redeeming qualities was his mastery of the rhetorical question.

Chamlon brushed his fingers through his wavy hair, which was severely parted on the right side.

"As you know, this is my final year at the Academy. Do you know what all Academy students dream of accomplishing in their final months of study? Well, I've been honored with a fellowship to complete my year as the apprentice in the Hall of the Last to Follow!"

By the end of his announcement, Chamlon had managed to stop Drethene by placing himself directly in front of her, his head cocked to one side, eyes wide and arms outstretched to emphasize the magnitude of his news. Drethene was uncomfortably close to bumping noses with him. She suspected the Academy was shipping him almost to the Far Reaches to keep him, well, a good distance from everyone else. Fortunately for the Academy, he was proud of this appointment and beside himself with excitement.

Drethene laid her hand on his arm.

"Chamlon, I'm so happy for you. I'll miss our conversations, but I know the Academy made the right choice in sending you on this honorable quest."

The energy in Chamlon's smile flowed through his body, raising him up on his toes.

"Yes, yes, a quest! Oh, all I'll learn of pedagogy and how to spread the Peace. How different will be my environment compared to the halls of the Academy! The challenges I'll face in learning to interact with those so new to the One People!"

Chamlon's monologue continued as Drethene felt a pang of envy. She was different and sent into the quiet of a library so as not to bring attention to herself. If only she could go somewhere else to share and learn more.

"Oh, Drethene, I'll miss our conversations as well." Chamlon must have mistaken her quiet jealousy for melancholy. "I'll write to you! I'll send correspondence to you here at the library to keep you apprised of my learning and experiences. I'll write so often you'll hardly realize we're not having our regular chats."

Drethene smiled at her friend. His ample lips accentuated his boyish face. He was not feminine, but there was a softness to his build and demeanor.

"I'm already looking forward to your letters, Chamlon. I wish you a wonderful adventure."

"Adventure, yes!" Chamlon was up on his toes again, this time heading out the door before Drethene.

She watched him shuffle along, talking to himself. Still smiling, she gathered her cloak around her and followed him until she was outside.

The cobblestones were slick and glistening from a recent light rain. The cool, damp air revived her body and her appetite. The street was busy with students running their final errands before curfew. Most of the merchants had closed their shops, but one set of tall windows still blazed with warm light.

Welcome fragrances beckoned Drethene to the door. As she approached, she could see the spotless glass jars filled with dried leaves and flowers, along with spices and powders, lining neatly spaced shelves with mirrored backs. Candelabra hung from the high tin ceilings constantly caressed by wafts of steam or smoke created by one of Doll's brews or stews.

As a young child, Drethene had often been sent to Doll's Apothecary to explain symptoms and receive remedies, mostly for Trem's sister. Doll always listened intently, her warm smile and encouraging eyes prompting Drethene to keep talking. As Drethene grew older, each visit to the shop lasted a little longer.

She could see Doll now, puttering behind the counter, looking exactly as she had ten years ago when Drethene first began her journeys to Doll's shop. She didn't know Doll's true name, but her nickname was well earned. Her earthen skin was smooth as porcelain. Her cheekbones were perfectly pronounced below large, beautifully tapered eyes, like the aloe leaves she kept to heal the woes of many customers. Her hair was long and swept back into a neat twist behind her head. She was lovely and well admired.

Whether from the herbs or the way she lit her shop, she apparently never aged.

"Drethene, my sweet, come in, come in. What're you doing in town at this time of night?" Doll polished her dark wood countertop with a rose-scented white cloth. "You're hungry and tired, I know it! Sit, and I'll fix you a bowl of the soup I made this afternoon."

Drethene sat on the well-cushioned, long-legged chair in front of the counter, thankful Doll's intuition was in perfect form, and she had food prepared. Doll set a bowl before her.

Drethene inhaled the steam from the colorful soup. She could see familiar vegetables and legumes swimming in the bowl. Doll's food always exuded an exotic aroma, the source of which was not to be found by poking around with one's spoon. Being an apothecary allowed her access to spices and other foreign goods considered overindulgent by the One People. Doll's stores of such herbs were accepted as purposeful in treating the ailments of those who walked in her door. She did her best to keep the shop open as much as possible. Having food available was also not seen as an extravagance but as a necessity for her and a service to those who might need strength and nourishment along with medicine.

"Daydreaming in the Gathering is one thing, but in my company? Well, that's just not allowed," Doll said. She'd reached the far end of her counter and was grinning at Drethene's reflection in a large mirror.

"Doll, how do you do it? You attend every Gathering, work a lot, and spend much of your time alone. What keeps you so happy?"

Doll continued wiping the counter while gazing at Drethene through the mirror. She tucked the cloth in her apron and turned around, hands on her hips.

"And you, young lady, are coming of age surrounded by loving family and friends, and have a special deal working in the library. What keeps you so *un*happy?"

Drethene's defenses engaged, but she tried something new. She breathed.

"I think I've finally found my happiness, but I'm to keep the reason to myself for a while."

"Well, I look forward to the day when you may let your joy shine."

Doll retrieved the cloth from her apron and polished brass handles and knobs as she strode behind the counter.

Drethene watched her while sipping the last of her soup. Doll tossed the cloth into a bin on the floor, leaned against the counter and smiled at Drethene, who returned a sheepish grin.

"I am happy, dear love," Doll said. "I have my responsibilities, but I also have my gifts and talents. I'm privileged too. Powerful heads turn the other way when they pass my shop. I'm well aware of my good fortune."

Doll dipped a ladle into her pot and refilled Drethene's bowl.

Suddenly, Doll's eye widened, and she stared at Drethene. She spoke quickly, "You will fulfill your calling, I know it! Do so with great care, for watchful eyes are not blind. All will walk in darkness until you can light their way."

Doll continued to stare into Drethene's eyes, unblinking. Drethene had experienced Doll's spontaneous "soul searches" before and knew to wait until Doll was looking less through her and more at her before speaking. She was concerned the ladle, now dangling from Doll's fingers, might hit the counter and startle her. Drethene slowly reached for the ladle.

"Still hungry?" Doll asked, blinking again. "Your bowl is full, let me find some bread."

As if nothing out of the ordinary had happened, Doll placed the ladle in the sink and searched a cabinet for more food.

Doll wouldn't recall her great insight. Drethene would take those words with her and never discuss them with her friend. She'd tried to gain clarification from Doll after similar instances and received nothing but frustration when Doll adamantly denied saying anything of the sort.

Doll returned with a slice of bread on a plate and another apparently shoved in her mouth in one bite.

She swallowed and said, "I'm famished. I just ate dinner an hour ago, but I feel as if I skipped two meals and then ran from here to the pond and back!"

The bells jingled, and Leader Crouglan entered, wearing his usual frown.

"Grand Leader, please join us," Doll said. "Your hardworking library assistant is catching up on a skipped meal before heading home."

Drethene studiously researched the contents of her soup bowl as Doll offered Crouglan the stool next to her.

Drethene managed a shaky smile. Crouglan's frown remained firm.

# tranquility

"I finished my curfew walk and noticed you had company in your shop," Crouglan said. "I was expecting a Watchman on break or a visiting leader. I'm surprised to see you in town so late, Drethene. Should you not be home getting needed rest to work on your garden with Trem?"

Crouglan's memory was impressive but his tone suspicious.

"My uncle surprised me with additional work today. You know how much I enjoy the library. I simply lost track of time."

Doll poured hot spiced tea in a glass bottle for Drethene to take with her for the walk home. She secured a glass stopper in the opening and wrapped the vessel in a cloth. She handed Drethene the tea and a bag of dried fruit to put in her satchel.

"How fortunate you have that cloak to cover your belongings," Crouglan said. "Even in our *Tranquility*-centered society, there are those who might take advantage of darkness."

"I'm blessed in many ways, Grand Leader."

Drethene's hands shook as she unfastened the satchel and placed the tea and fruit inside. Visions of the books falling to the floor repeated in her mind until her treasure was again secure.

"You should be escorted to the gate." Crouglan turned toward the door to summon a Watchman but found one already standing against the wall.

"Oh, greetings, Watchman. Your entrance went impressively unnoticed. Please escort this young lady to the gate. Drethene, once you've reached the wall, he must return to his duties. Be wary and avoid these late nights. I'll speak with your uncle about assigning you so much work. Perhaps he needs another assistant."

Drethene attempted a thankful smile and exited through the door being held open by the Watchman. She was doing her best to keep her secret without lying but regretted causing trouble for her uncle.

The streets were silent. The Watchman's footsteps syncopated with Drethene's, creating an awkward rhythm. Walking alone, the quiet wouldn't seem empty, but with a companion, Drethene felt a need for interaction.

"Maybe I'm out a bit too late, but the village is impressively quiet at night."

Drethene waited in a now uncomfortable silence for a response.

The Watchman continued his determined stride.

"We want to keep the Peace," he said. "Here is the gate."

He stopped and stared at the gateway leading out of the village to the surrounding farmlands. Drethene thought she caught an odd glint of gold from the eyes hidden beneath the brim of his hat.

"Thank you," Drethene said. "Have a good night."

The Watchman didn't respond but focused on the village exit through which he apparently planned to watch Drethene walk.

Drethene sighed and reconsidered the fear-invoking tales small children told one another about the creatures lurking under those hats in the guise of Watchmen. She walked alone toward the gate.

Outside the wall, the road home was dark. Drethene stopped to sip Doll's energizing tea, resealed the bottle, and stepped into the black night.

The crickets and frogs serenaded her. She looked to her left. Through the trees she glimpsed the white moon, rising as she walked, gradually lighting her return home. Hushed Pond was beyond those trees. Suddenly, the night song quieted.

Drethene would never recall what happened during the silence before the long, mournful cry rang out through the woods from across the water. After a few more noiseless moments, the crickets and frogs harmonized anew.

Drethene stopped. Her feet, no longer touching the dirt path, were engulfed in the grass of the meadow. She was facing the forest, heading toward the pond. What had just happened? She turned around and almost tripped over her headscarf and hair ribbon. She didn't remember removing them, but her hair was hanging loose. She was cold without her cloak, which was lying beyond her headscarf. She gathered herself and her belongings, quickly walked back to the path, and continued home.

Her pace was fueled by good tea, cold air, and her whirling mind trying desperately to remember how she'd veered off the path and begun to undress. Before long, she could see the lamp still burning inside her house.

Drethene reached the edge of the farm and nuzzled her favorite cow. An otherwise useless farm animal, she always stood vigil until Drethene came home.

As a little girl, Drethene had learned what happened to chickens who stopped laying and horses gone lame. She loved this cow, who gave not a drop of milk. At the age of eight, Drethene spent a cold November week sleeping in the barn so her father couldn't attempt the unthinkable in the wee hours of the morning. The only way her parents could get her to return to her bed was for her father to promise, while holding *Tranquility*, no harm would come to the cow.

Remembering her father's well-kept oath made Drethene smile as she watched the cow retire to the barn. She approached her house and opened the door as quietly as possible.

Her mother was asleep in her rocking chair. In her lap was a letter, sealed with the gold wax of the Halls of *Tranquility*. Drethene's heart skipped an extra beat as she shut the door behind her. She took one step on the creaky floor, and her mother's eyes opened.

"Ma, I'm sorry to have worried you."

"I was concerned, but not being able to open this letter has taken more of a toll on my nerves."

She handed her daughter the envelope, upon which Drethene's name scrolled in the superior cursive of the Academy.

Shaking hand to shaking hand, somehow the letter didn't end up on the floor.

Drethene opened the envelope, read the words and refolded the paper.

She looked into her mother's anxious eyes. "I've been summoned to the Honor Room."

# CHAPTER FOUR

The next morning, Trem stirred the contents of the breakfast pot. He breathed in the steam mixed with the smoke of the burning wood. The days were shortening, and the mornings were chilly. He lit candles and lanterns to light the way for his waking family. He took four bowls from the cupboard and filled his with porridge. Footsteps fell behind him as he sat down.

"Better grab a fifth bowl. Company's arriving early this morning," Trem's father said. He shook his head while filling the kettle with water.

"Dr. Larzimar again?"

Trem's father nodded, hung the kettle over the fire, and walked to the cupboard for cups and saucers.

"If your sister put half the energy she uses worrying about her health into baking bread, your mother wouldn't have to get up early to bake the loaves we owe to Drethene's family for those rugs."

Trem was displeased when anyone referred to fundamental statutes of *Tranquility* as if they were debts to be paid. The exchange of bread for rugs was a sharing of skills between neighbors, not bartering. Hearing such words from his father, Trem's prime example of how to live a life of Peace, would normally have been alarming. This morning's frustration was clearly about his sister, Taelmai, not his mother's baking obligations.

"Good morning, boys."

Trem's mother had a way of looking vibrant straight out of a short night's sleep.

"I love the smell of someone else's cooking." Noticing the extra bowl on the table, she added, "I see you've heard the doctor's on his way."

Just as she began pouring tea, there was a knock on the door. Trem greeted Dr. Larzimar, who showed no sign of early morning radiance.

"I wanted to get here early," the doctor said, removing his hat and running his fingers through uncombed hair. "Taelmai's anxiety only exacerbates her symptoms. I want to see her before her mind has time to make matters worse."

The doctor hung his hat on the peg and placed his bag on the bench with practiced accuracy.

"I'll get her," Trem said.

"No, Trem, let her wake up on her own," Dr. Larzimar said. "I might have time to make use of that cup and bowl."

Trem filled both and handed them to the doctor, whose sleep-lined face broke into a smile when Trem's father offered him a seat at the table.

"I know my most frequent patient won't be pleased if you speak on her behalf. How are all of you feeling today?"

The doctor relaxed into his chair as they answered him with nods and smiles and a series of replies of "Oh, just fine" and "Very well, thank you."

He'd finished half a bowl of porridge and begun to sip his tea when Taelmai entered the room.

Until this moment, Trem hadn't noticed her recent growth spurt. The length and slimness of her arms and legs were emphasized by her undersized shift, which was all she wore. Her long brown hair hung limp and unbrushed. She displayed a mix of relief and wide-eyed fear when she saw the doctor. Her distress was caused by a well-exercised struggle of outcomes. "Nothing to worry about," "something to worry about," or "wait and see." Worrying was her course of action, and Trem knew she'd stick with anxiety, regardless.

"Taelmai!" their mother scolded, spilling hot tea on the floor at the sight of her daughter. "You'll freeze. Go back into your room at once and get dressed."

"But I'm not even cold." Taelmai looked terrified. She turned to the doctor. "Should I be cold? Do I have a fever?"

"Come here, Taelmai."

Taelmai obeyed, trembling.

He touched her forehead and cheeks and stared into her eyes.

"No fever, my girl. Please sit down."

Taelmai remained standing, her eyes filling with tears. "Dr. Larzimar, thank you for coming again. I fear the day will come when you'll refuse to visit me."

"So many fears, dear child." The doctor stood up to guide her to a chair. "I'm here and will always come as long as I'm physically able."

The doctor smiled as Taelmai sat down. "You've worked yourself up again." He sat beside her. "That's why you're indifferent to the cold. Tell me what's going on."

"Yesterday, I was dusting a windowsill when I saw an orange and black striped bug on my arm, pointing a long needle at my skin. I felt nothing, but it could have bit me. I've heard about the disease-carrying bindrury fly. My arm has been aching ever since."

Trem and his parents stared at Taelmai. Their mother was smiling encouragingly. Trem and his father were simply waiting for more. There must be more.

Following a tense silence, Dr. Larzimar said, "Let me see your arm."

Taelmai cautiously lifted her arm toward him. "Show me exactly where you think the insect bit you."

She pointed to her forearm, closed her eyes, and tightened her lips.

The doctor placed his glasses on his nose, blinked a few times, and brought her arm closer to his face. He removed his glasses and looked at Taelmai, who wore the expression of someone waiting for the guillotine to fall. He held back a smile. "I see no sign of a bite."

Taelmai's eyes shot open, and she stared at the doctor.

"As usual, I can't prove the insect didn't bite you, but I see no evidence of a problem. Not having the actual insect on hand, I can't determine the species. The probability this was a bindrury fly is extremely low since they aren't found in this region."

Not to be toyed with, Taelmai said, "I'm well aware of their natural habitat, but I also know what they look like. Perhaps they simply haven't been documented around here. I'm specifically concerned about Striltzer Disease since once the symptoms appear, there's no known treatment. And we all know the outcome of that illness."

Trem didn't know the illness or the outcome, but he did know his sister's propensity to turn rare and horrific diseases into her own personal epidemic.

The doctor met Taelmai's determined look with sympathetic eyes.

"Taelmai, how many more days until you're certain you didn't contract Fonudlia from the stranger who coughed near you in town?"

"Four."

Trem rolled his eyes at his sister's ability to recall, without hesitation, the details of her myriad health concerns.

"It's unlikely you've contracted Striltzer Disease," the doctor said. "The unlikeliness is equal to that of you having contracted Fonudlia. I'm sure you already know the incubation period of ten to fourteen days for Stritzler. Let's make a deal. If you don't die from a cough within the next four days, you must accept you haven't been infected by a bug bite."

Trem and his parents stared at Dr. Larzimar, processing his strange logic. Trem hoped Taelmai, who could be quick-thinking as easily as illogical, would choose to accept the compromise. The doctor's thought process might have been just convoluted enough for her to feel comfortable.

Finally, Taelmai said, "I'll do my best, doctor."

She turned in her chair to face the table. She was quickly wrapped in a shawl by their ma and served a steaming bowl and cup. Taelmai smiled as she reached for the tea.

Everyone smiled and ate together.

When the doctor rose to leave, the family thanked him and bid him good-bye. Taelmai handed him a basket full of the goodness from their farm, covered in a woven blanket. Trem walked him outside.

"Dr. Larzimar, I'm planning an herb garden and would greatly appreciate your input regarding medicinal plants."

Trem spoke to the patient doctor for another hour. They bid each other farewell as the rooster called forth the sun's light and woke the rest of the farm.

Trem ran inside, scribbled down the doctor's suggestions, and hurried to tend to the neighs and brays of the hungry farm.

With his sister's worries momentarily at bay and the animals busy with their breakfast, Trem's excitement over his list of medicinal herbs fueled him on his way to the forest to forage for samples. As he walked down the lane, he reviewed the notes from this morning's conversation with Dr. Larzimar. Some of the plants were found in boggy areas. This meant he'd need to explore the far and unfamiliar side of Hushed Pond.

He crossed the meadow and entered the woods surrounding the pond. The journey seemed much longer without Drethene's company and a good race. He finally reached the water and walked along its edge. Mist hung in the chilly air above the still surface. Trem stowed his notes in his pocket as he kept his eyes on the ground ahead of him. Gnarled roots, long helping themselves to the pond water, made walking treacherous. His mind must have been playing tricks on him, though, as he kept seeing from the corner of his eye, a dark shape keeping pace with him just above the water's surface and under the curtain of mist. But every time he stopped to look out over the water, he saw nothing.

He was walking along a part of the pond he'd never explored. The saturated earth seemed to seep into the dense, damp air. The water's still surface was swirled with green film and sat stagnant in channels between tall grasses. There was an occasional dragonfly and croak of unseen bullfrogs, but otherwise, there was a lack of energy. The peacefulness was heavy and pungent.

Trem searched for a particular fungus growing near tree roots. He squished his way around the trees until he came across a particularly large willow with roots covered in orange hat-like growths. As he bent to take a sample, he noticed movement a few paces away. Something in the mud was attracting a host of flying insects. He worked his way along a thick root to get a closer look at this frenzy, apparently the bog's center of activity.

As he drew close, he heard humming and discovered a strange gathering of insects—dragonflies, horseflies, ladybugs, and termites, all constantly and quickly circling the same area. Through their flight patterns, he could see what looked like a black ball half submerged in the mud. He found himself being drawn to it as the insects must have been.

Upon closer inspection, he was able to distinguish some of the insect sounds. The hum was broken up into a percussive rhythm as the insects took their turns in their orbit.

As they passed in front of his nose, Trem heard each bug for a split second.

*Zim-zim-zim-da-da-dim, zim-zim-zim-da-da-dim.*

He didn't want to interrupt their repetitive dance, but he had to know what had them so entranced. He stuck his hand into the mud under the ball and began to lift slowly, hoping the bugs would continue their course. He held his head back to avoid the barrage of insect wings. As soon as his palm hit the bottom of the ball, he became instantly cold. His eyes widened. He raised his arm, elbow straight, palm up ... slowly ... and suddenly he had an eyeful of his own muddy fingertip.

"Ugh!" Trem covered his injured eye with his free hand and yanked his other hand from the mud. The ball, which barely had been lifted, resettled. The insects were unfazed.

Trem was not only in pain but was puzzled. How did his finger end up in his eye from a fully extended arm's length away?

He wanted to inspect his hand but could see nothing. Trem rebuked himself for being like his sister, fearing sudden blindness. As his open eye adjusted to the darkness, he could see his mud-covered hand in the moonlight. Moonlight? It was barely mid-morning. Removing his hand from his injured eye, Trem slowly wiped the mud from his other fingers. His hand didn't hurt, but he was apprehensive. Something was odd about this day, or night ... this place ... that thing. All appeared well, so he cleaned up more quickly and was pleased to see his healthy hand emerge. With the relief, he'd unintentionally opened his tender eye. He was seeing just fine.

Trem puzzled over his injury and the sudden night. Fear took hold. He fought the desire to run since impulsiveness had landed him in this situation. What had made him attempt to pick up a strange bug-infested object stuck in a bog? He was usually so analytical. He needed to leave before anything else got the best of him.

The moon was bright enough to light his way home. A thin veil of clouds was about to pass in front of it, as if someone were pulling a poorly knit blanket across the sky. His light source wouldn't be entirely obscured, but he could waste no time in case sister clouds were close behind.

Trem decided to double back along the shore until he came to familiar ground. The muddy trek was full of tripping hazards, but better to stumble than get lost in the bog of the body-bending-bug-ball.

Trem's trip around the pond impressed him with the size of what he'd considered a swimming hole. The ground finally felt firm, and he was glad to walk more swiftly.

Suddenly, the forest quieted. Trem hadn't noticed the songs of the insects and the frogs until they were silenced. A long, mournful cry came from across the water. Trem quickened his pace and finally recognized one tree and then another. He headed into the woods, hoping to see meadow soon. The forest swallowed the moonlight, but before long a brilliance emanated beyond the trees. The moonlight shone silver on the moist grass, and as Trem emerged from the forest, he saw a white image floating toward him. He hid behind a tree and watched. A girl ... laughing, no, cackling loudly and ... dancing?

He recognized the laugh and almost stepped out to stop Drethene, but as she came nearer, he couldn't bring himself to end this graceful and joyous moment. Her eyes were large and fixed, her hair long and flowing. As she waltzed, she laughed and threw back her head and arms in what appeared to be the utmost joy. This behavior was highly irregular and unacceptable. He'd need to talk to her.

The insects and the frogs gradually resumed their chorus, and Drethene came to a stop. She looked down at her feet and appeared confused. She turned around and picked up her belongings. As she hurried back to the road, Trem followed a good length behind her. He was glad for even the distant company and a more normal mission—to ensure her safe return home.

Drethene kept a quick pace, but Trem relaxed his, hoping to remain unnoticed. As she walked, a breeze went along with her. The wind never touched Trem, but he could see and hear it in the swaying of the branches and the rustle of the leaves. He stared up into a pine tree whose needles still quivered moments after she'd passed. He saw something moving in the dense protection of the tree. He couldn't make out a shape but was certain he saw two golden eyes before the tree became still and silent, hiding any inhabitants.

Trem matched Drethene's urgent stride until he saw her enter her home, then he returned to his. Trem's household was asleep. He was thankful he could slip into bed and put this odd day behind him.

Trem woke up to darkness, and he was hungry. He started a fire and gathered the ingredients for a hearty porridge. He lit candles and lanterns, set the table, and began making breakfast.

He sat down to the sound of footsteps behind him.

"Better grab a fifth bowl. Company's arriving early this morning."

Trem turned to his father, "Dr. Larzimar? Two days in a row! This is insanity."

"I know his visits seem constant, but the doctor hasn't been here in over a week, son."

Trem turned back to his bowl, his appetite gone. Something was very wrong.

"What's it this time?"

"Some kind of disease-bearing bug on the windowsill. We'll let the good doctor figure it all out. If your sister put half the energy she uses worrying about her health into baking bread, your mother wouldn't have to get up early to bake the loaves we owe to Drethene's family for those rugs."

This time, hearing these words from his father invoked panic from deep in his gut.

"Good morning, boys. I love the smell of someone else's cooking." Noticing the additional bowl on the table, she added, "I see you've heard the doctor's on his way."

"Good morning, Ma." Trem's stomach felt worse with every word he'd already heard. "Did Taelmai mention what the insect looked like? Was it orange with black stripes?"

"Oh, no. Did you see one too? This will add fuel to Taelmai's fire, and we'll be living the summer with closed windows to avoid a plague of these bugs."

Trem's mother began pouring tea. There was a knock at the door.

Trem got up to open the door. Apparently, no one else remembered doing this already.

Maybe his sister wasn't the only one heading toward insanity.

# CHAPTER FIVE

"The shores were dark,
The fog was thick,
The mother swam from the nest,
For what was that—hark?
An arm or a stick,
Oh, leave the eggs at rest.
An imp did emerge
From the wood black as ink
Pursuing a tiring fay,
A funeral dirge
And a mug full of drink
To toast the fairy's last day.
The Lady is on her way—
Haffey!
The Lady is on her way.
The Lady will be here soon—
Hafloon!
The Lady will be here soon."

Drithon did a jig as he sang the song from his childhood. Yesterday's many emotions connected to giving Drethene the *Sacred Writ* had settled into joy this morning.

"You thought yourself wise,
You thought yourself strong,
Enough to give me a limp;
Well, those were all lies,
Now you find you are wrong,
Your day's done! cried the cruel little imp.

# tranquility

The fay fell to his knees,
His strength had been spent,
His wings were touching the ground.
Tears fell from the trees,
To his heart they were sent,
He struggled to turn around.
The Lady is on her way—
Haffey!
The Lady is on her way,
The Lady will be here soon—
Hafloon!
The Lady will be here soon."

Drithon rhythmically stoked the fire, prodding his watched pot to boil. The amler root tea had worked. Last night, he'd been so comfortable and focused on his reading he'd allowed his fire to extinguish. This morning's tea would be later than usual. For shame.

"I was foolish, I know,
To challenge you here
To a duel so very one sided,
But what you do not know
And the prophecy's clear
I've won! the maimed fay chided.
The imp stared aghast,
The fay laid on a rock,
Both—were—still.
What had just passed?
A key to unlock
A most powerful will.
The Lady is on her way—
Haffey!
The Lady is on her way,
The Lady will be here soon—
Hafloon!
The Lady will be here soon."

Drithon thrummed his fingers on his thigh while he rocked on his chair, eyes closed. A chair leg landed on the trim of his robe, and as he rocked in the other direction, his eyes popped open at the tug of the material. Stitches ripped as he was knocked off balance and brought to the floor.

"The fay took his last breath,
The imp disappeared,
The mother watched from the pond.
She mourned his death,
In her eyes there were tears,
'Twas her egg he died upon.
She opened her wings,
And approached the fay,
Protecting him with her brood,
A mournful cry sings,
Night turns to day,
A brightening change of mood.
The Lady will come today—
Haffey!
The Lady will come today,
The Lady will see high noon—
Hafloon!
The Lady will see high noon."

Not even a fall could undermine Drithon's bright mood. If only the students of the Academy could be taught their history through melody, how much more they'd keep in their hearts and minds. The kettle began to steam. He rose from the floor and danced to the cupboard for a tea cup. Toe, heel, toe, heel.

"The sun it shone,
The mother awoke,
She lifted herself from her bed.
The eggs were alone,
No mirror, no smoke,
No fairy but ashes instead.
The other two eggs,

They wiggled and shook,
The chicks were hungry and lean.
Two beaks and four legs,
Wait, take a look!
The third little egg has turned green.
The Lady will come today—
Haffey!
The Lady will come today,
The Lady will see high noon—
Hafloon!
The Lady will see high noon."

Drithon burned his tongue, too anxious was he for his tea. Unfazed, he dreamed of a new song to celebrate his niece. Maybe the first song ever sung by the One People.

"The dust was no longer,
'Twas one with the shell,
A babe now laid inside.
She grew instantly stronger,
And made the egg swell,
The mother was filled with pride.
The egg burst like a star,
From all ends of the pond,
Came yodels of joy and love!
From the wood near and far,
And the heavens beyond,
Came music as white as a dove.
The Lady was born today—
Haffey!
The Lady was born today,
The Lady was born high noon—
Hafloon!
The Lady was born high noon."

Drithon sat, placed his feet on a stool, took a comforting sip of tea, closed his eyes, and rocked his head to the song's final stanzas.

"Her family from water
Swam quickly her way
With gifts of the loveliest fishes.
She was their daughter
As much as the fays'
Who brought flowers on porcelain dishes.
She ate of each gift,
And shared with the others,
Her mum kept a watchful eye.
She gave her wings lift,
Settled down with her brothers,
The birds and the fairies did cry
The Lady was born today—
Haffey!
The Lady was born today,
The Lady was born high noon—
Hafloon!
The Lady was born high noon."

Drithon kept humming the tune, as he added a log to the fire. The bells rang loudly. Bells?

Drithon gathered himself as he realized the bell at his desk was being rung repeatedly, calling him to his work. He put on his glasses and his robe. The tea should be the perfect temperature, he just needed a sip. Bells again! He ran down the hall, thirsting for his tea and tripping over the ripped trim of his robes. *Okay, all is well as long as it's not—*

"Leader Crouglan, how may I assist you this morning?"

"Late nights don't suit you, Drithon. I've been ringing for five minutes."

"My apologies, Grand Leader. Yes, a lot of organizing is needed to keep this library in order. I'll avoid the late-night work from now on so my responsibility to you and the students isn't compromised. May I help you find a book?"

*How did Crouglan know?*

"Not today. I came to discuss a meeting with you."

Drithon's desk was in its usual state of disarray. There were many notes and letters for him to push around while avoiding Crouglan's eyes.

"To what or whom do I owe the honor of a meeting summons?"

Crouglan's lips straightened from their usual frown. Was he amused?

"Since your library assistant has shown such dedication, I have an assignment to propose. I'd appreciate your input, as you've worked with her most closely."

Drithon bowed.

"Provide me the location and time, and I'll arrive prepared to assist."

Crouglan nodded.

"Tomorrow. High noon. The Honor Room. Get to bed early tonight. Keep the Peace."

Drithon felt a strange sensation building in his chest. No. Not now. Not at Crouglan. Not yet.

The power of the Realm, guarded and subdued in his mortal body, awakened as if the threat of an Honor Room hearing for Drethene were a physical attack against him. The power was released. Drithon feared opening his eyes, shut tight by his unsuccessful struggle to keep the power within him. Was Crouglan on the floor? Plastered against the far wall? Dead?

Drithon raised his head, opened his eyes, and watched Crouglan leave the library with his usual arrogance.

Drithon exhaled with relief and looked at his tidy desk. There was not a scrap of paper, stained teacup, or dripping inkwell to be found. He looked over the sides of the desk, hoping he might have simply swept the mess onto the floor as he struggled against his own power. The floor was bare. There was only one way his wreck of a desk could have become instantly spotless. He must have cobbled.

At least his internal struggle dampened the intensity of his power. Cobbling, in the face of a true threat, would be the equivalent of shining the enemy's sword. All parents in the Realm embraced this power to ease the broken heart of a babe. The petals of a flower could be reattached. A broken walking stick made whole. A melted snowflake reformed. And, apparently, a disheveled desk restored to order.

He hurried to his chambers. The *History and Prophecies of the Realm* were in a chest behind a tea set within a cupboard. The porcelain reminded him of his poured tea on the other side of the room near the fire. He looked longingly at the steam still rising from the cup, shook his head clear, and worked at removing the book from its hiding place. He found the verse he sought.

*The antithesis of darkest night,*
*The world is full of brilliant light,*
*Whilst tradition beckons under the moon,*
*Great change and hope take flight at noon.*

The words were ambiguous, but Drithon was well-versed in prophecy. The next day must be welcomed as a step in the journey Drethene was destined to make. Oh, how he needed tea.

Drithon returned the book to the chest and walked to the fire. He grasped the cup in both hands, his dry lips smiling, when the all-too-familiar summons rang an encore.

*Of all things to remain on that desk!* Leaving teacup and saucer reunited, he trudged back to the library. As he approached his desk and his visitor, he considered a cold cup of tea might be invigorating.

"D.D., I was delivering ointment to the student infirmary and thought I'd bring you these interesting teas I happened upon." Doll's radiant beauty was not brought forth by the lighting of her apothecary—unless she'd found a way to capture the warmth and carry it with her. Addressing him with her abbreviation for Dearest Drithon made her visit all the sweeter.

"You're living up to your name, Doll."

"You've been locked in your dungeon. I thought you might've run out of tea and passed out cold on the floor. At least this ridiculous bell is reliable."

Drithon tilted his head, pushed his glasses up his nose and smiled.

"I haven't been the best friend, customer, or librarian for that matter. I'm consumed by ... a project."

Doll squinted at him.

"Does this have anything to do with Drethene? She stopped in late last night, half starved, and had the great misfortune of an after-hours encounter with Crouglan."

Drithon stroked his eyebrows with the thumb and middle finger of one hand.

"She's not prepared. She needs time."

Doll pushed the tea at him.

"This is no place for us to talk, I know it. We're in a library, after all. You need to emerge from these halls once in a while, and I hope you choose to visit me when you do."

# tranquility

She strode out, leaving Drithon alone in his deep state of perplexity.

Drithon did need to leave the library, to keep an eye on Drethene and those who might stand in her way. He needed to observe first-hand what had taken place at Doll's. Caution was imperative. The blackness of last night should help. It was time to reawaken more powers of the Realm.

# CHAPTER SIX

Trem was confident this morning's *déjà vu* was his alone and was determined to live his second chance at this day very differently. After suffering quietly through a verbatim recap of his sister's health fears, Trem walked the doctor out and bid him farewell without a mention of medicinal herbs. Trem fed the animals and went to find Drethene.

She answered Trem's knock, and the two of them began telling their tales simultaneously at panic pitch while she pushed him back outside and shut the door behind her. They stopped speaking in unison moments after they'd begun.

"I don't know what you're going on about, but I've got a fistful of trouble we can't discuss here," Drethene said as she continued to shove Trem farther from her house.

Trem grabbed her shoulders. "I made time shift backwards."

"Jack rabbit! We've got to talk. Can we go to your house?"

"My family's in a good mood as long as my sister hasn't begun foaming at the mouth from making eye contact with a potentially rabid squirrel."

Drethene tilted her head and gave Trem a *be-kind-to-your-delicate-sister* look.

"Anyway," Trem said, "they're clueless about my predicament. My house is as safe as any other place."

The friends kept a solid, silent pace and arrived at Trem's door unnoticed.

"Let's talk in my room."

Trem led the way past the lunch pot simmering in the fireplace. They entered his room, and he shut the door.

Before he could speak, Drethene said, "We have to tell my uncle."

"Tell him what?"

"About what you did."

"Why would I tell the librarian of the Academy I went into a bog, touched a strange black ball surrounded by bugs, poked myself in the eye with my distant finger, and returned home to the night before this all happened?"

"Listen, that librarian is also my uncle. He knows a lot about strange things, and I think he is one of the few people who wouldn't report your experience to Leader Crouglan."

Trem closed his eyes and swallowed. He needed to understand what happened without jeopardizing his image in the eyes of the leader.

"Okay." Trem opened his eyes and looked at Drethene. "We'll go see your uncle, and I'll tell you both everything. Now, what's going on with you?"

"My questions have been answered in a book. The doubts I've voiced over the years have been validated."

Trem was silent. *The only library Drethene should enter is one with* Tranquility *on every shelf.*

"There's a small glitch." Drethene looked apologetic. "I was summoned to the Honor Room."

From outside the room they heard, "No! Oh, please no!"

Trem's bedroom door burst open, and Taelmai ran arms extended toward Drethene, toppling them both onto the bed.

"I see you're feeling well enough to eavesdrop," Trem said as he peeled his sister off the stunned Drethene. "Shouldn't you be in your room counting how many times your heart skips a beat?"

"How did you know I've been having heart trouble?"

Trem rolled his eyes.

"Have I been looking pale lately?" Taelmai asked, her voice tightening. "I thought I've been a bit sallow."

"Yes, yes, you have," Trem said.

"And my breathing," Taelmai gulped air, "it's been a little shallow, hasn't it?"

Trem nodded with mock sincerity and said, "I noticed yesterday."

"Oh, no! So did I!" Taelmai gasped, grabbing at her chest and looking as if she might faint.

Drethene punched Trem in the arm.

"Taelmai, don't listen to him. You look just fine."

"But you don't know," Taelmai whimpered, grabbing Drethene's arm, "such ailments might develop gradually. You really need to pay attention every day to appearance, breathing, eating habits, general demeanor ..." She trailed off, clearly calculating what was certain to be a trend of degradation in all of these.

"Well, then, you might as well begin digging the grave," Trem mumbled, knowing his sister was too deep in her thoughts to hear him but earning himself another punch from Drethene.

Taelmai closed her eyes, released Drethene's arm, and sank to the floor. She must have remembered Drethene's plight, for she stood up with surprising strength and a flush of color to her cheeks, quite uncommon for someone with such a serious ailment.

"When, Drethene? When do you have to go?"

Drethene seemed momentarily more apprehensive about Taelmai's potential reaction than her impending visit to the Honor Room.

"Tomorrow." Drethene winced and prepared herself for impact.

The room remained quiet, except for a soft thump. Trem crossed his arms, shook his head, and watched Drethene tentatively open her eyes. Taelmai was in a heap, not unconscious but crying so hard her weeping was silent. She finally inhaled. The impending wail was certain to bring their parents running.

"So much for our safe place," Trem said.

He gently helped his sister to her feet and brought her to her room as his mother walked into the house. Trem shut Taelmai in her room and stood beside Drethene, prepared for questions.

"Trem, what's wrong?" his mother asked.

Trem's mother always appeared calm in the face of his sister's outbursts, but the deep concern was ever-present.

"Drethene's been summoned to the Honor Room, and Taelmai's taking it pretty hard."

His mother's eyebrows relaxed, and then worked their way up her forehead into a *that-was-bound-to-happen-sooner-or-later* expression.

"When do you present yourself in the Honor Room, Drethene?"

"Tomorrow."

"When did you receive your summons?"

"Last night."

"My, they're moving quickly on this one."

Drethene's mouth worked as various retorts feuded with her better judgment. Trem's mother waited patiently, wearing the expectant look of a parent certain the next word from a child is going to be worthy of punishment.

It was Trem's turn to do the pushing out the door. He grabbed Drethene's arm and led her out of the house while giving his mom some *she's-just-worried-about-tomorrow* gestures. Trem closed the door behind him and turned to find Drethene embracing Drithon.

"Your ma said I'd probably find you here." Drithon looked directly into Drethene's eyes and smiled. He was the only person Trem had ever seen find joy, not discomfort, in making eye contact with her. "Looks like I arrived not a moment too soon."

Drethene looked down and said, "I've been summoned to the Honor Room."

"I know. Come with me." Drithon began walking away from the house.

"I made time shift backwards," Trem added.

"I know," Drithon said without looking back. "Don't give yourself too much credit. You're coming with us as well."

Trem and Drethene shrugged at one another and struggled to keep stride with Drithon's quick and strangely graceful pace.

"Uncle Drithon, I have a question, but I think I know the answer," Drethene said.

"We'll soon have all the time we need to discuss questions, but you may ask."

"Where are we going?"

"You'll soon find out."

Drethene looked at Trem.

"I should've known not to waste my breath."

They continued their fast-paced jaunt from the farm and headed away from town in a direction Trem had never explored.

They crossed a meadow from which they could see tall peaks of mountains in the far distance. Trem stared, mouth agape. Drethene smiled at the sight.

"Enjoy the view, younglings," Drithon said. "We're about to enter a darker forest than either of you has experienced."

As the unfamiliar woods filled the horizon, Trem stopped short. "I need to know where we're going."

"You wouldn't believe me if I told you," Drithon said.

"What happened to me in the bog shouldn't have been possible, but it happened, and you knew before I told you." Trem was pointing his finger at Drithon. "I'm not moving until you tell me why my little time issue didn't even make you blink. And," he added, taking full advantage of Drithon's quiet calmness, "I want to know where we're going and why I should trust you."

Drithon took a deep breath and gently pushed Trem's finger away from his nose.

"I'm well-educated in the ways of the world before *Tranquility*. Remember, Trem, I'm the source from whom Drethene gets her history books."

Trem scowled and shook his head. He despised those books.

"Right now," Drithon continued, "you may well wish you'd read one or two of them. For what you stumbled upon in the bog is nothing new to Unemond, just forgotten. Where we're now headed is the dwelling of ignored and neglected neighbors. How we're getting there is akin to a long unused gate in an old hedgerow."

Trem realized whatever they were about to do was certain to be well outside what was considered acceptable by the One People. He fell to his knees. He looked at his companions, who regarded him not with shock but with understanding.

"*Tranquility*. I dishonor *Tranquility*."

Trem felt Drethene kneel beside him and put her arm around him.

"Your experience with time wasn't a random foible, Trem," Drithon said. "This event was foretold and has set you on your current and truly right path. Take heart and know you don't stray."

Drethene and her uncle helped Trem to his feet.

Trem sighed as he looked at Drethene. "I always knew you'd eventually involve me so deeply in your trouble I'd get stuck in something I couldn't escape."

Before Drethene could come to her own defense, Drithon said, "Ignorance, children, is fodder for blame. Let's proceed swiftly and without argument, so we may all learn and understand what now feels like chaos."

They entered what appeared to be an ordinary forest. Within moments, the undergrowth thickened and was as high as their knees, slowing their pace. One hundred more steps, and the vines covering the trees hung so low the three walked hunched over. Soon the encroaching branches prevented them from raising their heads at all.

Trem and Drethene followed Drithon as he climbed out of the brambles and crawled along the lowest tree branches creating a mesh floor beneath them. All light was gone. The blackness was palpable, as if they were moving through cold pudding. Breathing became difficult, but they continued on their path, trusting Drithon hadn't led them to their doom.

Trem was the last to push through the thickness with a slurpy-sounding pop. He fell to the ground, gasping for air. The space they'd entered was empty, still, and silent. Drithon sat calmly as Trem and Drethene caught their breath. Trem could see nothing but his companions' faces, lit by an unidentifiable source.

"We now have all the time we need," Drithon said.

"Where are we?" Drethene asked, squinting into the darkness as she forced herself up to a kneeling position.

"For now, all you need to know is we're safe."

"What is this place?" asked Trem rubbing his hand over the cold stone of the floor beneath them.

"Okay, then," said Drithon. "We are in a Flow, but you both must understand why we are here. Let's begin with an ancient friendship between two worlds."

"Please," Trem said, "someone wake me up. I'm having a nightmare that I'm trapped in a dark cave with a rebel and a librarian."

Even in the dark, Drithon was quick enough to catch Drethene's hand before she struck Trem.

"Children! Please button your mouths and put on your listening ears."

They stared at Drithon incredulously.

"Show me."

They both rolled their eyes and made halfhearted button-fastening motions in front of their lips.

Drithon waited.

More eye rolls and they each used their fingers to represent bunny ears atop their heads.

"Thank you. There was once a strong relationship between Unemond and the Realm. The Flows were busy arteries connecting the two worlds, giving passage for each people to visit the other. They've been quiet for generations. I believe Drethene's summons to the Honor Room is Leader

Crouglan's attempt to avoid what's already begun. Drethene, what you've read, and Trem, what you experienced in the bog have opened gateways for you to walk your paths. Your unique physical characteristics do have meaning beyond the annoyance they cause you."

Drithon pulled from his satchel a glass jar filled with tiny phosphorescent stones which acted as an impressive source of light. Trem could now see his companions in their entirety, not just their faces. Drithon removed a book from his satchel.

"Drethene, do you have the *Sacred Writ?*"

Drethene opened her satchel and displayed the two books.

"Give one to Trem."

She did.

"Drethene, this is the *History and Prophecies of the Realm*. Read this while Trem reads the *Sacred Writ*. These books will answer questions, Drethene, you constantly ask, and Trem, you will never admit you've had. There's no doubt you wonder why the two of you look different from everyone else following generations of enforced intermarriage."

Trem looked at Drethene, who was avoiding his eyes and hiding a smile.

"The Trint!" Trem said.

"Don't start," Drethene said.

"The what?" Drithon asked.

"Never mind," Trem and Drethene said.

"Okay then. Prophecy tells us," Drithon sang,

*The blood of the Realm is strong,*
*And not so easily hidden,*
*Babes will be born of the throng,*
*Displaying features forbidden.*

Trem shook his head in the silence. His Trint joke was over, but he now felt like he was being taunted. For once, he wanted one of his companions to keep talking to chase those words out of his thoughts.

"Your blood of the Realm runs strong," Drithon said, "and the beauty of your ancestry shines in your faces. *Tranquility's* hold on the One People forces your parents to try to hide what can't be denied. You've fulfilled

Prophecy simply by being born. Your recent experiences call for you to learn more about what's been foretold."

Drithon gestured to the books in their hands and began singing indiscernible words—low, quiet, and comforting.

Trem watched Drethene smile and open her book. Could she actually be accepting the librarian's story about magical passageways to another world?

Trem longed for normalcy, to be at the farm planting seeds in his herb garden. Should he have been listening to Drethene instead of stifling her all these years? He'd never before been confused about what was right and true, and he found the mindset unsettling.

Trem looked at the foreign book in his hands and opened what was not *Tranquility*.

Drethene looked up only after she'd read every word. Her uncle sensed her movement. He opened his eyes and shared a smile with her. He closed his eyes again, never breaking his chant. Trem still read.

Drethene was not sore this time, although she was certain this book was as lengthy as the *Sacred Writ*. She was neither thirsty, nor hungry, nor fatigued. She looked at Trem.

Trem looked up and said, "Jack rabbit!"

They both smiled. Drethene couldn't help herself, she nearly toppled Trem over as she ran to him and threw her arms around his neck. Trem awkwardly embraced her, gently patting her back.

"Don't misunderstand me, Dreffy. That was a lot of interesting reading, but I can't simply abandon all I've ever known to lead my life by words I don't fully understand."

Drethene pulled away from him, and Trem thumbed through the pages, shaking his head.

"You must admit it's nicer to read than *Tranquility*," Drethene said.

"Oh, many of the words paint a very pretty tale, but the rest is a huge riddle."

Drethene frowned and said, "The words are poetic, not a 'tale'. There is more meaning inside one page than all the stagnant rules of *Tranquility*."

Trem sat up straighter. "There's plenty of good intention, if you read with an unbiased and open mind, behind the smart and simple prose of *Tranquility*."

"If you'd read at least one other book in your lifetime, you might've found other, more meaningful writing styles. Allowing the reader to be thoughtful along the way is an attribute of something well written, as opposed to *Tranquility*, which erases the desire to read by providing nothing but mindless laws!"

Drethene and Trem continued to hurl insults. Drithon had resolved his chant and placed a hand on Drethene's shoulder. He did the same to Trem. They were almost nose to nose, shouting in their fury. Drethene had just called Trem a pompous pumpkin, which meant nothing to either of them but had optimum spitting potential. Drithon's gentle touch eased them both into huffing, puffing silence.

"My younglings, take a breath and listen to me. Trem, no one except Drethene, apparently, expects you to put aside all your beliefs after one reading of the *Sacred Writ*. Drethene, your passion is understandable, as you've read many books containing bits and pieces of the inherent knowledge contained in the *Sacred Writ*. Remember, even you admitted to not having grasped a full understanding after one reading. Talking to one another will be much more profitable than yelling. Allow us now to continue our journey. We have a visit to make."

"We don't have time for a visit," Trem said. "Drethene needs to get to the Honor Room."

"Time is of no concern here," Drithon said.

Trem shook his head and continued to fume.

Drethene followed her uncle as he began to walk. She didn't bother looking to see if Trem followed. She knew he would. The darkness became substantive once again but never oppressive like their bizarre forest voyage.

Once they'd pushed through the blackness, Drethene tumbled onto moist ground. The world around her was white, not bright, but rather blank and silent. She was surprised by how well she could differentiate between ground, sky, and trees—all of one, or rather, no color.

"The trees look like cauliflower," Drethene said.

At her words, a tear rolled down Drithon's cheek. Drethene was puzzled by his emotion, and then noticed he was not wearing his glasses. She was about to question him when she heard a familiar yodeling.

Drithon grabbed both Trem and Drethene by the hand and bowed his head. The two friends imitated him.

There was a cacophony of fluttering and stumbling. Drethene began to raise her head, but the strong squeeze of her uncle's hand returned her chin to her chest.

"Do not spend your tears, my son. If your love alone were enough to show her the Realm, she would see all of its glory. Her senses will be strengthened as her knowledge and acceptance grow."

The voice came from a bright white glow directly in front of them. Drithon reached into the brightness and lifted to his lips a hand draped in a black garment dotted with white. Drethene searched where she imagined a head should be. Her eyes had to jump up a span further to meet a warm smile and two eyes. Red eyes!

Drethene threw back her head and released a cackling laugh echoed by the creature in front of them and a multitude of voices in the distance. Suddenly, a layer of veiling dropped for Drethene, shattered by the contagious guffaws. She looked in astonishment at the beautiful figure. The contrast between black feathers and ivory skin made her slip her pale fingers through her own midnight hair. The creature's arms were long and graceful, but her legs were unseen. From the midst of her shoulders, two huge black wings, covered in lines of white squares and dots, still worked to settle into a comfortable position.

"Drethene and Trem, welcome home," the Lady said. "You are filled with new knowledge and many questions. As you learn and accept, more and more of the Realm will be open to you. You are surrounded by color, sound, joy, and beauty you've never imagined. They are out of your reach for now. Continue on your journey with trust in each other and the promises written in our history."

Drethene ran forward and embraced the Lady, who emitted a loud and warbling laugh. She returned Drethene's hug, even wrapping her wings around her, quelling any fear she was not pleased with Drethene's sudden affection.

Trem's face was a pool of confusion. "What's going on? I can't see anything. Who are you talking to?"

"You can't see her?" Drethene asked.

"See who? Can we go now? I think I'm ready to sit in the dark and ask questions."

Drethene looked with longing at the Lady, and squinted as she peered around her, hoping to catch at least a glimpse of what lay behind the remaining veil of white.

"Never mind, my dearling," the Lady said, "this visit was necessary to simply show you the Realm is a true place. You will all come again, with more ability to experience life here. Until then, spend time together in contemplation and discussion, and you will know how to begin by the time you return from whence you came."

# CHAPTER SEVEN

Back in the Flow and accustomed to the light of the glowing jar, Trem was becoming comfortable in this dark, quiet place. He read the *History and Prophecies of the Realm* while Drethene and her uncle discussed the Lady and their ancestry.

Trem drew a deep breath, handed the book back to Drethene, and listened.

"The Lady and I agree you and Trem are the first found of the Sworn Seven," Drithon said. "Your physical appearance is significant. More importantly, you've both been experiencing, without fully understanding, calls to the Realm."

"Are you some kind of Realm spy?" Trem asked.

Drithon laughed. "Such an imaginative accusation from someone who's never read a child's tale. Does this mean you accept the Realm exists?"

Trem was regretting his question.

"I have ties to the Realm," Drithon said, "but I prefer to see myself as a concerned uncle, not a spy."

Drethene surveyed her uncle, gave him a relaxed smile and said, "No, he's no spy. My uncle has always been mysterious, though."

"If you have such a strong connection to the Realm," Trem said, "why don't you look as out of place amongst the One People as we do?"

"A fine question, Trem. Not all descendants of the Realm stand out amongst the One People. At least one of your parents is descended from the Realm and still fits right in. There's purpose in the two of you shining through your unique appearances."

Trem recited,

*When the first are found,*
*Sing praise to heaven,*
*For they will be bound,*

# Tranquility

*To gather the seven.*

"Trem, for the first time, your ability to recite what you've read doesn't annoy me," Drethene said.

"I look forward to hearing him sing what he easily memorizes," Drithon said, smiling at his niece.

"Your family shares the same wit, I see," Trem said. "Why's there so much rhyme in this book?"

"Most of the prophets were minstrels who portrayed their messages through rhyming melodies. In addition, there's much more to the pages of both the *Prophecies* and the *Writ*. Drethene, may I have the *Prophecies*?"

Drithon opened to a random page and laid the book on his lap. He beckoned them closer, took the corner of a page between his thumb and forefinger, and rubbed the page between his fingers. Soon, deep blue smoke began to rise. There was a sizzling sound and finally, a pop, and the corner of the page divided.

Trem looked at Drethene. They'd overlooked a good deal of information if every page they read had actually been two stuck together.

Once Drithon separated the pages fully, their faces glowed in the radiance of what lay before them. Indeed, they'd missed something extraordinary during their first reading.

"These images are illuminations, created by scribes of the Realm," Drithon said. "It's believed if one hears the music, reads the words, and looks at the images, the intended meaning of these books will be well expressed."

Prior to this moment, Trem had seen only stained glass and the few paintings in the Hall. Here, gold, silver, and the deepest shades of blue, red, and purple formed something quite special. The details were clever and exact, as if the scribe had used a single hair to paint them.

This illumination showed a weeping owl in a nest, its wings stretched toward the ground. An owlet was falling from the tree toward a dark chasm, its wings chained to its body. In the chasm was a horrific creature, laughing, arms stretched up, awaiting the falling owlet. In the midnight blue sky were seven bright lights like huge stars, each a different color. A single ray shone down from each of them and touched the head of the distraught owl in the nest.

"It's about hope," Drethene said quietly. "It's very sad, but there's hope."

Drithon smiled at his niece, although tears stained his cheeks.

Trem flipped the page back to read the words preceding the illumination. "The prophecy cites nothing more than the loss of a young one to darkness. How did the scribe come up with this image?"

"There's a saying in the Realm," Drithon explained. "'Draw near to those closest to the truth, and your talents shall bear fruit sweeter than that of the Messengers.' Scribes and prophets, or Messengers of Truth, were inseparable. The scribes were inspired to create images to illuminate the meaning of the prophets' words. Many prophets didn't remember saying anything and had to read the words of the scribes, just like the rest of us. They appreciated the artwork as much as everyone else. That artwork, as is the case here, was often more definitive than the words. You might say, their fruit was sweeter than that of the Messengers."

"This image is so specific," Trem said. "What if the scribe is wrong and the prophecy unfolds differently? Everyone will be waiting to see this scenario and might miss the true fulfillment."

"I can tell you," Drithon said, "this prophecy is being fulfilled, and this image is very true to its unfolding."

Drithon wiped his eyes and closed the book. His tone made clear there would be neither further conversation about the meaning of the artwork nor its effect on him.

"Uncle, what you just said about prophets forgetting their own words reminds me of—"

"Doll," Drithon finished for Drethene. "Yes, I suspect she has prophetic blood flowing in her veins."

"I always called what she did 'soul searches,'" she said, sounding a little embarrassed.

"You're not incorrect. What Doll says isn't universal like the prophecies of the ancient Messengers of Truth. Her words are personal and meant for the one to whom she speaks."

"I wish I had a scribe to draw me an image of what she means."

"Doll gave her words to you. I have a notion the prophets, just like Doll, didn't remember what they said, because the words were never theirs to keep. Now the words are yours. Sharing them might help you gain understanding."

"I've been hearing her over and over again in my head. 'You will fulfill your calling, I know it! Do it with great care, for watchful eyes are not blind. All will walk in darkness until you can light their way.'"

"Her words aren't unclear, dear nieceling. I suspect you fear understanding them, for indeed, your calling is considerable, and those who watch are formidable."

Drithon put his arm around Drethene and patted Trem on the shoulder with his other hand. "If Doll reveals a 'soul search' to either of you again, I recommend you memorize well, as you've done, Drethene, and ponder."

Drithon released Trem and Drethene. "I want the two of you to experience the power of the *History and Prophecies* heard from the mouths of Realm folk. The two of you need to open your hearts to the Realm. These might help."

Drithon opened his hand, revealing two rings. Each held a glistening stone, shimmering impressively in the dim light of the jar. Drithon handed a ring to each of them. Drethene's had a turquoise stone, and Trem's stone was black.

"Is this ring made of wood?" Drethene asked.

"The texture and appearance seem wooden, but this is harder than any tree I've ever known," Trem said, examining his. Etched into each ring were images of creatures he'd never imagined.

"The carvings are tiny, yet so detailed," Drethene said. "The stones are glorious. Thank you, Uncle."

"The stones have belonged to you since before your birth," Drithon said. "They were born of the Realm and kept in the lands of your respective mortal ancestors. At the Great Council, they were surrendered to the deep pond in the center of the Valley of Hrithto. That night, the Lady dived to the pond's depths, retrieved all seven and has kept them ever since. Five more are still in the Realm. The rings were forged by the wood nymphs of the Realm in preparation for the fulfillment of prophecy."

Trem's lingering doubts made him frown at his ring.

"Trem, I ask a great deal of you, I know. To truly experience the Realm, you must already believe it exists. You need to believe before you see. I'll help you, but you must begin by trusting me."

"I welcome the help. I just hoped reading the *History and Prophecies* would clear everything up. Now you say I'm a part of fulfilling these predictions, which makes it harder to believe any of this is true."

"Don't try to understand. Even I don't comprehend everything written in those pages. Use them as a map. If you want to reach your destination, you must trust and follow the map's direction. Otherwise, you'll remain adrift."

Trem stared at his ring, feeling quite lost.

"Now might be the time to discuss Trem's experience in the bog," Drithon said.

"You never did tell me the whole story," Drethene said, furrowing her brows at Trem, who answered her with a helpless shrug.

Drithon smiled at their exchange. "You were drawn to a Flow, Trem, because of your innate connection to the Realm. Your fumbling about rattled through all the Flows, shaking those of us with access to them. After we regained our balance, there was great laughter and celebration."

Trem recited,

> *The ways are dark and still,*
> *Traveled by a meager few.*
> *No more young ones try the thrill*
> *Of pushing their way through.*
> *An abrupt and sudden shake*
> *Echoes after countless years.*
> *If any slept, they are awake,*
> *And join all Folk in cheers.*

"Your memory and ability to connect Prophecy and fulfillment will be a great service to you, Trem," Drithon said. "With us, you experienced your first Flow entry—a bit uncomfortable even in the company of an experienced navigator. Your solo foible knocked you backward both physically and in time. Ease will come with practice."

Trem looked at Drethene. "I'm running out of arguments, my friend. I don't know if it's because there's truth in this, or I'm just exhausted."

Drethene smiled. Trem drew closer to her.

"I'll make an effort to accept more and argue less, if," Trem said, "*if* you'll admit *Tranquility* isn't pure poison. You've fought against our ways as long as I've known you. I've been on the defensive. Can you expect me to change swiftly without my own fight?"

Drethene's smile faded. She looked to her uncle for help. He smiled and nodded his encouragement. She took a deep breath and thought for a moment.

"*Tranquility*," Drethene said, her voice shaking, "helped build a strong bond between our families."

Trem nodded his agreement.

Drethene cleared her throat. "It gave good direction when there was conflict. Our families were never harsh with one another. Instead, *Tranquility* allowed us to live in Peace, more like one big family than two neighbors."

Drethene took another deep breath. "Trem, my argument is mostly with the people who twist *Tranquility's* words. No, *Tranquility* isn't poison. The sickness is how it's manipulated by people. An apple is a good fruit, but people can still gather arsenic from the seeds."

Drethene stopped and looked at Trem hopefully.

"That's the best I'm going to get, isn't it?" Trem asked, looking at Drithon.

"I think so, Trem," Drithon said.

Drethene looked hurt until Trem smiled at her.

Trem looked at his ring, which he wore on the third finger of his right hand. Drethene wore hers on the same finger.

"Okay," Trem said. "What do we do with them?"

"Allow the rings to do what they're meant to," Drithon said.

All three stared at the rings as they glimmered with tiny points of light. Beams from every point in Trem's ring reached out and showered the surrounding darkness with a multitude of swirling stars. The blackness broke into scattering pieces. Or were they fleeing shadows? Drethene's ring serenaded them with pleasant tones and harmonies to match the myriad sparkles in her ring. This timeless place was not endless. There were walls made of stone hung with tapestries and extravagantly framed artwork.

Trem was drawn to one large chaotic painting. From a distance, splashes of color appeared haphazardly tossed upon the canvas. Upon closer examination, the painting comprised miniature images of countless human acts. The detail reminded him of the illumination. There were moments of kindness—a young woman feeding a feeble elderly man. Those of horror—a man eating the leg of a murdered woman. Those of disinterested souls—two lavishly dressed women laughing and strolling past a man dressed in rags, crawling and leaving a trail of blood. Those of love—a mother nursing a babe. Throughout the work, one image appeared repeatedly—a white unicorn. Wherever the creature was, its horn touched the ground and there was a pool of gold. Every image following the beautiful beast was delightful.

Trem stood in front of the painting, taking full advantage of the freedom of time in this place. His companions were engrossed in other wall hangings. There was no need to talk, since the song of Drethene's ring serenaded them.

Trem understood the tapestry better than he understood the windows of the Hall. Drethene's ring sang a wordless rhyme helping him remember.

Drethene was radiant with the joy of the painting she admired.

"I'm ready, Uncle."

Drethene and Drithon looked at Trem.

"Okay."

With the darkness abated, there was no need to force their way. The path they walked was clear. They simply entered the Realm.

Drethene looked disappointed. Trem guessed she must not have been able to see much more of the Realm than their last visit.

Trem could still see nothing. He was unsurprised and uncomfortable.

"Do not be discouraged, children," the Lady said. "It is far better to build your belief slowly with truth and answered questions than to have it be instantaneous and ill-founded."

Trem stared blindly—eyes wide and mouth agape. He couldn't see her, but with the gift of the ring came his ability to hear in the Realm.

Once he heard, he was taken aback just enough to crack the foundation of his disbelief and to allow him to see a bit. He could only see the Lady, as if the sun had burned through the fog just where she was.

Trem gathered himself. "Drethene, you really look like the Lady. I was wondering why she seemed familiar when I read about her. You must be related."

"Yes."

"So, you've got fairy blood."

"I do."

"And duck?"

"That would be loon."

"I guess your annoying laugh and your talents in the water all make sense now."

# tranquility

The Lady's red-eyed gaze was naturally intense, but Trem could feel the tenderness with which she looked at him. Trem added one color—red—to the short list of those he could see in the Realm.

"I'm sorry, my lady. I didn't mean to speak as if you weren't here."

Trem trembled in her presence and stared at his feet. Beautiful, tiny, red flowers surrounded him. He tried to move off those he stood upon but could find no place absent of them.

"They're hardier than clover, Trem," Drithon said, "and there's hardly a patch of open ground not covered in them. They're magnificent. Feel free to pick one."

Trem looked up at the Lady, who nodded her approval. Trem knelt and pulled upon a single bloom. He held the finest stem he'd seen on any plant. He pulled gently, so as not to tear too close to the flower. The stem continued to exit the earth, but the root held tight. Trem got to his feet. The stem displayed impressive length. Trem stood to his full height, his hand level with his nose. The roots of the strangely tall plant still remained in the ground. He raised his hand to eye level and drank in the beauty of the flower.

The plant trembled, and a tiny face peeked from between the petals. There were giggles, and four more minuscule heads popped out in succession to look at Trem. As the final tiny face emerged, she tumbled and landed straight in his eye.

"Again with the eye!" Trem cradled his injury with his free hand.

All disappeared except for one, who sang,

> *He shall return to them,*
> *The brother from afar,*
> *He'll pull the passage stem*
> *And find them as they are.*

"You see, Trem, your family traits run strong as well," Drithon said. "The Groundlings always speak in rhyme, and most of their words quote prophecy. You apparently have inherited the ability to memorize and recite, in addition to your propensity for cultivating the earth."

Trem held his relatives in his hand. They squinted in the light. Their hair was shockingly blond, and their eyes were all brilliant blue. Each embraced a finger of his hand.

"Wow, I think I was less shocked to find out Drethene is part waterfowl. I'm not exactly a small guy. How did … I mean, at some point someone this tiny had to … oh, forget it. Now the bird thing is really getting weird."

"The blood of the Realm is strong," the Lady said, clearly amused. "The One People have blended their mortal features. Still, some carry our ancient blood. The genealogy is immortal and different from your mortal understanding but not so shocking as you may think, Trem. Most importantly, the Sworn Seven emerging from the One People cannot be ignored."

"Of all the One People in Dale, Trem and I are the only ones who look different," Drethene said. "If the rest are scattered, how can we ever fulfill the prophecy and find them? We haven't even come of age. I can barely get a snack at Doll's without finding myself escorted home by a Watchman."

Drithon and the Lady exchanged glances.

"Prophecy will be upheld," the Lady said. "You will gather with the other five. We do not know how or when, but it will be done."

*Seven will unite,*
*Rings join gleaming bright,*
*The darkness they destroy,*
*To reestablish joy.*

The Lady reached out to Trem and Drethene, who approached her and offered their hands adorned with the rings. The Groundlings still clung to the fingers of Trem's other hand.

"Dear fledglings," the Lady said, "I will help as best I can to unite you with your five brethren. I sense the two of you sharing through the rings. Once all seven are united, you will be able to accomplish what you are destined to achieve."

She released Trem's hand and took both of Drethene's in hers. The intensity of her eyes deepened the meaning of her words.

"You must gather strength from the truth. There is great change awaiting you in Unemond. Accept this with courage, faith, and hope."

The Lady tucked Drethene's hair behind her ears, tilted her head as she stared in Drethene's eyes, and tenderly kissed her forehead before turning to Trem. She took his free hand in both of hers. The Groundlings held in his other hand regarded the Lady with admiration.

# tranquility

"Your doubt will continue, especially away from this place. You must return to your home and keep what you've learned here quiet in your heart. Feed this new knowledge, like a seed in your garden. Show the new life sprouting forth only to those who have shared the truth with you. They will help you cultivate a crop to feed many."

She released Trem's hands and spread her wings. Two fairies took hold of each wing and began to move her backwards into the pond. The Groundlings in Trem's hand released each of his fingers and jumped to their flower, which returned to ground level via its quickly retracting stem.

"Return to your land, and trust what happens there is right," the Lady said as she floated effortlessly in the water, folding her wings as her fairy helpers circled above her head.

She suddenly dived beneath the still waters without causing even the smallest ripple. This delighted the fairies, who darted along the water's surface in an apparently familiar game. The three companions watched the fairies swoop and reel their way out of sight.

"This is a fine beginning," Drithon said as he tapped his foot and slapped his leg to a rhythm unheard by Trem and Drethene.

# PART TWO

# CHAPTER EIGHT

The bells jingled. Doll looked up from the poultice she was applying to the burnt arm of the village baker. She wore her customer-ready smile, unable to see who entered due to the glare of the rising sun filling her windows. Once she recognized her newest visitor, her expression melted into a relieved and comfortable grin.

Doll washed her hands as Drithon sat down at the counter. She placed a cup of hot tea in front of him and returned to her patient.

"Remove the cloths tomorrow afternoon and begin to apply this three times a day," she said, handing a jar of pale yellow salve to the baker, who removed the cork and winced at the smell.

"I increase the potency for each return visit. I recommend shoulder-high gloves for removing large loaves from the oven."

"Thank you, Doll." The baker shoved the cork into the jar with the heel of his hand. "I'll visit the tannery first thing tomorrow morning."

Doll smiled as she patted the baker's uninjured arm. She shook her head a little as she watched him leave.

"This tea is lovely, Doll," Drithon said. "Something's familiar, but then again—"

"One cup is all you're getting, D.D. I enjoyed three cups one day last week and regretted them for three wakeful nights."

Doll scrubbed the area of her counter where she'd just treated the baker's arm.

"The tea came with a shipment of fonlond root from the Far Reaches," she said. "They love to mix leaves until they're not even certain what they're drinking."

Doll tossed her cloth in the bin on the floor and leaned on the counter in front of Drithon.

"Something is heavy on your heart, D.D., I know it. I, too, have been feeling a strange burden."

Doll brought her hand to her now tense brow, and the bells sounded on the door. She winced.

"Ah, Drithon, I'm glad to see you choosing early mornings over late nights. Taking my advice and keeping a tidy desk—mind you don't try too hard to impress me," Crouglan said, his mouth caught up in a smirk.

Yes, a true grin, nasty as could be.

"Grand Leader, I was lured by a cup of tea poured from a pot other than my own."

"Not quite a vice but getting close." Crouglan sat on the stool vacated by the baker. "I'll need to keep a closer eye on you, Drithon."

"Grand Leader, may I interest you in a cup?" Doll asked.

She had the pot and cup in hand, and her gracious smile back on her face.

"No, Doll, no time. I have but one question for you. The night before last, I assigned a Watchman to walk Drethene to the gate from your shop. A report must always be filed following any assignment, and I have yet to see one. I realize they're not the most social men, but I was wondering if you're familiar with the Watchmen of your neighborhood."

Doll worked to maintain a calm exterior as she fought the headache accompanying Crouglan's presence.

"The occasional Watchman stops in, Grand Leader, but as you know, they're difficult to distinguish from one another. I didn't recognize him. I wish I could help you."

"Very well." Crouglan stood up. "I guess the secretive manner of the Watchmen must occasionally hinder even my quest for information. I'd appreciate your questioning any Watchmen who enter your door about their duties that night. If you identify the one I seek, please recommend he see me as soon as possible."

"So be it, Leader Crouglan." Doll bowed her pounding head and avoided eye contact with Drithon.

"Drithon, I'll see you at noon. Too much of my time has been focused on your niece recently."

Crouglan walked out the door. After she made certain the leader was out of sight, Doll glared at Drithon.

"'Tidy desk?' Something's wrong, D.D., I know it! What's Crouglan talking about?"

"You're right, Doll. Crouglan caught me off guard yesterday morning, and I might've unintentionally cobbled in front of him."

Doll allowed Drithon to sweat under her silent glare.

"You remember what cobbling is, yes?" he said. "Kind of a funny name, really, since things might've been undone instead of put together."

Doll wasn't laughing.

"I'm hopeless when it comes to Drethene." Drithon planted his forehead in his upturned palms. "Crouglan began talking about her and a meeting in the Honor Room. I was doing my usual paper shuffle as he spoke, when suddenly there was hardly anything on my desk, and what was there was neatly in place. The last time I slipped up was our first autumn picnic. Remember? You held my hand, and every leaf on the ground returned to its rightful branch above us."

Doll shook her head in disbelief.

Drithon couldn't stop talking.

"I think Crouglan's sniffing around to see if I had anything to do with the missing Watchman paperwork. There's no reason for him to ask you to be his lookout. He spoke to you in front of me, to let me know he'll be watching. He's right, of course, because I was the one who walked Drethene to the wall that night. Those Watchman uniforms do stink. Anyway, I'm rusty, and reworking time is much messier in Unemond than in the Realm."

"Stop! Drithon, just stop talking before it gets any worse!"

Drithon obeyed.

"That man carries ill tidings," Doll said. "Recently, the closer he is, the worse I feel. The longer I'm in his presence, the more difficult it becomes to mask my discomfort."

Doll's head throbbed with pain and confusion.

"I witnessed Drethene feeling the pull of the Realm," Drithon said. "That discovery alone was well worth a bit of risk-taking, right?"

Doll did not agree. All she could do was shake her aching head.

The bells jingled, and Doll forced her smile back onto her face.

"Good morning, Trem," Doll said. "What brings you into town so early?"

"Good morning, Doll. My mother is hoping you have more syrup for stomach upset. My sister has worked herself into quite a spell over her latest parade of worries."

Trem sat next to Drithon.

"Absolutely, Trem. That's a staple on my shelf. I'll fix you a large bottle."

Doll disappeared into a back room.

"What brings you here, Drithon? Getting yourself all 'Dolled-up?'" Trem asked, very pleased with himself.

"Well, Trem, visiting and talking is one way to find out what a friend has been up to. But not everything is shared across the counter of the apothecary."

Trem smiled, hoping he was about to be the one to make Drithon confess the affection many suspected.

"For instance, I doubt she'd tell me she dances by the water in the dark." Drithon stood up. "I guess I could secretly follow her home to discover more."

Trem's smile sank into confusion, and the soundless "How" on his lips brought a smile to Drithon's face.

"The Lady instructed you to cultivate new life. Fill your heart with fresh wisdom, not old gossip."

Trem's confusion and surprise were laced with shame.

Drithon snatched Trem's cap from his head and ruffled his blond curls. He replaced the cap so it sat too low, covering Trem's eyes, and gave him a friendly shove in the shoulder.

Trem hid for a few moments under the safety of his cap.

Doll returned with the bottle of medicine.

"Remind your mother not to give her more than three tablespoons per day," Doll said. "We want your sister to feel better, not sleep for a week."

Trem was reconsidering Drithon's spy status. How many more secrets did this Flow-traveling, Realm-visiting, clumsy, nearsighted librarian hold? He adjusted his cap and turned his attention to Doll and his mission in her shop.

"A week, did you say? Ah, yes, I'll be certain to remind her."

Trem reached for the bottle, but Doll pulled it back.

"Okay, I promise to tell her the correct dosage."

Doll offered Trem the bottle and said, "You should plant ginger root and mint in your garden. They might save you a couple trips into town."

"Good suggestion, Doll. I think I'll be spending time with the herbs today to keep my mind occupied."

Trem took the bottle. Doll grabbed his hand and examined the ring on his middle finger. Trem looked at Drithon apologetically and received a raised eyebrow and a shake of the head in response.

"This would be a lovely time to enlighten me as to what's going on," Doll said.

She continued to examine the ring, keeping Trem's hand firmly in her grasp.

"Apparently, neither one of us is particularly good at going about our business covertly," Drithon said, looking at Trem's ring and its adoring audience. "Let's hope our blunders are in service to prophecy and not the recipe of our undoing."

Drithon leaned between Doll and Trem. With his ear hovering just above Trem's hand, and his face inches from Doll's, Drithon did his best to regain her attention.

He said loudly, "Drethene's been summoned to the Honor Room. There has been a recent surge in prophetic fulfillment. Doll, are you listening to me?"

Doll was staring, unblinking, through Drithon to where the ring sat on Trem's finger. Her lips were working, and her finger moved slowly toward the black stone. Drithon removed himself from between them, abandoning his useless attempt to distract her. As she touched the stone, her eyes closed, and a tear rolled down her cheek. She grabbed Trem by the shoulders and brought his face close to hers. Her eyes were now open, intense.

"You will protect her, I know it! You must help her, even in darkness, so she may light the way for others."

Doll stopped speaking but held fast to Trem. She still peered into his eyes.

Hesitant to turn his head but needing Drithon's guidance, Trem strained his eyes to look as far left as possible. Drithon signaled to wait a quiet moment.

Doll released her grip on Trem, blinked, stepped back, drew a long breath and said, "Anyone for bread and jam? It's early, I know it, but I'm famished."

Doll headed into her store room.

Drithon looked at Trem, who remained in an awkward position, as if Doll still had him in her grip.

# tranquility

"I'm sorry, Drithon. I'm worried sick about Drethene, and with this ring on my finger, I can, well, sense her. I know she's okay. On my own, I may be good at memorizing, but with the ring, I share her understanding and some of her self-confidence. Removing the ring makes me feel blind."

"She needs you too, Trem, I'm sure. I know you want to watch over her. However, I recommend you go home and stow the ring somewhere safe. Keep it hidden until we know the outcome of this afternoon in the Honor Room."

Crouglan rounded the corner past the apothecary and smiled. Quickly, his smile melted into a mediocre frown. He didn't want to bring attention to his unusual mood. Underneath that mask, he was almost giddy with anticipation.

He'd sniffed out the players in a threat to the Peace and the very fiber of *Tranquility*. His was an awesome responsibility, but success was near.

*Tranquility's* words rang in his ears. "To ensure a community of Peace, members must be similar in appearance, values, and abilities, so as to avoid conflict or bias between individuals."

He had to remove this malignant blemish from Dale—a girl whose mere appearance, not to mention her questionable values, disturbed the Peace. He'd be even more pleased to be done with her odd uncle, as well. If *Tranquility* didn't provide a clear plan, a new Defining Action might be in order. No matter his course, once he was successful, Crouglan would be even more well-regarded and respected in his leadership. His teachings of *Tranquility* would be neither questioned nor ignored.

Crouglan entered the Academy's main hall. He returned the bows of students with a proud inclination of his head. He walked up the rounded staircase and down the corridor toward his chambers. He entered his private sitting room and closed the door behind him. *Tranquility* lay on a reading table near the room's one window.

Crouglan was crossing the room when a sizzling sound stole his attention from the book. The volume and pitch increased, culminating in a loud *thunk*. The room in front of him disappeared in a sea of blackness. He spun around to escape through the door, and the same process unfolded again. The door, the walls, and the honors hanging on them were swallowed in nothingness. Crouglan felt panic rise in his throat as he stood alone in the dark. He could feel the smooth tile floor beneath his feet take on the unevenness of stones.

"What you do in the name of *Tranquility* is commendable. Feel my presence and power. With this strength leading you, your good work will spread beyond your imagining."

The voice came from everywhere at once. Searching for the source was futile. The following silence was even more frightening.

Feeling deaf and blind, Crouglan spoke to fill the maddening void. "I'm impressed with your obvious strength and command of this place. Show yourself so we may speak as equals."

Laughter rang out as if from a hundred souls, and Crouglan sank to his knees with his hands over his ears. As the hilarity diminished, he looked to the front and saw a tall, slender man with ivory skin. His long black hair was tied with a silver strand and covered one shoulder. His torso was naked, and his feet were bare. His pants were made of woven silver. Each arm wore six tight silver rings, the first just below his shoulders and the last at his wrists. A silver chain connected each ring along his arms, and a thicker chain ran across his chest between the two uppermost rings.

"Never will you be my equal. My offer of power is to accomplish our shared belief in an absolute adherence to the laws of *Tranquility*. I cannot rest until every obstacle in the way of perfect Peace is removed. You will help me, and I will enable you. You will be rewarded for success but will never obtain my full power."

The terrified Crouglan nodded in acceptance of what had been presented to him as inarguable fact.

"Very well," the stranger said. "I see you are not a dull man, and you acknowledge this choice is not yours. Your willingness reflects well upon your nature and our relationship. You need no power beyond your mortal intentions in the days ahead. I will be watching and will provide you only with what you need as you continue to make progress. You will be made a powerful man as long as you continue to serve our common interests."

Crouglan bowed low, and when he arose and opened his eyes, he stood in his well-lit sitting room. He blinked and noticed something shining on the floor. He picked up and examined a tiny link of silver chain. He watched, unable to react, as the metal sank beneath the skin of his hand. A chill ran through him, and he knew he'd never be alone again. He walked to the window, looked out on the world, and laughed.

# CHAPTER NINE

Drethene sat in the haunting quiet of the hall outside the Honor Room, flanked by her parents, awaiting her summons. The light shuffling of slippers caused the three of them to turn their heads as an Academy student rounded the corner. Based on the cream color of his oversized robes and the nervous intensity of his stride, he was a new student. He continually glanced at the scroll in his hand and occasionally in the direction he was going. He disappeared around the next corner, stumbled to a stop, and soon returned to stand in front of Drethene and her family.

The student's head was buried in his scroll as he chanted, "Your summons to the Honor Room must be confirmed. Please hand me the document summoning you to this place."

As soon as he finished, he stood tall, looking above Drethene's head, waiting with his hand outstretched.

Drethene placed the letter in his hand. He stowed the paper in his pocket and returned to his script.

"The reason for your summons will be revealed to you during your time in the Honor Room. Remain here until your escort arrives."

He placed the scroll under his arm, then resumed his purposeful glide down the corridor in the direction from which he'd originally appeared.

"Pleasant fellow," Drethene's father said, not lifting his head from the study of his fingernails.

Drethene had hoped his comment would lead to an exchange of smiles between them. Hers went unanswered.

Her mother patted Drethene's hand and said, "This might take a while, dear. I see no harm in walking this section of the corridor a bit. I think we'll be unable to miss the arrival of your escort."

Drethene stood with her mother and accepted her arm. They walked slowly.

"Ma, how angry is he?"

"Drethene, you know your father's tone always kept you children from crossing him."

Drethene nodded.

"That's just your father's way. There's rarely emotion connected. He is often serious but seldom angry."

"Oh, I don't know, Ma, I think he wasn't too pleased when I asked you both to read," Drethene looked around, remembering where they were, and whispered, "the book."

"You received an Honor Room summons, and your first response was a history lesson and a list of prophecies. Then you told us to read a book denser than *Tranquility*. We were given a lot to consider. Today, we sit with you in front of the Honor Room. You can't expect this to be the moment your father begins to chatter like a squirrel. Plus, he couldn't find *Tranquility* this morning. Let him be. He's here because he loves you. Nothing said or read can change that."

They'd reached the window at the end of the hall. They stood in silence looking over the red rooftops of town toward Hushed Pond, the mountains rising behind the water, and the long path home. The pale blue sky was covered with just enough clouds to catch the sun's rays and form them into hazy arms reaching for the ground.

"Drethene, I've worked my entire life to maintain the Peace. At this unlikely moment, I feel truly at ease. No matter what happens today, I know it's right. Thank you for sharing with us what you did."

She swallowed hard before continuing, "If I look at you, I'll cry, dear love. I'm proud to call you my daughter."

Drethene was not sharing her mother's emotional control. She held fast to her mother's arm and pushed her cheek into her soft yet strong shoulder. She shed tears of thanksgiving, love, and relief. Her mother caressed her cheek and kissed the top of her head.

"I've always known there must be more to a well-lived life than existing without conflict," Drethene said. "No rule book can conjure eternal peace. Do you think Pa understands as well as I think you do?"

"Drethene, I know you feel a sense of urgency, but you can't rush your father into accepting something so foreign to him, no matter how true. You've planted the seed. I embrace what you've shown me, Drethene, but instantly transforming the thinking of two parents may be too great an achievement, even for you."

Drethene and her mother returned to sit next to her father. The three were sitting quietly when they heard a loud clang from behind the immense bronze doors of the Honor Room. Three more clangs and a snap, which caused them all to jump, were followed by the ominous opening of the massive entryway. The portal led to a dimly lit hall, the width of the open doors. In front of each door, an academy student took his post and stood at attention—one dressed in pale blue, and the other in orange on the verge of red.

Footsteps approached from the dark depths. Drethene wished for Trem's ability to usher comforting words from the *Sacred Writ* or a prophecy. Nothing came to her. Frustration mixed with anxiety and anticipation didn't treat her stomach kindly. The footsteps grew louder. She began looking for an acceptable, but unfortunately nonexistent, place to be sick. She glanced toward the hall just in time to recognize Uncle Drithon walking toward them. She nearly ran to him, but he put his hands out to keep her from moving. He must have seen her green complexion, for he approached her, held her hands, and whispered in her ear.

*In places of darkness,*
*Imagined or true,*
*Keep peace in your heart,*
*And light will find you.*

Drethene closed her eyes and could almost hear the music of her ring, which was stowed in the satchel at her side. She knew peace didn't mean silence, and she used the memory of the ring's serenade to cleanse her heart of sickening worries. She opened her eyes and nodded to her uncle. He gave her hands one last squeeze before releasing them and turned to embrace his brother. Drethene's father welcomed the affection. She thought she saw a smile on his face and was certain there was a tear in his eye. Drithon kissed Drethene's mother on each cheek and squeezed her shoulders encouragingly.

"I am your escort. Follow me to the Honor Room. You are expected."

After giving his mother the medicine from Doll, Trem headed to his herb garden. With Drethene in the Honor Room, he could think of no better place to pass the time. He still needed a plant or two to cultivate.

# tranquility

The crunch of the leaves underfoot and the chill air reminded him fall planting was drawing to a close. His search for bog-loving mushrooms hadn't worked out well, so he'd decided to focus on something simpler. Doll had suggested ginger and mint. Mint was familiar and prolific.

Cropland butted up against the trees serving as their property's perimeter. Trem skirted the fields, searching for the plant's green textured leaves. In between the fading pest-repellant marigolds, hearty mint had flourished. Trem squatted with his back against a tree to dig up some herbs. He carefully placed a mint plant in his bucket, which he'd half filled with dirt, and stood to return to his garden.

He took a step and sensed movement in the woods. He looked more closely but saw nothing except the sun reflected in a tiny pond ebbing and flowing from its current state to nothing but a muddy hole for as long as he could remember. He drew closer and found the water perfectly still, providing a stunning reflection of the trees and sky. He almost believed the water to be the true place, and what hung above, the duplicate.

Trem bent over the water and saw himself even more clearly than he'd seen in his sister's bedside mirror. He raised his left hand and pushed his hair away from his eyes. He saw his own consternation as his reflection lifted not the mirror image, but its own left arm. Trem slowly lowered his hand. He raised his right arm, stopped at eye level, and quickly brought his hand to his side. Once again, his reflection was synchronized with his movement, but lifted the unexpected arm.

He leaned to his left, and his reflection bent in the opposite direction. Trem touched the water. He winced, certain he was inviting another eye poke. No fingers emerged. While Trem's hand created a ripple, his reflection's touch caused a hole. He drew his hand across the water. His reflection did the same, cutting a slit along the surface.

Trem put his hand in the middle of the opening and attempted to grab one watery side as if touching cloth. He drew his clenched hand closer to him, causing nothing but more surface disturbance. His reflection's hand pulled one side of the slit back, revealing a farm and woods exactly like the one by which Trem knelt. He lowered his head into the hole. His head rose from a pool on the other side, and Trem heard the thunder of hooves. Startled, he lost his balance, felt a rush of water, and found himself swimming in this other pond, much deeper than the one at home. He grabbed a branch and pulled himself to shore.

The approaching hooves grew louder. Trem looked in the direction of the sound and scrambled behind a tree to avoid the approaching beasts. One stopped for a drink from the pool.

Trem would've thought he was on his own farm, if it weren't for the unicorns.

Unicorns?

Trem searched for someone who might have been involved with, or at least understood, what just happened to him. And why was he perfectly dry after just emerging from a pond? The only person he saw was a small boy approaching from the lane.

"They're unicorns," the boy said.

"Yeah. I didn't think they were real."

"They exist. They're not nocturnal."

"Okay."

Trem studied the boy.

"By the way, who are you?" Trem asked.

"I have a rock," the boy said, digging in his pocket, and displaying an ordinary stone.

"Wow," Trem responded without much enthusiasm.

"You're rude!"

The insulted boy folded his arms and stomped a few paces away.

"I'm sorry. Can I get a closer look at that rock?"

The boy harrumphed.

"I used to collect rocks when I was your age," Trem said, approaching the boy.

"You were never my age."

The boy reluctantly opened his palm to reveal his treasure.

"What a nice-looking rock." Trem hesitated before speaking again. He pointed across the fields, needing something simple and certain to discuss. "That's my family's farm."

"No, my young man," the boy said. "Things are different in this place. Those who reside here aren't the One People."

Trem furrowed his brow at this response and the turn in the boy's personality, suddenly mature and informed.

"Ooh, a pretty flower," the boy said, skipping to a nearby tree. "Ooh, purple, my favorite color!"

Trem couldn't help but overstate his own enthusiasm about the flower. He stood wide-eyed and open-mouthed in response to the little one's similar look of amazement. As the boy examined the plant, Trem stared at him as if there might be some physical explanation for his bizarre shuffle in maturity.

"It looks just like one of the flowers on your ring, Trem."

"Hey, how did you know about my ring? And how do you know my name? Would you please tell me who you are?"

On the verge of either tears or a smile, the boy looked shocked by the tone of Trem's voice.

"I'm Klindyn, and she told me your name, and … What was your other question?"

Klindyn looked thoughtful and tapped his chin with his first finger. "Think, think, think. Oh, never mind."

"What do you have on your finger?" Trem asked.

"Oh, she gave me this when I visited the big pond," Klindyn said, twirling a ring much like Trem's but with a translucent, brown stone. "It's amber. Where's yours?"

"Drethene and I agreed not to wear them today. She can't risk hers being discovered, and if only one of us is wearing ours, that person feels terribly lonely."

Trem grinned at his willingness to share with Klindyn once he'd revealed his ring.

"She told me such connections would grow between those who have rings," Klindyn said, staring at his.

"So, you met the Lady. Did you read any books? Meet any long-lost family? Are you on board with this whole Sworn Seven thing?"

"You've been to the Realm, met the Lady, and emerged from a pond to be greeted by unicorns, and you're still doubting the legitimacy of who we are?"

Trem was speechless.

"You were led here by whatever force has brought me here for countless ages," Klindyn said. "I travel here through the hollow trunk of a tree. Whenever I return home, I'm sticky from head to toe. I think there's something in the tree sap keeping me from looking any older than I was the first time I came here."

"You don't live here?"

"No, I live in Unemond like you. I spend a lot of time here, which may be why the visit to the Realm and the revelation of the Sworn Seven were less shocking for me."

Klindyn's eyes shone with a childish brilliance.

"What should we do, Trem? Do you want to go for a walk? This place looks just like home, right? It is, but it isn't."

"I guess so."

Trem decided exploration might answer his questions and odd company was preferable to none. He was beginning to accept experience without immediate understanding was sometimes necessary. He was amazed by how Klindyn sounded like Drithon one moment and a four-year-old the next. Had this boy truly stumbled upon the key to endless youth?

"Let's follow the unicorns," Klindyn said. "They're my favorite."

Klindyn skipped through the woods. Trem followed. They took a path leading toward town. The unicorns traipsed ahead of them.

As they approached town, the road became busier. Children dressed in brightly colored clothing skipped past them, singing songs and laughing. Trem was fascinated by how very different they all looked from one another—long brown hair, short black hair, curly blond hair; eyes of all colors; noses of all sizes.

"I live by the sea," Klindyn said. He worked hard to keep stride with Trem, all the while examining his precious rock. "People come from across the sea to my town, so I see lots of people who look different."

"Am I gawking, or are you trying to make me feel better about my own appearance?"

"No. Light hair and eyes aren't bad. I've looked the way I do now for almost four hundred years. Or is it four thousand?"

Trem stopped to consider his companion. Klindyn had reddish hair made more vibrant when compared to his almost black eyes and dark skin. Were any of these traits of the Realm? Trem shook his head at his consideration of the Realm as a real source of heritage.

Klindyn continued walking, eventually turning around and doubling back.

"Oh, there you are," Klindyn said. "I was looking for you."

As Klindyn skipped toward him, Trem watched the boy with more fascination than he did the unicorns.

"She told me about you and Drethene, so I'll tell you about me. I live with my fourteenth, or is it one hundred and fourteenth, generation granddaughter, disguised as her son. Her oldest daughter is seven years old and will take her mother's place as my guardian when she comes of age. I've been a family heirloom all my life. Just as your village ignores your light eyes and hair, my family's little boy who never ages has no attention brought upon him."

Klindyn stopped in front of Trem, smiled up at him and said, "Well, come on! You want to see the town, don't you? I want to show you my sculptures."

The unicorns galloped playfully across the meadow and into the woods surrounding Hushed Pond. Klindyn led Trem to a tree not far from the path.

"Do you like it?" Klindyn gestured hopefully to the old pine.

"Are you able to make trees?" Trem's voice was an octave higher in reaction to Klindyn's return to boyishness.

"No, silly. Look at the sculptures."

Trem moved closer to the tree and noticed the branches were adorned with wood twisted and carved into fantastic shapes. Tiny wooden flowers seemed to swirl around the branch and turn into fish on their next go-around. These transformed into fairies, who flew around the branch and emerged as owls soaring through a starry night. Trem touched the wood, which was as hard as rock.

"Remind you of something?" Klindyn pointed at his ring, hand held high, his eyes diverted from Trem's to emphasize the covertness of his clue. "Oh my," Klindyn's eyes were frozen on something or someone behind the tree, and his voice was filled with surprise. "What are you doing here?"

Trem was hoping to see the Lady. He had questions for her, so he waited with great anticipation for her to show herself.

Slowly, carefully, and elegantly, a lone unicorn emerged. Her coat, mane, and even her hooves were pristine white. She had large, sad, amethyst eyes and a golden horn. She ignored Klindyn and slowly approached Trem.

"Do you have any idea how rare this is?" Klindyn whispered.

"My sense of what's rare, real, or imaginary isn't what it was a few days ago."

Trem was curious and strangely disappointed. A unicorn didn't hold answers but created new questions. At the same time, he was in awe of the lovely creature walking toward him. He was very used to horses, but this beast had a horn, a beautiful but potentially piercing weapon.

"Stay very still," Klindyn whispered.

"Thanks for the warning."

The unicorn came within a foot of Trem, looking straight into his eyes. Her horn pointed diagonally from her forehead, above Trem's head. Should she look down, he feared his face would be sliced in two.

Suddenly, she hung her head, causing both boys to jump. She was apparently accustomed to distancing her horn safely and caused Trem no harm. She nuzzled Trem's legs with the top of her head. When he didn't do what she wanted, she pushed harder until he had no choice but to sit.

She knelt beside him. Sitting next to the kneeling unicorn was much less intimidating than standing face to face with her. Trem allowed his breath to escape, and the unicorn nodded her approval. She touched her horn to Trem's palm and pushed toward him causing his fingers to curl around the horn. His hand became very hot, and he inhaled quickly. She continued to put pressure against his hand, but he was sure he could have pushed her away. Certain she was using a gentle force, the choice was his, and he chose to accept whatever was happening between them. She lay against his chest, and he patted her cheek with his other hand.

Silver tears fell from her eyes, and the emotion was so strong Trem wept with the beast. Klindyn cried into his hands at the beautifully sorrowful moment.

The unicorn gently lifted her head, and Trem's hands fell from her. She rose, as did he. He went to embrace her, but she shook her head and snorted, bowing instead. Trem returned the farewell bow. She galloped off in the direction of her herd.

"She loves you, Trem."

"Why?"

"This place is different. Love can be felt with great strength between two creatures simply because love is big. There are a lot of constraints in Unemond. Here, there aren't, so what I create when I'm here exists in ways its counterpart in Unemond can't. I don't understand how, but my creations exist in both places, just differently. They're much subtler and static in Unemond. Love is free to roam and grow as it's meant to in this place."

"Why was she sad?"

"I don't know. But a unicorn approaching a boy," Klindyn laughed, "and offering her horn? Something special just happened."

Trem and Klindyn looked at one another, and if Klindyn weren't small and young in appearance, Trem would've been certain he was looking into a pair of kind, wise, old eyes.

"I work in stone, too," Klindyn said. "I'll show you when we get to Dale."

They continued on and entered town, which was bustling in quite unfamiliar ways. Musicians were strolling the streets, playing stringed instruments and singing ballads. A puppeteer had set up a makeshift stage. His puppets were hitting each other on the head with magic wands, much to the delight of the children and adults gathered around. Artists were selling paintings displayed on easels. What stood out most was the laughter, frequent and true.

"I made those." Klindyn pointed at the huge stone lions flanking the library.

"They've been there as long as anyone in my family can remember," Trem said.

Klindyn pointed at a girl wearing a bright red hat with a feather sticking straight up. "Bet you've never seen them do this."

As the girl walked past the first sculpture, a huge paw whacked the hat off of her head. The girl, unhappy but not frightened, picked up the hat and tapped the lion's nose with it. The lion shrunk back, ashamed. The second lion roared as she passed him. One stern look from the girl, and he licked his paw and returned to his pose.

Trem knew this was not Unemond, but the lions, the laughter, the joy, all gave the town fresh life, which he quite liked. He thought he might rather stay in this Dale.

"So, you've been coming here an awfully long time," Trem said.

"Indeed."

"I grew up with that pond. Why haven't I been here before? If I had, I might've had an easier time believing all this Realm, magic ring, time-shifting stuff."

"Everyone's journey is different, ring or not. This Realm, magic ring, time-shifting stuff is happening to you now, and you're still struggling with belief. If you'd come here a year ago, would you have come back?"

Trem thought for a few moments.

"No. No, I wouldn't have. I would've thought I'd had a dream, or I was going insane. I would've avoided the pond for the rest of my life."

"Well, then, this is the right time for you to be here."

Trem watched Klindyn's eyes transform once again from those of a wise man to those of a curious child.

"Look at him!" Klindyn said, pointing over Trem's shoulder. "I've never seen anyone dressed like that."

A tall young man approached. He had long black hair, wore neither shirt nor shoes but brandished pants made of some sort of mesh.

Trem averted his gaze. He'd never seen anyone walking down the street so scantily clad. If this had been the Dale in which Trem lived, everyone would've ignored this man's indecency and allowed him to pass in peace. But this was not that Dale. Trem looked up as voices spoke and fingers pointed.

Trem tried to watch the lions instead, but they, too, were staring at this man.

"He's looking at us, Trem," Klindyn said in a small, frightened voice.

Trem felt Klindyn press against the back of his leg, peering from behind him.

"Hey, you're the one who knows this place. I should be hiding behind you."

Klindyn embraced Trem's leg. Trem shook his head and gave Klindyn's shoulder an unconvincing pat of reassurance.

The man's pants caught the sun, and Trem could see they were made of metal, most likely silver. He also had six rings, with chains connecting them, on each arm.

The man smiled. Hot pain seared Trem's finger where his ring ought to be.

"Klindyn," Trem whispered between clenched teeth, "keep your ring hidden."

The man stopped before Trem and said, "Trem, come with me. Your doubts are well founded. I will provide you with knowledge and power over your destiny."

"I don't think you should go with him," Klindyn said into the back of Trem's leg.

"Once again," Trem whispered, "your warning has already crossed my mind."

# tranquility

The man held out his hand to Trem.

"What's your name?" Trem asked as he fought against the pain in his finger.

A flash of anger passed over the man's face.

"Phovul."

Phovul was not pleased to see Trem's ringless finger and being questioned stoked his anger.

He remembered his master's words, "Let nothing but truth fall from your lips into my ears."

Phovul had squirmed when this command was given, amusing his master, who laughed and said, "Yes, yes, all your words will be true to me. There may be others who will hear falsehood from you. Should anyone else be powerful enough to question you directly, only truth may answer them."

Phovul had intended to maintain an overwhelming presence so mortals were too intimidated to ask questions. Apparently, Trem had a bit of fight in him.

The sound of galloping hooves distracted Phovul from his thoughts.

From behind Trem and his young companion came a herd of strong white unicorns. The most pristine specimen led the way. Trem faced the herd running full-force toward them. Everyone else in the street fled for the safety of buildings and alleyways. The lion statues pressed their chins to the ground and covered their heads with their paws.

Phovul was amused by Trem's confidence as the boy stood with one hand outstretched toward the oncoming unicorns and the other on the head of his small, trembling friend.

Phovul came to stand behind them, slowly raising his arms on either side of Trem.

The lead unicorn bent her head low as she approached.

Trem remained motionless, his hand still held out to her.

Phovul closed his eyes and turned his palms to face the unicorns. The earth trembled with the intensity of the galloping herd. Phovul released his power, and the ground quaked beneath them.

Phovul reveled in his strength as the earth before them began to crumble, allowing huge rocks to work their way to the surface. The first unicorn reached them in just enough time to shove her head under Trem's little traveling companion and toss him an impressive distance behind her as the rocks boiled up from the earth. The boy landed on the back of another steed. The unicorn immediately left the herd to take the frightened child to safety. Phovul suspected he had just lost an opportunity.

The lead unicorn nudged Trem to the side and scrambled to get to Phovul, her horn aimed at his heart. The rocks spewed upward, and she rose with them. She struggled to get down, not to escape but to plunge down the other side and put an end to Phovul. Unicorns, like their equine cousins, are no mountain goats. Her hooves slipped, and her legs gave way, breaking, and sending her tumbling backward to her herd circling the growing tower of rock.

Phovul and Trem were alone within the stone structure. The building had no roof, so there was ample light.

Phovul panted and sweated from the effort of creating their enclosure.

"Okay, Phovul," Trem was clearly working hard to maintain a false sense of calm. "What did you just do?"

"I am willing to share this knowledge with you, Trem. I think you will find it compelling and unquestionable."

"Is there a way out of here?" The pitch of Trem's voice confessed his anxiety.

"There will be, when we are ready to leave."

"I need to get out."

"Allow me."

A long hall appeared behind Phovul.

Trem's eyes were wild. Phovul smiled as he watched him calculate the probability of escape.

"If we are going to work well together," Phovul said, "we should walk together."

Trem made a mad dash for the hallway.

"Your ignorance does not serve you well," Phovul said calmly. "I had hoped to lead you by the hand, but the wrist is not far from it."

A silver bracelet appeared around Trem's wrist attached to a chain connected to a ring around Phovul's upper arm. Trem landed on his back, his arm yanked above his head by the taut links.

"Our time together will reveal your true potential," Phovul said, as Trem was dragged on the ground toward him by the retracting chain. "You will forgive my use of force to get you started on this road. You've followed many people down different paths leading only to more questions. I'm the last one you will follow. I will help you become the leader you were meant to be."

Once Trem lay in front of him, Phovul yanked him up until he stood. Phovul began walking toward the hall, knocking Trem to the floor once again. Phovul didn't stop but looked back to see Trem eventually scramble to his feet and follow, scraped and bruised.

"You've seen a few Flows," Phovul said. "Tedious and limited means of travel. From now on you will move about on my coattails, experiencing magnificent power. Our first destination together will be to visit mutual acquaintances who are gathering in the Honor Room."

Trem stumbled, and Phovul tugged the chain upward to keep him upright and moving.

"Here, catch." Phovul tossed a link in the air and turned to watch his power increase.

Trem instinctively reached to catch it with his free hand. He looked at the silver ring half submerged in his palm. Phovul kept Trem's other arm outstretched by the pull of the chain. Trem was about to bite at the link, but it disappeared into his hand.

Trem laughed. Not the joyful laughter heard in the streets of this Dale, but an uncontrollable dark and diseased chortle belched like a poisoned meal.

# CHAPTER TEN

The hall was long, and the smell of oil-soaked torches unsettled Drethene's stomach once again. The Honor Room was in one of the village's oldest pre-War buildings. Shadows of hooks and nails flickered in the torchlight like spastic inchworms. No one had bothered to pull out the metal bits once the paintings and tapestries were removed from the stone walls of the dank corridor.

The party came to a stop. Drethene wanted their march to continue. A few hundred miles more, and she might feel ready to face what was to come. Avoiding the inevitable, she examined the stone wall directly beside her. Between two torches, she could see the vague outline where a large painting had been, the ghost of its perimeter framed by slightly darker, smoke-tarnished stones.

"Drethene, this is where you must part ways with your parents," Drithon said.

Drethene turned toward his voice and jumped at the sight of two gold doors twice the size of the bronze ones they'd used to enter this hall. Her parents were equally captivated. There was no extravagant decoration, the gold appeared to be simply hammered. Upon closer inspection, that pounding had been the defacement of the doors. The occasional ghostly image of a unicorn head, drum, or dancer's torso could be discerned, but always severely disfigured by the hammer. Apparently, the Academy supported destructive expression instead of the creative sort.

Drethene smiled bravely as her parents embraced her. The two Academy students who'd accompanied them led her parents to another entrance. Drethene and her uncle stood together in front of the immense gold doors.

"Uncle—"

"I know no more than you, my nieceling. Keep heart. What happens beyond these doors is necessary to the fulfillment of prophecy."

His tone betrayed his anxiety. Drethene took strange comfort in knowing she was not alone in her fear.

Drithon took her hands in his and said,

*Once these words become truth, the brave journey begins,*
*The friend may be foe, and those feared become friends,*
*Undaunted, the travelers must persevere,*
*The journey itself may be dark and unclear,*
*Truth, love, and light in the end will appear.*

Drithon squeezed Drethene's hands encouragingly. She smiled a little, in thanks for the hope in the prophecy. He released her hands and picked up a wooden staff leaning against the wall. He knocked on the door with it seven times.

From behind the doors, they heard a small chorus of "Keep the Peace." Drethene was thankful the doors opened slowly, as this allowed her eyes to adjust from the dark hall to the brightness of the Honor Room.

"Jack rabbit!"

Drithon shouldered her. She was to remain silent until questioned.

Drethene kept her mouth quiet but open in awe. The overwhelming light source was a ceiling constructed entirely of glass. The walls were covered with paintings and tapestries depicting battles, ancient tales, and romance. Bejeweled swords, scabbards, and daggers hung in the narrow spaces between the works of art. Pedestals held statues of ancient creatures, warriors, and dancers. Cases held stringed instruments, drums, and horns.

Drethene remembered reading the Honor Room was once the repository for forbidden ancient artifacts. She'd always wondered what had kept them from being destroyed. She now felt confident the presence of these objects, considered disgraceful expressions of folly and ego whose mere existence could disrupt the Peace, was an excellent source of controlling most visitors to the Honor Room through fear and discomfiture.

Instead, Drethene was inspired. Those who'd created these treasures had been bestowed their abilities as a gift. They understood hoarding their talent would be the equivalent of a fruitful farmer refusing to share his grain. They channeled their energies into these creations to be shared with the world.

She hoped whatever she'd do or create would honor her ancestors and inspire others to search for their talents. She was encouraged by words of the *Sacred Writ*.

*A gift that's been given must always be shared,*
*Not one in this world can claim it as theirs,*
*With each individual's traits it is paired,*
*Forging grace, love, and glory not to be ensnared.*

Wise, comforting words. Maybe, somehow, Trem had shared his gift of recollection with her. Upon thinking of his name, her finger burned where her ring should be. There was a raw, red circle around her finger. She tested it. *Trem?* The burning sensation increased and the angry area on her skin visibly pulsed and deepened in color. Was something wrong?

"Who takes us from our good work and seats us in this gathering?" asked an anonymous voice.

"Drethene Bidalind," Drithon responded.

Drethene jumped at the sound of her surname. Last names were used only in the most formal occasions as verification of one's identity. Otherwise, they were avoided, directing familial allegiance to the One People.

A wide corridor split the sea of pedestals, allowing Drethene to see a portion of the Council seated at the far end of the room. Her view was suddenly blocked by billowing midnight-blue fabric worn by a senior student of the Academy. He was tall and slim, his dark brown hair was almost straight, and his skin was slightly milkier than most of the One People. He glided up the corridor with purpose and none of the nervousness exhibited by the younger student who'd greeted them in the hall. He looked directly at Drethene. She raised her chin and met his gaze as a challenge.

"Are you called Drethene Bidalind?"

"I am."

"Is it your concern that gathers the Council?"

The mixing of words gnawed at Drethene. She had plenty of concerns, but the Council would be the last group of people she'd gather to deal with them. She closed her eyes, desperate to let her defensive thoughts spill from her lips. She understood the ritual and these questions were testing her temperament, not verifying why they were all there. Following a few deep breaths, she said, "Yes."

"Are you prepared to answer truthfully the questions posed by the Council?"

"I am."

"Are you prepared to fulfill all actions requested by the Council based upon the synthesis of their recommendations in response to your answers?"

Drethene looked at her uncle, who continued facing forward to avoid the *you've-got-to-be-kidding-me* look on her face. He was right—no good could come of eye contact in this situation.

A few more deep breaths were followed by, "I am."

"Drethene Bidalind, your honor gathers us here. May these proceedings guide you down a tranquil path leading you to Keep the Peace."

"Keep the Peace!" echoed from the Council members and through the Academy students.

The Questioner studied Drethene for a moment, an eyebrow raised, before bowing slightly. Drethene returned the bow. The blue robe grazed her skirts as he pivoted to lead her down the aisle. She followed, full of thanks for her uncle's footsteps following hers.

They arrived at the Council Table. The Questioner performed a militaristic right turn and made his way to the only empty seat. He sat and attempted nonchalance as he shimmied his lanky legs under the table. Apparently, the Council included a student representative.

Drithon was at Drethene's side. They both faced the Council which was made up of seven leaders from across the land of the One People. They wore gold-trimmed gray robes. Small gray caps adorned each of their heads. Thickly braided golden ropes hung from these caps on either side of their heads, and a tassel at each end rested below their shoulders. For a moment, Drethene was amused at how these ropes, representing prestige and wisdom, resembled the braids of young flaxen-haired maidens from stories of long ago.

The screech of chair legs against the floor returned her focus to her present situation. A student was pulling another chair beside the table. Every Council member had a copy of *Tranquility* open in front of him. Each book was opened to a different page, evidenced by the thickness of paper on either side of the binding. Fear for her life was briefly replaced by fear of boredom as she hoped she wouldn't be the recipient of seven lectures describing her law-breaking history.

"Our advisor, Drithon Bidalind, will now join us at the Table," a Council member commanded.

Drithon obeyed, taking his seat at the end of the table.

"Drethene Bidalind," Crouglan said. "I doubt anyone who learned of your summons here today was greatly surprised. Why is that?"

Drethene didn't expect her first question to require a confession as an answer. She'd hoped to be asked for a confirmation of lineage or date of birth.

Drethene reminded herself what was about to happen had to be so, to make right what was now wrong. That was the key. There was right and wrong. Wrongdoing couldn't be bred or indoctrinated out of them. Each individual must make the conscious choice to do what is right.

"Grand Leader, I'm different. Is anyone ever surprised when the one who receives sidelong glances and is the subject of whispered conversations is brought before the Council for questioning?"

The sounds of shifting weight and shuffling papers filled the room. The Questioner struck his knee hard on the bottom of the table, evidenced not only by the sound of the impact, but by how he bit his lip. Drithon's head was bowed. He was rubbing his forehead with one hand, and thumbing papers with the other. Drethene couldn't tell if he was hiding a smirk or a grimace.

Crouglan said, "Be reminded, Drethene Bidalind, *statements* answer questions. Should we find allowing you a question appropriate during this session, we'll inform you."

Crouglan scribbled as he spoke and nodded to his neighbor when he'd finished. Crouglan strained his eyes to look at Drethene without lifting his head.

"Drethene, you're about to come of age," the next Council member stated. "Have you considered an appropriate celebration?"

Drethene tried not to focus on her tender finger. She took a moment to scan the faces of those gathered in search of comfort and encouragement. She easily located her mother's smile. They'd spent many evenings by the fire, sipping tea and discussing Drethene's dreams for her coming of age.

"My talents are in research—my passions are reading and exploration. I'm thankful for my opportunities in the library. I hope to come of age by expanding my strengths in service to the One People."

Every Council member fervently scribbled in agreement. Drithon stopped rubbing his head and grinned. The Questioner's brow was raised again.

Drethene was pleased. She'd maintained truthfulness without prematurely revealing her intentions. Then she frowned as she caressed her increasingly sore middle finger.

A sickly grin crept up Crouglan's face. He stopped writing to look at Drethene.

Drithon rose slightly from his seat in response to the turn in his niece's demeanor. He looked at Crouglan, whose snickering did nothing to comfort him. He perused the faces of the other Council members, who were too busy writing and nodding at one another to notice the odd energy entering the room.

Total darkness, however, couldn't be ignored. The brilliance of the Honor Room was blotted out with an inky black, causing Council members to gasp and many in the audience to scream. The light returned as quickly as it had gone, and all eyes turned to the odd pair walking up the aisle.

Drithon's stomach sank. He'd expected to see Phovul, eventually, and he'd anticipated a trying reunion no matter the time or place. Having Trem in the mix was a surprise he could have done without.

Perthin, the Questioner, who was surely on the path to a Council seat, turned his attention back to Drethene and rose from his seat as she whimpered and seemingly clutched her belly.

Drithon saw what she did and knew better. She was reaching for her satchel.

"No, Drethene! Not yet!" Drithon yelled.

Drethene looked at her uncle, then at the pair walking toward her.

"Trem," Drethene asked, "what are you doing—"

"She has something pretty in her bag, I've been told," Phovul said. "Let her show it off. Girls like to do that."

"So, Phovul, he's let out your leash," Drithon said, walking toward the chain-clad man.

"Have you met my new friend?" Phovul said, with a mock gesture of polite introduction.

Trem shared Crouglan's expression. Their eyes were wide, blinking rhythmically and simultaneously. Their smiles were reminiscent of someone in extreme pain trying to convince loved ones they're fine.

"Young boys and old men," Drithon said. "These are your conquests? I see nothing pretty on your fingers. Are things not going as planned?"

Drithon was hoping Trem had listened well and didn't have the ring when he ran into Phovul. Based on Phovul's reddened face and glaring eyes, not all was lost.

"Leader Crouglan," said a gruff-voiced Council member, "where are your Watchmen? How did these men enter the Honor Room?"

Crouglan slowly faced his colleague. His blinking was too frequent and steady, his smile sickening.

"Never before have the Watchmen or the Honor Room been faced with the evil now in our presence," Drithon answered, seeing Crouglan was overwhelmed by the presence of his master. "This same evil has permeated more than the walls surrounding us."

Avoiding certain mayhem, Drithon chose not to reveal Crouglan's allegiance.

The Council members, unhinged by Drithon's cautious words, all began talking. Phovul's annoyance at the commotion and delay threw Crouglan into action.

"Fellow Council members," Crouglan said with troubling calmness. "These are my guests. Don't hinder their purpose. They're here to rid us of our main problem this morning."

The fire no longer raged under Phovul's skin. Instead, he looked pleased with Crouglan and ready for action.

"So, you're here for a big catch, eh?" Drithon asked. "Ah, well, harpooning a whale is quite different from wallowing in the shallows and scooping up tadpoles, my boy."

"Do not call me that," Phovul said through clenched teeth.

"What? Has your master given you a pet name you prefer?"

Phovul looked away from Drithon without responding.

"Drithon, how do you know this man?" the gruff-sounding Council member growled. "Crouglan, have you lost your mind? Why'd you invite this chain-clad—"

"I need quiet," Phovul said.

# tranquility

Phovul closed his eyes, and Drithon moved as near him as he dared, not wanting to be shut out. A shiver went through Phovul's body, and his fair skin turned a paler shade. He grasped his hands in front of him, pulled them into his middle, and crouched down to the floor. Indentations the shape of large chains appeared all over his skin as he grimaced under the strain of the power he held. His head snapped up, his eyes wide as he released the energy at the stones underfoot.

The room shook as thick rock walls erupted from the floor. Screams echoed as people were sent tumbling down hills of rubble where tile floors and benches once had been. As the four walls grew taller, Drithon, Trem, Phovul, Crouglan, and Drethene were now quarantined. They could no longer hear the panicked yells of those outside the fearful prison.

Drithon looked up as he heard a familiar voice screaming in chorus with others being carried skyward by the growing walls.

"Ma!" Drethene cried.

"Oh, please, no," Drithon whispered.

The crush of the glass was followed by the silence of the victims. Trem's smile faded for a moment.

"Fight him, Trem," Drithon said.

Drethene fell to her knees and wailed, breaking the weakened ceiling. Crackling and tinkling accompanied the echoes of Drethene's grieving call. Large plates of glass spun toward the floor, many shattering against the rock walls. Trem walked toward Drethene in a shower of glass shards.

"Oh, Trem. My ma!" Drethene said, reaching for his embrace and protection from falling glass.

Drithon spoke loudly, "Drethene, Trem isn't your friend right now. It's time to use the gift of your people."

Drithon turned to find Phovul watching Drethene with a mix of anger, anxiety, and a splash of something like empathy.

"Resurrecting tough memories, my boy?" Drithon said.

"Quickly, Trem," Phovul hissed.

The slime of Phovul's voice quickened Drethene's movements. She'd streamlined the access to her satchel and easily slipped the ring on her finger. Trem was in the room, yet without his ring—she felt his absence, and the emptiness was overwhelming. Drethene's confusion and sadness were clearly smothering her senses and her ability to use the ring.

"Think of your ma, Drethene," her uncle called.

Drethene obeyed and allowed grief to take over. The ring joined in her emotion and emanated mournful tones, waking the musical instruments trapped within Phovul's walls. The large drums intoned slow, deep rumbles. The thickest strings of the fiddles tall and small joined their percussive brothers with their dark droning. The horns tilted upward and sang a sorrowful fanfare. The reeds wailed, and Phovul's one mistake in the construction of his tower undid his plan.

Drethene looked up as the harmonies filled the tower and rose to escape through the opening once sealed by glass. Phovul tried to contain the sounds with a ceiling of rock. The vibrations, full of passion and strength, crumbled the stone before his creation could take shape.

The music caressed the walls, absorbing the blood of Drethene's mother and the others who'd met a similar end. The slow, roiling tones mixed with crimson blood. Drethene watched sound enter the sky like weightless lava.

The birds of the air joined their voices in the funeral dirge. They darted around, and under the musical stream, caught red on their backs and wings and flew off.

Drethene looked at Trem, who simply stood and stared at her.

Phovul chained Trem and dragged him through the corridor he'd created as an escape.

Once they were gone, Drethene looked at her uncle, who watched Phovul's exit with a mix of sadness and approval.

As Drithon approached Drethene, the light in the room dimmed. Drethene looked up at what appeared to be the flat underbelly of a cloud but was actually an immense, silvery blanket. Carried by a hundred blackbirds, the gleaming, diaphanous material was being lowered over the survivors of the tragic day.

Drethene's grief stole her ability to speak—she merely looked at her uncle for explanation.

"This is a Peace Quilt, sewn in the Realm," Drithon said, "made of the essence of loved ones who have passed to comfort mourners of the newly departed."

Ten meters from the floor, the birds released their grip and returned to the sky in single file, creating a swirling vortex toward the heavens. At what appeared to be a predetermined height, each bird went its separate way. From the ground, the birds appeared as black droplets released from a spinning, ink-soaked lasso. The quilt danced down to cover everyone in the Honor Room. As Drethene was draped in the unearthly material, she felt the embrace of her grandmother who'd passed away years ago. She could smell her perfume and feel her cool, soft skin. She was also comforted by her grandfather's stranglehold of a hug from behind her.

Then she heard the familiar voice of the Lady say, "Drethene, your mother has gained immortality because she embraced what you shared with her. She will find her place in Valndana. Now you know what every member of the One People needs to experience. They tried to be one with each other in their own world, but mortals are on a journey to join with all others for eternity. They will live in peace and be one with each other only after they have traveled their right path and have departed the mortal world, just as your mother has done."

Drethene smiled through her tears. Sweet snapshot memories of her mother flashed past her eyes. Thoughts of the remainder of her life, devoid of her mother's presence, sank her deep in a thick, black mire. She trembled and found breathing difficult. Primal, guttural moans erupted from her as she clenched her middle and rocked herself. The lonely rocking reiterated her mother's absence. The quilt, filled with familial love, wrapped her in a soothing embrace. The countless emotions left Drethene numb.

The Lady's voice returned, "Few, yet immense, have been the steps of your journey thus far. This Peace Quilt is to comfort all who mourn this day. It is of the Realm and will overwhelm the unbelieving One People. Those touched by the fabric will sleep and then awaken with no memory of this afternoon's events. The destruction cannot be reversed or ignored. The One People will blame you, youngling, if they were in this room or not, if they remember the destruction or not. Even in their ignorance and misguided blame, we give them comfort. Remember this act of grace when you must decide how best to use the power given to you. Have courage, stay strong, and be faithful."

The shouting quieted and everyone fell asleep. The quilt melted away into a silvery liquid that quietly destroyed Phovul's walls and disappeared into the floor. Drethene joined the others and slept.

Drethene felt herself gently lifted. Her head lay against a strong shoulder. Her eyes opened slightly, and she saw nothing but deep blue fabric. She heard men arguing. Paralyzed with fatigue and grief, she had no choice but to endure being wrestled from her cradle of comfort.

She was thrown over someone's shoulder. Her head dangled and her stomach was pushed against a sharp shoulder and the edge of her satchel. She surrendered to exhaustion.

# CHAPTER ELEVEN

Crouglan had the prisoner's cart parked outside his window before sunrise so he could enjoy Drethene's last hours in Dale. Yesterday afternoon, following the Honor Room debacle, he'd called a special Gathering to explain the girl's crimes to the One People. The news had created the stir he desired. He announced there was to be no gossip in the Hall. Instead, he gave permission for discussion and expression of concerns at the cart. The phrase "take it to the cart" soon became a common response to an unwanted complaint or accusation.

Gossiping and the spreading of rumors were strictly forbidden by *Tranquility*, but Crouglan allowed this morning's liberties as an appropriate recompense to the crime of murder. The cart would take away the criminal along with the ill will, allowing the One People of Dale to return to an even more peaceful life. He had a corps of Watchmen distantly surrounding the cart. Passers-by were comfortable doing and saying what they dared. Crouglan had instructed the Watchmen to exercise leniency regarding acceptable public treatment of prisoners—all part of meting out just punishment for Drethene's deeds.

"Do you think she's really in there?" a woman asked her friend.

Sholvon, owner of the cart, eavesdropped on the small crowd gathered around his charge in the morning sun.

"I was told so. They're getting the horses ready to hitch, and we'll finally be rid of her."

"I heard fire spewed from her eyes in the Honor Room," a man said. "She always tried to hide them, but I'd seen those red rings in her eyes. I always knew they were evil."

Those gathered backed away, squinting at the cart as if they expected plumes of fire to spray out of the cracks between the wall boards.

"To think she killed sweet Zivasa. How did a wonderful woman raise such a wicked girl?" the man's wife asked.

"The girl's motherless now," the man said. "This is fitting. Horror should have no mother."

"I heard she's possessed. The demon left her body, and together, they destroyed the Honor Room," another man said. "Good riddance!"

He picked up a stick and threw it at the cart.

Others followed suit and threw whatever they could find. The Watchmen did nothing.

"Enough, enough!" said Sholvon, from behind the mob. "That's my cart and my prisoner, and both need to make it to my destination, or I don't earn my living."

The crowd might not otherwise have given way, but the horses he led were tall, thick-legged, and strong. Snorting and trying hard to peer past their blinders, the steeds were agitated by their master's displeasure.

"Is she in there?" a small boy asked.

"I certainly hope so," Sholvon replied. "There are gaps in the wood you can see through. I'll check."

He walked toward the cart. The boy's curiosity made him follow.

Sholvon stopped and acted as if he were trying to look without getting too close. The boy stood next to him, squinting at the spaces between boards.

"Did you see a flash of red?" Sholvon whispered.

"No," the boy said, moving a little closer. "Where?"

Sholvon pointed.

"Right, there. Why, she's looking at you!"

He turned quickly on the boy, leaned down close to his face and whispered, "Be careful. You heard what she did to her own mother!"

The boy screamed and took flight. His parents ran after him, and the crowd dispersed.

Sholvon approached the cart.

"You okay in there?" he asked through a crack in the door.

"I guess," responded the sniffling Drethene.

"I don't know what you did, young lady. I gathered the part about your ma from what was being said by those folks. We transport many prisoners, but we're no judges. I just want to make that known."

"Okay." After a short pause, Drethene added an uncertain, "Thanks."

# CHAPTER TWELVE

Since he'd lost his family three days ago, Drethene's father hadn't moved beyond the main room of his house. The bedrooms were too personal, and his emotions too taut. This morning, he'd awoken in a chair in front of the now extinguished fire. He faced the cold hearth and finally came close to shedding his tears. He'd cared for that fire like a living thing created by his wife's hands. Now the embers too had grown cold.

He still clenched the unopened letter he'd found in the cupboard atop the soup bowls. "Juznyn Bidalind" scrolled across the envelope in her handwriting. They'd used their full names when addressing one another as an expression of heightened affection. Now that the fire had died, he needed to read her words to feel her presence.

My Dear Husband,

So, you've found this letter, and I'm gone. I write this knowing our daughter's day in the Honor Room will be life-changing. After reading the *Sacred Writ*, I fell asleep with questions whirling through my mind. Until we had our beautiful daughter, I never questioned *Tranquility*. As Drethene grew up, I answered her questions and defended our ways.

Last night, my dreams were like none I've ever had. I woke up early and refreshed. My mind was quiet. One truth stood out clearly. Drethene wouldn't be returning home after the Honor Room. I prepared to do the same and began to write.

I believe in her and in what she's revealed to us. I can't return to a life of *Tranquility*. I'll be gone if she is.

Please know my love for you is strong and true. If I'm able, I'll return to you. Under whatever circumstances you read this letter, all that's happened is right. Please open your heart to that truth, as I know we'll be together again.

In faith and hope,

Zivasa Bidalind

P.S. I know you were looking for *Tranquility* before we left for town. Well, I hope you've been enjoying the stew I prepared for dinner. The words ruling our life together kindled a lovely flame beneath the pot. Please forgive me.

Juznyn folded the letter, tucked the paper in the envelope, and glared at the ashes beneath the pot. "It was a good fire, dear wife. I forgive you only for being the quicker one to the flames with that wretched book."

Without revealing his true intent to his family, he'd searched for *Tranquility* to destroy every page as a display of his faith and trust in their daughter and what she'd shared with them. Reading the letter and knowing the fate of the missing tome didn't accomplish what he'd hoped, though. His tears held fast, unwilling to escape and provide him the grieving his heart craved.

He heard the sound of heavy boots on the steps outside his front door.

Juznyn quickly tucked Zivasa's letter in between the pages of the *Sacred Writ*, which he placed in his satchel.

"Bidalind, are you in there? There's work to be done."

Juznyn opened the door, faced Tomus, and said, "Good morning, neighbor."

"You'd better be crying now or done with it," Trem's father said. "'Shed tears for two days following a tragic loss. Those closest to a deceased person must lead all others in returning to normalcy following a death. Public grieving rekindles strong emotions in others, inciting a breakdown of the Peace.'"

"Thank you for the reminder."

Tomus studied his friend's face as he handed Juznyn a covered bowl. Juznyn welcomed him into his house with a nod.

"'The One People must enforce the words of *Tranquility* with one another ensuring none fall short of their promise and duty,'" Tomus said.

Juznyn closed the door and motioned for Tomus to have a seat at the empty table.

He faced his friend, took a deep breath, and began, "Methinks we're in for some grand changes—"

"Methinks?" Tomus interrupted. He remained in an uncomfortable half-seated position, his hands clenching the edge of the table. "Methinks? I know you're grappling with an incredible loss but reverting to the old tongue is a slap in the face of *Tranquility*. I'm your friend. I'll help you through this, but there's only so much even I can do without calling a Discussion, and we both know where that'll inevitably lead."

Juznyn placed the bowl on the table, removed the lid, and was distracted by the fragrant steam of oatmeal with warm fruit and nuts. His desire to keep the fire blazing had him eating overcooked stew for a couple days.

"I could use your help," Juznyn said. "I need your friendship, your work ethic, and also your confidentiality."

Tomus sat heavily in his chair. "If I agree to such an absurd request, what am I to expect to hear? You're arming yourself, burning *Tranquility*, and beginning a new life?"

Juznyn had ladled some of Thleana's porridge into a smaller bowl and was about to eat a spoonful. With the spoon dripping before his lips, he watched his friend take note of the bulge on his hip under his shirt. Tomus squinted at the naked mantle where *Tranquility* had always resided and studied the cold embers under the stew pot.

Tomus stood up as slowly as Juznyn placed the spoon back in the bowl.

"Tomus, hear me. We've both experienced unthinkable loss this week. Something is changing in our world, and the leaders will attempt to make the unfamiliar go away in the name of *Tranquility*, an impossible feat."

Juznyn placed his hand on his friend's shoulder before Tomus could take a step toward the door. Juznyn spoke to the back of his head.

"I haven't wept. I can't. Losing my wife and my daughter in one day is too much. I need time. *Tranquility* doesn't allow time for healing. There's much necessary for mortal existence *Tranquility* doesn't allow. The One People are hardly alive. We need more than sustenance and peace. My daughter always knew this. Her passionate desire to understand more than we were ever taught, and this disaster, finally opened the eyes of her stubborn old Pa."

Tomus looked at Juznyn. "I'll continue to teach my children, not the other way around. Drethene always had a strong will, and as we learned the other day, an evil one. She's affected you, neighbor. I need to remove myself from your presence to collect my thoughts as to how I must conduct myself to keep the Peace."

"How'll you continue to teach your children, Tomus? You can't teach a child who's disappeared or one who is quite irrational."

The two men looked at each other, jaws set, minds whirling, hearts breaking.

A startling knock at the door was followed by unsettling words.

"Arguments are rare and forbidden. Allow my entrance to eradicate the pestilence in the lives of two men held in high esteem as keepers of the Peace."

The neighbors glared at one another and each silently mouthed, "This is your doing."

Juznyn gestured toward the door and said, low and quiet, "You're closer."

Tomus's eyes squinted. "It's your door."

Juznyn growled, and Tomus stepped aside. The two men nodded to each other as was the custom when one gives way, and Juznyn approached the door. Everything in his life had been predictable. He shook with a fear he'd never before experienced. His senses were edgy. The metal of the lock sparkled from his wife's polishing. Termite damage had churned the wood allowing him to smell the pine as keenly as when he'd cut the panels years ago. The handle felt frigid in his grasp as he prepared to allow this next uncertainty into his home. The weight of the knife at his side provided little comfort. He'd wielded it successfully at a loaf of stale bread, the extent of his combat experience.

Juznyn pulled open the door to discover a tall, hooded figure standing unusually close and filling the entryway with his height and flowing robes. Juznyn stepped back and clumsily grabbed for the shirt-covered hilt of his weapon.

"Self-defense won't be necessary," the stranger said. "If I intended to be forceful, you'd have to be much defter."

The man walked into the house as Juznyn continued his backward gait. Tomus had moved to the far side of the table.

The man sat down, uninvited, and kept his head covered, another impropriety. The neighbors stayed still, silent, and uncertain. Juznyn could request he depart in light of his rude behavior and for causing them unsettled feelings, a breach in *Tranquility* doctrine. Yet he was filled with curiosity, and that tinge of anxiety was giving him a keenness and sharpness of senses not altogether reprehensible.

"Might I offer you a drink?" Juznyn asked, deciding to forgive his visitor's transgressions and welcoming whatever he brought to this day.

The stranger shot a faceless glance at his host, who met his hidden eyes with confidence.

"Much better," the stranger said. "Stand strong in the face of uncertainty, as there will be plenty in the days ahead. If you shrink back and attempt to defend yourself from every new and frightening happenstance, you will learn nothing and never move forward."

Juznyn looked at Tomus, who shrugged.

"How about that drink?" Juznyn asked, trying out his perseverance. He believed he saw a smile beneath the hood.

"Very well, I'll have tea," the man replied.

Juznyn reluctantly removed the stew pot from the hearth, swept the ashes, and prepared a fresh fire for tea. He considered collecting the ashes in a tin but decided ridding himself of the relic was a more meaningful tribute to a new beginning.

Tomus remained standing, and the stranger still sat in silence.

"Tomus," Juznyn said, startling his friend. "Fetch cups and spoons. You know your way around here."

Tomus looked at the stranger. The hood nodded, and Tomus obeyed the command, muttering to himself about *Tranquility*, taking orders from neighbors, and "methinks."

The stranger watched Tomus, allowing Juznyn to seat himself next to him without notice. Discovering Juznyn close at his side, the newcomer jumped. Juznyn smiled.

"I'm most interested," Juznyn said, "in how you plan to 'eradicate the pestilence.'"

Tomus had returned to the table and noisily placed down a tray, eliciting another jump from the stranger whose hood slipped, revealing his identity.

"I know you, boy," Juznyn proclaimed. "You questioned my daughter in the Honor Room. You're making your way to a seat on the Council, if I'm not mistaken. Perthin, I believe. Is this some bizarre rite of initiation?"

Perthin shook his head causing the hood to fall down his back.

"I act on my own. Intimidation was the best plan I could conjure to get me inside quickly and convince anyone within earshot I was here to uphold *Tranquility*. I apologize. And as for my future with the Council, well, a few days ago, you would've been correct about my path. Recent occurrences have altered my course significantly."

The kettle whistled, and Juznyn fixed tea. He put a cup and spoon in front of each of his guests and finally, himself.

"I want to help Drethene," Perthin said. "Until I heal, I beg your assistance."

Perthin revealed his hands—two mangled, bloody specimens. The neighbors winced.

Tomus filled a bowl with water from the pitcher on the stand. Juznyn retrieved cloths of various size for washing and binding.

"What happened to you, son?" Tomus asked.

"I made choices in the Honor Room leading to my being detained. The only way to freedom was first releasing my hands. The One People are not experts in prisoner restraint but breaking free was not easy."

"After the Honor Room, I was confused," Juznyn said, placing the cloths next to the bowl in front of Perthin and taking his seat beside him. "My brother had to control himself and not steal Drethene away from the mayhem. If he had, he also would've been treated like a criminal. He still has his place at the Academy, where he can be most helpful to her. I know as well as the rest of Dale she's being transported from the village. But do you know any more?"

"I tried to save Drethene," Perthin's voice was full of apology. "As you know, there was great confusion in the Honor Room. No one could remember what had happened, as if we'd all fallen asleep and forgotten the last few hours of our lives. I saw Drethene lying on the floor, and shadows of memories of what had just happened flickered in my mind. She looked helpless, so I picked her up. I had her in my arms, sir, but my attempt didn't go unnoticed. Watchmen took her exhausted body from me, and I haven't seen her since. I was quickly and rather painfully admonished for my actions."

Tomus said, "No member of the One People, especially Council members, would bring physical harm to anyone. I don't believe this tale."

"Then what I tell you next will definitely challenge your sense of reality. Crouglan Bonhyn administered my punishment. Once Drethene was taken from me, I was still confused and too dismayed to find my own escape. I saw many from the Council pushing themselves up from the floor or discovering themselves still seated but slumped over the table. They appeared to be as disoriented as I was. Crouglan suddenly loomed in front of me, seething with anger. He accused me of breaching *Tranquility* and ultimately, depriving him of his prize.

"He was spitting in his fury. I asked what prize I stole from him. Blinded by his wrath, he said, 'The girl was mine!' He never touched me, but I was overcome by pain and then darkness. When I awoke, I was propped up against a wall outside the hold, wearing chains. The only benefit of his attack was the awakening of memories of what had passed in the Honor Room. Please understand, I don't treasure these memories but am glad to know what happened, or I might not have had the fortitude to break free."

Tomus looked dumbfounded.

"The restraints were shoddy and locked imperfectly enough for me to force my hands out, but not without causing myself a good deal of damage. Once I was free, I sneaked down the hall while the guards fumbled with the cell door lock. They were unaccustomed to having a prisoner, therefore they focused fully on the prison. Tears streamed down my face. Not screaming in agony took immense effort. Lifting my arms up and covering my head with my hood took all my strength. The destruction of the Honor Room created a great enough frenzy I was able to simply leave the Academy and walk out of town."

Juznyn's emotional barricade crumbled, and he sobbed into the cloths he'd brought for Perthin's hands. He blew his nose and said, "Perthin, you did rescue my daughter. You brought the Council's attention upon her before Crouglan could snatch her up. Better the Watchmen and their protocol than Crouglan and unknown evil. No matter how sad and horrific that day in the Honor Room was, what occurred was right."

A new flood of tears escaped Juznyn as he heard his wife's words fall from his lips. Tomus walked around the table and placed his hand on his friend's shoulder.

Juznyn grabbed his hand and said, "I'm glad you're here."

"I'm glad you finally weep, neighbor, still I fear your accomplishment is ill-gotten. This boy has escaped captivity and needs help. Of course, he comes to a man weak from the loss of his family. How easy. And from the looks of you, he was right to try to convince us evil has permeated the hierarchy of our people and we must stand strong against them. You play with our emotions, young Perthin, and I'll not allow your lies to separate me from what I know is true and right."

"Know this, sir," Perthin said. "I was a student of the Academy and the Questioner of the Honor Room. Not only was I about to graduate, but I was to be one of the youngest members of the Council. I forfeited those opportunities, and almost lost my life, because I picked up a girl from the floor of a disaster. I don't regret trying to help her. I respected Drethene's strength from the moment I met her. Most people melt into tears or literally collapse under my gaze, their fear in the Honor Room is so great. Her knowledge and faith shone bright."

Tomus remained silent, looking unconvinced.

"She impressed me with her resolve in front of the Council," Perthin continued. "I admired her responses to their questions. She didn't have a chance to answer many, but I believe most Council members would've been interested in hearing more from her. When the stranger entered, I suddenly wanted to protect her. He wanted to stop what I wanted to continue. I want to know her."

"If you'd listened to her, Tomus," Juznyn said, his pride and faith in his daughter strengthening him, "instead of passing judgment on her every action, you might just have experienced the truth and joy in what she knows."

"Enough," Tomus said, drying Perthin's hands and wrapping them in fresh cloths. "Besides needing bandages and a safe place to heal, why are you here, boy?"

"I want to help Drethene," Perthin repeated. "I thought her home might be a good place to start."

Tall Perthin looked ostrich-like as he was forced by his useless hands, now well-bandaged and cradled on his lap, to bend his head to his cup and slurp his tea. Juznyn smirked and caught Tomus's eye. Tomus merely shook his head and added sugar to his own tea.

"Crouglan will want to keep my escape quiet. If he shows he's displeased with me, questions will be asked. He'll create a benign story to excuse my sudden absence. I'm sure he'll convince everyone this was my choice. If I had just one trusted confidante within the Academy, I'd be able to contact faithful friends and gather more help from inside those walls."

"Well then, Perthin," Juznyn said, "you've come to the right house. My brother's choice to maintain his place at the Academy will indeed help Drethene. We must go to him, but first, join me in finally eating this delicious breakfast Tomus brought. We need more than tea to begin this day."

# CHAPTER THIRTEEN

Doll had stopped walking. The cool hints of autumn in the morning breeze chilled her. The walk from town had been long and brisk, and the resulting sweat lay cold on her skin. She knocked lightly on the door. Although she'd been asked to come, she still felt as if she were trespassing. Actually, she intended to intrude beyond her invitation, and this was unsettling her honest soul, adding a few more beads of sweat to her skin.

She'd volunteered herself into this situation. She was already making a delivery to Taelmai. Logically, she could also retrieve something of Trem's from the house. This sounded right when Drithon said it. After all, the item would be given to the rightful owner, and he was a member of the household. She'd convinced herself this truly was not thievery.

She wanted to abandon the plan. She'd included written directions for each remedy in her cache. Leaving the box near the door would provide all the family needed. She stooped to put down her burden, prepared to walk away as soon as she stood up, but the door opened.

"Doll, thank you for coming," Thleana said. "Let me take the box from you. Come in, come in. I have tea and biscuits and no one to join me. My husband is visiting our widower neighbor, Trem has been missing for three days, and Taelmai's in a state of shock. For my own sanity, please be my company for a while."

Doll's anxious thoughts quieted in favor of comforting her friend. She followed Tomus's wife inside and sat at the table. Thleana poured tea and took biscuits from the oven.

"Is Taelmai talking?" Doll asked.

"Oh, Doll, she is, but it's all nonsense. She swears she saw Trem disappear into a pond, a puddle really, near our fields. That pool has always been a mystery and a good meal for her imaginings."

Thleana put jam and cream in small metal dishes. She placed these, and a wooden bowl filled with honey, in front of Doll.

"Anyway, no one can disappear into that tiny shallow. The rest of her story is about a little boy emerging from the water and some madness about unicorn horns. Her mind isn't right, Doll. I can't find my son. I can't lose my daughter too."

Doll placed her hand on her friend's arm. "Thleana, I'm no doctor, but I'm happy to talk to her."

"Thank you. I realize the good doctor has more pressing issues in town. The horror of the Honor Room hasn't hit me beyond poor Zivasa. At least Drethene's gone. I've always known she'd bring us pain, but I never imagined something like this."

Doll breathed deeply. Thleana was hurting. She'd lost her best friend, her son was missing, her daughter appeared to be losing her mind, and her husband was busy tending to their mourning neighbor, leaving her with no company but her own dark thoughts. Thleana's sole sense of relief was not hers alone. Drethene was an easy and obvious scapegoat for the shocked and hurting citizens of Dale. Righting that wrong was not Doll's calling today.

"Shall I go to Taelmai?" Doll asked.

"Yes. I will stay here. She's frustrated with me, as I refuse to listen to her rambling, and she'll speak of nothing else."

"I'll take her some of your delicious tea and biscuits."

Thleana smiled for the first time since Doll had arrived. "Yes, they're her favorite, and she hasn't eaten much. If you can get her to begin making sense and to eat something, I'll be most grateful. Do be careful of your success, as I may just call upon you next time, even if the doctor's available."

The two women enjoyed the fleeting reprieve of a shared smile and a quiet laugh.

Doll picked up the tray and walked to Taelmai's bedroom.

The door was ajar. Doll put her lips to the opening and said, "Taelmai, it's Doll. May I come in?"

"Oh, yes, please do."

Doll was impressed by the energy in her voice. She entered the room and was taken aback to discover a well-groomed, fully-dressed Taelmai busily packing a satchel.

"Hi Taelmai, you look well. What are you doing?"

"I'm going to help my brother."

"Oh, my. How?"

"Do you want me to tell you the truth, or do I need to create a story you'll believe?"

"I'll take the truth. You might be surprised by what I believe."

Taelmai stopped her packing and looked at Doll. "I need you to promise me something."

"Okay."

"Nothing from your box has or will find its way into the tea or biscuits."

"Taelmai, I promise."

Doll placed the tray on Taelmai's dressing table and handed her a biscuit. Taelmai did something extraordinary. She took the biscuit from Doll's hand and took a bite. She didn't avoid the spots where Doll's fingers had been or pull the biscuits apart to search for foreign particles and undercooked sections. Something big enough had happened to squash her fear of contamination and food poisoning.

"The day of Drethene's Honor Room visit, I followed my brother into the fields," Taelmai began.

She'd just finished licking jam from her finger. Typically, she'd have been holding the biscuit in a cloth to avoid contact between her food and her potentially pestilence-covered hand.

"He was worried about Drethene, and I was worried about both of them, and about myself too, of course. Trem was fascinated by this small pool of water. Suddenly, he fell in. I ran to help him out, but he was gone. There was nothing in the pond. I sat beside the still water and cried. Either my brother had mysteriously disappeared, or I'd finally lost my mind."

Taelmai shook her head, remembering the emotion, and took a huge bite of a biscuit and swig of tea. Apparently, her fear of choking had subsided as well.

"I calmed down and moved closer to the water. I've heard of quicksand and thought maybe he'd sunk beneath the bottom of the pool. I lay near the edge and pushed my hand into the silt. I inched closer to reach a deeper section.

"Suddenly, a hand grabbed mine. I pulled back with all my might, hoping it was my brother. Instead, out tumbled a little boy, right on top of me."

Taelmai shuddered while wringing her hands.

"He frowned and said, 'What was that for?' I think my shocked expression scared him a bit, and he said, 'Never mind.' He asked if I was looking for Trem. I nodded yes while wiping off my hand. I didn't know where he was from, and you never know what disease a stranger may carry. Plus, we don't know what symptoms to watch for, and we may have no resistance—"

"Taelmai, what happened with the little boy?"

Taelmai smirked at Doll and told her the story the boy had shared about him and Trem in the altered Dale, including his rescue by the unicorns, and the death of the one who had communed with Trem.

"Finally, the other unicorns surrounded their fallen friend, and the boy, Klindyn, joined them. They touched their horns to the dead unicorn's and bade Klindyn place his hand there as well. Through this union, he was told, 'Evil took your friend and ended the days of our sister. A loved one must force our sister's horn into the place where evil entered your friend. He will return to you, and her death will not be for naught.'

"I told him this was all impossible and couldn't have happened in the five minutes between my losing Trem and finding Klindyn. He responded, 'I've had to accept a very different view on time' and went on to describe his family. He lost me when he said he was his granddaughter's son. He explained he'd made a hilt and scabbard to protect the horn and the one who used it. I told him Trem was my brother. He handed me this."

Taelmai produced the gift from her satchel. The dagger's hilt and scabbard were made of the same stuff as Trem's ring, for which Doll still needed to search. The intricate carvings illustrated running unicorns and rocks erupting from the ground. Taelmai pulled the hilt from the scabbard, and a brilliant gold horn emerged, smooth and reflective as a mirror. The base was as wide as the hilt, and the tip was needle sharp.

Doll was drawn to the weapon, but Taelmai returned the horn to the scabbard and then to her satchel.

"I'm going to find Trem and help him," Taelmai repeated and returned to her packing.

"Did you show the dagger to your mother?"

"Of course not. Although it would prove the truth of my story, my parents would confiscate it as a threat to my safety. I need the dagger to help my brother. I just don't know where to find him."

"I know someone who can help you. He's an avid traveler and has been places and seen things I sometimes still find hard to believe. Your quest sounds just right for him."

"He sounds perfect, but my greatest challenge may be escaping this house."

"This isn't what I expected to be doing today, but I'll help you. Before I do, I need your help, Taelmai. Your brother has a special ring I suspect is still at home. Does he have a spot where he might've stashed it?"

Taelmai smiled wryly. "I spend more time in this house than all of my family combined. I know everyone's hiding places."

Taelmai put her satchel over her shoulder and opened the door. She motioned for Doll to follow. They easily entered Trem's room without notice. His bedchamber was simply furnished—there was a bed in one corner, a desk near the window, and a small wardrobe near the door. *Tranquility* rested in the middle of the desk. Taelmai pushed the book to one side and revealed what appeared to be an empty inkwell. Taelmai hooked her finger through the hole and pulled forward. A tiny drawer slid silently toward her—inside was a small leather pouch. Doll gestured to Taelmai to remove the pouch, which she did. Doll opened the small sack's bunched neck, peeked inside, nodded to Taelmai, and pulled the pouch strings closed.

They quickly returned to Taelmai's room. Once inside, Doll reached for Taelmai's satchel. Taelmai tightened her grip.

"You must trust me. I want to do my small part in helping Trem," Doll said.

Taelmai hesitated.

"If you carry this bag, your ma will be suspicious. I was carrying a huge box when I arrived. She wouldn't have noticed if there was or was not a satchel on my hip."

Taelmai put the little pouch in the satchel, tucked in two bottles and a tin of tea, and handed the bag to Doll. Apparently, Taelmai was not entirely cured of her health anxieties. They left her room arm in arm and walked the short hall to the main room of the house.

"Taelmai, you look so well," her mother said, looking pleased.

"I always feel better dressed and clean," Doll said. "So, I suggested the same for Taelmai, along with a long walk in the fresh air."

"By all means," Thleana said, "take all day if you wish."

Doll hoped Taelmai was as strong as she looked. They walked out the door. Doll quickened their pace and gave Taelmai another encouraging pat on the arm.

# tranquility

"Phovul, you are trying my patience. Your power over two is acceptable. Returning here without a third is not."

From the darkness, ice-cold claws touched the back of Phovul's neck and caressed his long hair from underneath, grabbing hold of the ends of his tresses and yanking Phovul's head back.

"Listen well. I want more success from you. I don't trust you can control your charges when you are away from them. Keep the boy close and restrained. I can feel how he pulls away from you. He is strong and will be useful to me. You must learn to control him. Continue to give the leader his freedom. He is doing my work by his own nature. Watch him closely and pull him back if he strays, but I think he won't."

Phovul's head was released. He gasped for air, and tears of pain streamed down his cheeks.

"The chains you fear are nothing compared to my plans for your eternal existence should you fail me."

The voice surprised Phovul, as its source was suddenly nose-to-nose with him. He could smell the foul breath and feel the moist warmth, yet there was nothing but darkness before his eyes. His neck and scalp still ached.

"There will be no more mistakes, master."

Phovul's voice shook, and the tears continued with the thought of what could be even worse than a return to bondage.

"Go back to your pets and gather more, quickly and quietly."

The voice was whispering in his left ear. Phovul turned his head, always in pursuit of a glimpse of the source, no matter how foul. Two icy claws cupped his face, nearly piercing his skin.

"I am tempted to scar you permanently, but your beauty may still win me more power. Use this gift, Phovul. No more grand entrances. They don't impress me. They only make me suspicious of your intentions. You don't want me to begin doubting your motives, Phovul. Use subtlety and quiet power to win your next captive. Prove your worth to me, and my anger may subside."

Phovul's head was thrown back and struck the stone wall. The wicked gift of unconsciousness overcame him, useful for dark dreams of how to win his master's favor or at least, how to lose his attention.

# CHAPTER FOURTEEN

*By land they're separated,*
*All so different from their kin.*
*So long they have awaited,*
*A connection from within.*
*They sense the others' presence,*
*When they wear gifts of the Realm,*
*Unlocked immortal essence,*
*Powers not before beheld.*

Drithon had gone without sleep for three nights, thanks to a tea from Doll and a knot in his stomach. He studied prophecy to preserve, at least, a hope-based connection to his niece. He maintained his status as librarian by taking full advantage of the confused state of the Council and returning to the Academy as soon as Juznyn was reasonably settled at home.

Drithon supplied library space and resources to the Council, whose members were most grateful. Even if Crouglan had tried to get rid of him, Drithon made himself too valuable to their recovery plan to be dismissed.

Drithon knew he needed time in the Academy to gather friends and to prepare. He'd always known as prophecy unfolded, and the Sworn began to assemble, he'd have to relinquish his role as Drethene's protector. Staying put allowed him to keep his eye on Crouglan and gained him the confidence of the Council.

After reading this most recent passage, he fell asleep with a smile on his face, seated upright in his chair.

The sudden, loud ringing of a bell startled him, causing him to tip back in his chair, perform a remarkable backward somersault, and somehow land on his feet. Once he recovered from the surprise of being upright and in the sudden company of friends, he bowed to his clapping and laughing audience of two.

"D.D., I see even in dark times, you maintain your endearing qualities," Doll said as she stepped toward Drithon to straighten his glasses and smooth his robe.

"I'm pleased to entertain the woman who just interrupted my first nap since I began sipping her latest tea." Drithon affectionately squeezed her shoulders.

"Here's your key and your bell."

"You keep the key."

Taelmai stared at the floor.

Drithon added wood to the fire and water to the kettle.

"Taelmai, how wonderful to see you here," Drithon said. "What brings you into town?"

"I need to find my brother, so I can help him."

"Trem's in trouble, Taelmai."

"I know, and I can help. Finding him is the challenge."

"Well, now, this is working out nicely. If you and Doll brought more than your sense of humor with you today, I think I may know how to find Trem and Drethene."

"Indeed," Doll said, "Our visit has more ring to it than your silly old bell."

Doll handed the satchel to Taelmai, who revealed the contents of the leather pouch.

"Now we have something to work with!" Drithon said, snapping his fingers.

As he reached for the ring, the kettle began to hiss, reminding Drithon he still had to prepare his teapot and find cups and spoons. He was frozen, arm outstretched, eyes darting between the ring and his tea service.

"D.D., you're a ridiculous man." Doll grabbed the ring from Taelmai's hand and slapped it into Drithon's. "I'll fix the tea and find us lunch."

Drethene yawned and stretched. She toppled over as the cart rounded a bend in the road. This brought reality crashing into the slowly lifting fog of sleep. Her heart raced, her mouth was dry, and her empty stomach lurched as she opened her eyes.

Two slits created by the poorly hung door added late afternoon light to the clouds of road dirt suspended within the cart. Before her nap, she'd wondered what section of Unemond they were racing through and just managed to get a look out one of the openings. The beating her temple had taken from the bumps and jerks of the cart as she peered through the gap had cut her curiosity short.

Drethene sat in the center of the cart, her arms wrapped around her knees and her head bowed. Travel had been a dream of hers. Two days in a cart was spoiling the adventure she had imagined. She wished to be in her father's arms. His embrace was now as impossible to receive as her mother's. She wouldn't blame her father if he were as pleased as the rest of Dale to see her gone.

The cart came to a stop. The horses needed water, food, and rest. Drethene and her escorts could stretch their legs.

They'd been traveling day and night, changing horses at various points. Sholvon and Sneafan, the couple in charge of this efficient transport, took turns driving and sleeping. They weren't from Dale, and they were kind to Drethene.

Their coffin-like sleep chamber was directly behind the seat of the cart, and Drethene had overheard their conversations as one bade the other to sleep well.

"Those Dale folks can't be right about this sad girl. What devil would mourn the death of its victim with the tears she sheds?"

"I don't like not knowing where we're going. I feel like a child on a treasure hunt, picking up directions to our next stop at every resting point. In all my years, I've never heard of such a thing."

"You saw the torches in Dale. An unnatural death took place there. She must've done something horrible, but I just can't imagine this polite, thankful girl doing anything of the sort, no matter how strange she looks."

Drethene was not the typical passenger of the Horse Force, as the husband and wife were known. *Tranquility* didn't allow for corporal punishment. When serious offenses occurred, the guilty were sent far away, quickly. The Horse Force ensured this speedy deportation, keeping teams of horses available along every major route for rapid changes and almost nonstop trips. On this journey, the pair took decent breaks.

"Halloo, Drethene! Time to come out. We'll have a good stretch and a bite to eat here and enjoy the salt air."

Sholvon struggled with the rusty bolt, the door shook and swung open. Drethene shielded her eyes from the sun. The large sky was uninterrupted by the hills and trees of home. She took a few deep breaths and coughed and sneezed the road dirt out of her nose and throat. An unfamiliar odor filled the open air. Drethene wrinkled her nose.

Sholvon chuckled and said, "Your first experience with the sea, eh? You'll find it an exhilarating fragrance with time."

Drethene's eyes adjusted to the light, and her nose accepted the briny scent. She stepped onto the dirt road. On one side, there were scrubby brush and small prickly plants covered with red bulbous growths. On the other side were sandy hills spotted with sparse grass.

Drethene reached her arms toward the brilliance above, shuddering with delight at her ability to move about freely.

"You spoke of the sea, Sholvon. I'd love to see so much water."

"Let's walk between the dunes." Sholvon handed her a piece of bread and a hunk of cheese. "I don't think you'll have trouble spotting an ocean."

Drethene was pleasantly surprised by how soft the dry sand felt. She was used to the silty bottom of a pond and expected this coarse-looking sand to feel as gritty as the paper her father used to smooth the edges of his woodwork.

As she continued through the dunes, eating her lunch, the roar of the ocean became louder. Although her legs felt better, she walked more hesitantly. She was not sure how close she was to this powerful water. The dunes ended, and Drethene was greeted by an impressive expanse of beach as far as she could see to either side of her. The distance between her and the ocean was no more than the breadth of her farm's largest bean field. The endless water was the turquoise color of the stone in her ring.

"We'll rest here," Sneafan said as she lay back against the dune, her eyes closing as soon as she was fully reclined. "Be certain you can always see us and return here within an hour's time. We shall reach our final destination before tomorrow's sunrise."

Sholvon sat next to his wife with a grunt and a long groan of pleasure as he stretched his back against the soft sand.

"We'll be watching you," he said, his eyes also closed.

Drethene walked as close as she dared to the crashing water. She was honored to be treated as royalty by such a majestic body constantly bowing and prostrating before her. She smiled and curtsied in return to the frequent waves until she felt familiar with the movement of the sea. She felt embarrassed as she remembered her audience of two. She looked behind her and saw they weren't watching her but were facing each other.

She couldn't tell if they were engaged in quiet conversation or deep sleep. She was too drawn to the water to walk back to check. She'd assume they were keeping a close eye on her.

She walked along the water's edge not noticing the moon in the sky until she spied its reflection following her in the wet sand. She headed back, and unsuccessfully attempted to outrun the moon's terrestrial twin.

Breathless from her race, Drethene stopped running. Walking had a way of making her mind work, as if gears were connected from her legs to her brain. Following the tragedy in the Honor Room, she'd been isolated. She longed for her uncle's wisdom to help her understand what had happened. Putting the ring on her finger had stopped the wall's growth, although not soon enough. Wearing the gift of the Realm now caused a crushing weight of solitude, reminding her Trem did not have his, but she endured the discomfort in the hope of avoiding any more tragedies.

Drethene walked away from the water and sat in dry sand. Since her time in the Honor Room, she'd been shuffled around a great deal, but thankfully, no one had removed her cloak. Her satchel still hid beneath, and she retrieved the *Sacred Writ*. Soothed by this place, she decided to accept the final stretch of this journey as a new beginning and to celebrate by reading the final paragraph.

*The people of Unemond could not remember a time without war. There were those who felt they were no more than the trampled grass between fighting beasts. As the warriors succeeded in fighting and killing, they failed to remember the reason for battle. The violent desire to win had supplanted the passionate upholding of beliefs. War's end was forced by exhaustion and lack of purpose. Sadly, the love and joy needed for lasting harmony were never planted in the ravaged fields. Today, the people of Unemond are quiet and free from battle, but still lack the passion and intention lost by their ancestors. Not until they look beyond themselves will the promise of true peace be revealed to them.*

Drethene shut the book, envisioning her mother as a trampled blade of grass in the start of a new wave of war. Drethene prayed the Lady was right, and her mother was living in the true peace for which she'd always striven.

A particularly loud crash of sea water sent foam to touch Drethene's toes and soak the end of her skirt. The water was warmer than she expected.

# tranquility

As the waves receded, bubbles balanced on the wet sand. Drethene lifted one with her toe. The orb refused to pop. She placed it back on the sand. Another round of sea foam came forth and returned to the ocean, having delivered a new bevy of bubbles. The one she'd touched, along with its original companions, had grown larger.

Drethene looked at her ring. Through it, she'd begun to feel the coming and going of another presence, like light seeping into a dark room when a door is open, leaving a paper-thin memory when it's shut again.

The largest bubbles began floating up from the sand, and the ring sang like the wind. Startled gulls cried, unable to clench the floating balls in their gaping jaws. Frustrated webbed feet kicked the bubbles out over the sea.

Drethene watched the shimmering orbs float over the water and continue to grow. Once they appeared to be about half her size, she began seeing shadows and movement inside them. Pelicans took over where the gulls had left off, but now the spheres were too large for them to scoop into their bills, even with their potato sack chins. Drethene could see creatures flipping and stretching inside what now appeared to be diaphanous eggs. Her ring was accompanying the cacophony of movement with more intense tones and harmonies. The creatures struggled to be free of their levitating confinement.

One finally sent a spiky limb through its bubble egg, causing the glistening shell to pop and disappear. The creature fell into the water with a small splash. Sounding like muted fireworks, about fifty others did the same thing, and suddenly the bubbles were gone, as were their young. The water became very still. Tiny waves barely lapped at the shore.

Drethene's ring sang a soothing tune, reminiscent of a lullaby. Fifty heads popped out of the water, smiled, closed their eyes, and hummed along with the song while bobbing up and down and swaying side to side. Their faces were child-like. Iridescent feathers of deep blues and greens covered their heads. As they played, Drethene saw diminutive silver wings on their backs with long feathers connected to their fish-like tails. Their fingers were webbed, and their elbows were covered in a hard, protective shell. When they bent their arms, a dagger-sharp fin protruded from those elbows. They looked like decent weapons and were apparently what the creatures had used to escape their eggs.

Drethene watched as they hummed, played, dived, and jumped. They were joyful and innocent, beautiful and spirited. In an instant, they were gone.

"Child, what're you doing?"

Drethene spun around quickly, stumbling in waist-high water. She wore nothing but her shift. Sneafan held Drethene's clothes in her hands, and Sholvon held the *Sacred Writ* and her satchel.

"Get out of the water. There's a big group of something swimming out there, and they might enjoy a tasty morsel like yourself," Sneafan said, nearing the water as close as she dared, squinting at the waves and motioning for Drethene's return.

Drethene obeyed. The Horse Force looked bleary-eyed. They must have dozed off to have missed the amazing creatures hatching from giant bubbles over the ocean.

Sneafan wrung seawater from Drethene's shift and wrapped her in her sandy dress. Drethene thanked her, taking care not to expose her ring. She had no place to stow it now Sholvon held her satchel. He was flipping through the *Sacred Writ*.

"Where did you come across this?" Sholvon asked.

Drethene felt a wave of relief. They didn't know the book was hers.

"I found it while I was here on the beach."

Not a lie—she did find it in her satchel.

"Well, I better bring it with us. Our final destination has been revealed, we're aware they have a library. We'll leave this with your caretaker."

Sneafan nodded in agreement with her husband's wise decision, and the three began to walk to the cart. The Horse Force might not have been the quickest wits on the road, but they were kindhearted. Their lack of deductive reasoning was working in Drethene's favor. Now, she needed to figure a way to recover her belongings before they parted ways, but her mind was still full of the beautiful sea creatures and her strange habit of losing herself, only to find she'd been drawn to water in some state of undress.

She rubbed her hands together as she became aware of the cool autumn air on her wet skin and clothing.

Drethene climbed into the cart as Sholvon and Sneafan perched themselves on the driver's seat. The refreshed horses lurched forward and found a comfortable trot.

After a short time, Drethene's ring glowed white and hot as she heard voices approaching. Grasping her burning finger, she looked through the lower slit, bumping her head as the horses and cart came to a sudden stop.

"Greetings, travelers. Who have ye in the cart there?"

The voice sounded somewhat familiar.

"Our charge is known to us and those who have the proper papers. No one else is privy to the information," answered Sholvon.

"You have interesting reading material, madam. May I take a look?" the familiar voice asked. "My apprentice is studying literature under my tutelage. May I use your text as a test of his accomplishments?"

"Since it's already in your hands, sir, you might as well," Sneafan replied.

"Here you are, Trem. Give this a read."

Drethene held her hand over her mouth, capturing Trem's name before it could leave her lips. With the cart stopped, she was able to position herself to peek out of a crack and see right between the seated Horse Force.

Trem stood in front of the cart. The *Sacred Writ* was in his hands, but his muscles seemed stuck. Sweat beaded on his brow.

She now recognized the voice as Phovul's. He said, "My apprentice is a perfectionist, an admirable quality. He fears sounding sophomoric and, therefore, refuses to even open the book."

Phovul took the book from Trem and offered it to Sholvon.

"Please, continue on your way. You are brave to risk your lives transporting such a forbidden tome."

Sneafan shot Sholvon a worried look. Sholvon accepted the book and comforted his wife with a pat on her leg.

"We're bringing it to the proper authorities," Sholvon said. "They'll hear our explanation, and all will be well."

Drethene remained quiet, impressed with and feeling protected by Sholvon's steadfast calm. This encounter could easily go bad. Fortunately, accomplishing their delivery and keeping information confidential weren't only Sholvon and Sneafan's profession, but also their gift.

"We're honored with the charge of enforcing the peacefulness of *Tranquility*. If we may assist you with our words, ask now, and we'll answer you as best we can within the confines of our oath of confidentiality. If your need is beyond our ability, we must wish you well and continue on our journey."

Drethene heard a snap, a slap, and the galloping of hooves diminishing into the distance. The pattern repeated.

"I am not confined by the laws of *Tranquility*," said Phovul. "I also have a goal, and the contents of your cart will allow me to attain it quickly. Open the door now, or I will kill you and then open it."

Drethene heard a muffled whimper of fear from Sneafan.

"I'd prefer you to live to proclaim my story," he continued. "But I am bored with this delay. Murder would lighten my mood. Either way, the cart will open. You decide."

A moment later, the door of the stranded cart swung open with a muttered apology from Sholvon. Even the Horse Force was overwhelmed by Phovul's ill will.

Drethene had focused on what Phovul had done in the midst of the horror of the Honor Room, not on what he looked like. Before her now stood a beautiful man, staring directly at her. He had long, black hair and green eyes set in a perfect complexion. His skin was almost too smooth—a feminine quality stretched over a masculine jaw. He was tall, thin, and strong. He reminded her of the warriors from the histories she'd read, adorned in nothing but metal. He must have come to rescue her. She wanted to run to him, but she was frozen.

"What is this fog? Is there no one in this cart? What have you done with the girl?" Phovul was confounded and irritated.

*What fog?* Drethene could see clearly. She was drawn to this man. She tried to move toward him but felt as if she were walking on a log rolling in a pond. Her attempts took her nowhere, and the harder she tried, the farther she slipped from him.

He peered more closely into the cart and attempted to enter. There was an audible sizzle. He screamed in agony and drew back his arm, minus a few layers of skin.

Oh, no. She'd hurt him. She screamed. No sound came from her mouth, but her ring vibrated violently and silently, as if absorbing her voice.

"Trem!" he yelled. "Go in there and find her."

Trem barreled in and knelt before Drethene, who was about to remove her ring. He grabbed both of her hands. Drethene looked at him through teary eyes. He fastened his lips with the imaginary button of childhood. Her tears fell as she imitated him.

He gently took her hand and pushed the ring firmly back on her middle finger. He didn't let go. The tangible emptiness haunting her was filled with his essence. The relief was satiating.

Trem didn't move his lips, but Drethene clearly heard him say, "The ring is of the Realm and protects you, Dreffy. Never remove it."

Trem let go of her hand. Loneliness washed over Drethene. She scrambled and clawed at Trem to regain the comfort he'd brought and quickly taken away. He firmly sat her on the floor and left the cart. Drethene's sense of loss was renewed, increased, sickening.

"Where is the girl, Trem?" Phovul's teeth were clenched in pain and exasperation.

"She's out of reach." Trem looked at Phovul's arm and said, "I have an herb for that."

Trem led him away.

# CHAPTER FIFTEEN

"Oh, dear me, what did they do to you, child?" Sneafan embraced Drethene, rocking her gently.

She combed her fingers through Drethene's hair and wet her forehead with tearful kisses. The innocent and honest concern and affection calmed Drethene.

"I'm fine."

Sneafan brushed hair out of Drethene's eye and kissed her forehead once more.

"Let's get some air."

The sun was lower in the sky but still bright. Although they hadn't traveled far, Drethene now saw they were approaching a wooded area. Sholvon was studying the forest. Sneafan approached him, linked her arm to his, and patted his hand. When he saw her smile, he gave a sigh of relief and nodded at Drethene.

"The horses ran into the woods," Sholvon said. "That's the direction we're going anyway. We must abandon the cart."

Sholvon handed Drethene her satchel, heavy with the *Sacred Writ*.

"We all must carry our share of the burden. I hope this and a bag of blankets won't be too much for you."

Drethene accepted her part of the provisions. She was uncertain if Sholvon had reasoned from recent events these items were hers. She hoped he was pleased to rid himself of them both, abandoning his plan to hand them over to someone of authority.

They shouldered their loads and began walking toward the woods. Drethene could still hear the crashing waves, and she was reminded of the beautiful sea creatures. She looked at her ring and wondered what other surprises were in store.

Upon entering the forest, the ocean sounds were snuffed out as simply and fully as a candle is extinguished by a breath. The air was moist, and all was dark and silent. Drethene breathed deeply to fill herself with the piney scent of the trees. The ocean and its inhabitants were fascinating, but a misty pond surrounded by trees such as these was home to her.

As they walked, the possibility of escape dawned upon Drethene. She was not shackled. She could easily outrun the Horse Force. She had even been reunited with her valued belongings.

Nevertheless, she wouldn't abandon them. They'd surrender their livelihood, if not their lives, if they lost her. They were experienced with transporting people who wanted to escape from them. Their trust in her was steadfast, and her ultimate goal was to gain the trust of all. If she deceived this couple, she'd be off to a poor start.

Sholvon saw a horse in a small clearing in the distance. Once they were close enough to see it wasn't theirs, Drethene and her escorts were discovered by the horse's true owner.

"Drethene! Is it really you? This isn't at all how I imagined our next encounter."

The familiar voice and the unmistakable pronunciation of her name were unexpected comforts to Drethene. A friend from home who appeared pleased to see her was a welcome surprise. However, if he hadn't spoken, Drethene didn't think she'd ever have recognized Chamlon. This was not the overambitious, nervous Academy student who pursued the uninterested with endless conversation. This was a seemingly taller, much calmer, almost regal version of the young man she'd befriended. Was that a crown on his head?

"Chamlon, I'd never have recognized you." Drethene stepped forward to greet him. Sneafan and Sholvon each grabbed one of her arms and held her back. Apparently, they hadn't forgotten she was still a prisoner.

"State your name, please, sir," Sholvon said. "We're charged with the transport of this young woman to a nearby Hall. We've been waylaid and can spare no time in idle conversation, as we must deliver our charge as quickly as possible."

Chamlon closed his eyes for a few moments as if hoping upon opening them, he'd wake to a happier reality. When he opened his eyes, beyond the initial hesitant squint, they shone with a mix of sorrow, pity, and disappointment.

"I'm Chamlon of Dale. There's only one Hall in this region and not far from here. I can escort you there myself, as it's my home."

Sholvon bowed low and said, "My apologies for speaking harshly, Leader."

"There's no need. I'm no leader. The people of the Hall of the Last to Follow have a leader, and I was placed there by the Academy to assist him. This Hall's members are unique and in need of transitional leadership as they become accustomed to the ways of the One People."

Chamlon hadn't lost his knack for verbosity.

"I ride often into these woods. My sojourns began as recreation, but since this crown was presented to me and placed on my head, I am expected by the Hall's membership to patrol the surrounding lands and guarantee their safety. Again, these people have needs unfamiliar to the One People. I'm pleased to fulfill their desire for comfort until they find the solace and security of *Tranquility*."

He gestured toward his horse with undeserved grandeur.

"You may place your burdens on this steed, and we'll walk together to the Hall."

Drethene and the Horse Force tied their bags and bundles to the beast. Drethene kept her satchel over her shoulder, hoping to appear as if she didn't notice its weight now the majority of her load had been lifted from her.

Chamlon led the way. Drethene approached him as they walked, with no interference from her chaperones. The work of the Horse Force was practically accomplished. Drethene was feeling much more at ease knowing the Council had unknowingly sent her into the hands of an old friend.

"So, Chamlon, a well-deserved honor has been bestowed upon you by the membership of your Hall."

She found herself in the ironic position of scurrying after her friend.

"It's really a symbolic gesture." Chamlon removed the crown and swung the circlet around his wrist like an oversized bracelet.

Drethene could now see it was woven from long dried leaves and gold and silver fabric.

"The lands from which our membership originates still follow the laws of old," he said. "They still recognize kings and queens in addition to religious leaders. Their transition is smoother if they see their leader as a spiritual guide and me as their law enforcer and protector. Eventually, they'll learn *Tranquility* is both."

# tranquility

Chamlon ran his fingers through his hair and bent forward slightly into his familiar stance. The crown seemed to hold a dash of magic for him, or maybe he'd learned the only way to keep the circlet on his head was to walk tall. He stopped walking, so Drethene did too. The Horse Force paused a distance behind them. He looked at Drethene's forehead, his old conversational habit allowing him to engage people without seeing the frightening truths in their eyes.

"There's something else very different about our Hall. We're the only one with an active prison. Again—because it's nothing shocking to our membership. Being the keeper of the law, I'm in charge of the jail."

Chamlon took in a few quick inhales through his clenched teeth—a clear indication he'd said something he found discomforting.

Drethene's stomach lurched as she realized the reason for the return of Chamlon's familiar signs of interpersonal unease.

Chamlon replaced his crown on his head. "*Tranquility* allows for imprisonment for only the boldest offenders. There's need for only one such place for all of the One People. A messenger from Dale informed me I was to receive my first new prisoner since my tenure here. He explained the Horse Force and the need for secrecy until the arrival of the guilty one. Drethene," Chamlon looked, perhaps for the first time, directly into her eyes and asked, "what did you do?"

Drethene was about to attempt an answer when she saw a brilliant flash of green light in the woods. She saw others throughout the surrounding trees.

Fully distracted, Drethene said, "Those are the brightest fireflies I've ever seen."

"Oh, those are no fireflies, Drethene. Thankfully, the creatures you see are far away. They're one of the reasons my visits to the forest became patrols. The lights you see are the result of a predator's sting. The powerful shock disables the victim and allows the creature to feed at its leisure. Normally they feed on frogs and mice, but recently their prey have grown to rabbits and badgers. Livestock has disappeared as well. We're trying to determine if they've begun to hunt collectively, which is unlikely since more than one sting emitted simultaneously has been known to kill predators and prey instantly. We fear a larger breed has entered the forest."

"Chamlon, many frightening changes are taking place throughout the land of the One People. I'm here because terrible things happened when

I was in the Honor Room. I was blamed for everything and sent away. I wasn't given a trial. No one told me exactly why I'd been summoned in the first place. Would you blame me for these stinging creatures and their new habits? If you did, the Council would probably add the transgression to my list of offenses."

The bright flashes made the forest appear pitch dark, even though the sun was surely an hour from setting. Each flare announced the demise of another woodland creature. One particularly bright light was accompanied by a sickening zap.

"Although I uphold the law, I'm in no place to judge you," Chamlon said. "I wish I could change your fate once we enter the village, but I have no power to do so. I must honor *Tranquility* through adhering to the decrees of the Council.

"Before I knew you were my prisoner, I'd eagerly anticipated this moment. That same messenger I mentioned guaranteed if I accomplished the imprisonment, I'd be highly considered for the position of Questioner in Dale, a most prestigious appointment."

Chamlon's excitement almost made Drethene feel she should happily enter the prison to guarantee him his most recent, greatest desire. Notwithstanding, the realization of the pains taken by the Council to make her go away helped her refocus on her purpose. The fate of the Questioner who'd examined her also entered her mind.

"What I'll do," Chamlon continued, "is change my plan for your entrance into the village and the prison. I'd intended a parade of sorts, with the Horse Force cart being flanked by the children of the village to emphasize how *Tranquility* ensures the safety of our future. Instead, we'll simply enter the village as we are now, with no fanfare. Folks will be inside preparing for supper by the time we arrive. We'll walk to the prison and quietly enter. Your successful imprisonment will be announced at tomorrow's Gathering."

"Thank you."

"What happened to the cart, anyway?"

"You might as well add its disappearance to my offense list too."

She heard the zap of another sting and couldn't decide if she felt sorrier for the creature turned prey or for herself.

# CHAPTER SIXTEEN

Drithon relaxed and studied the ring. Taelmai watched as he turned it slowly. Closing his eyes, he took a few breaths, and said, "Nothing, nothing at all."

"I love how the animals dance and the plants grow as you rotate the ring," Taelmai said.

Drithon looked at her thoughtfully.

"Here." He handed her the ring. "Take a closer look and tell me more about what you see."

"The birds are flying and flowers bloom. I can hear the birds' calls and smell the fragrance of the blossoms."

The stone's deep blackness was rich and endless. Her finger entered the gem as she touched the ring's surface.

"It feels like pudding."

The birds began to circle Taelmai's finger. The longer she kept her finger submerged in the stone, the farther up her arm the birds flew. She smiled and cooed at the creatures.

Doll started walking toward Taelmai, looking very concerned, but Drithon stopped her.

"Taelmai, slip the ring on your finger, look into the stone, and tell me what you see."

Taelmai placed the ring on her finger. Doll and Drithon smiled. They all could see, smell, and hear the ring's activity. The birds were breaking off flowers from the trees and placing them in Taelmai's hair. The stone grew, not increasing in weight or mass, but blossoming in reach.

Taelmai looked into the stone. "I see something."

A bird landed on her shoulder, opening its beak near her ear. Taelmai could barely see her friend in the ring's shadowy depths, but she clearly heard Drethene's voice whispering, "Trem, Trem is that you? I'm wearing the ring, just like you said, is that you?"

"No, Drethene, it's me, Taelmai!"

Drethene continued to quietly chant Trem's name. She couldn't hear Taelmai.

Taelmai was about to touch the stone again when she saw another, clearer image. Klindyn reached toward her. Taelmai touched the stone, which expanded to allow her hand full entrance into its depths. She grabbed Klindyn's hand and pulled him. The stone stretched as if birthing Klindyn into the room. The ring flew off Taelmai's finger and landed on the floor beside Klindyn. The birds and plants returned to their miniature sculpted state and the stone resumed its original size.

"What was that for?" Klindyn cried, rubbing his wrist.

"Just déjà vu, I guess." Taelmai rubbed her overexerted shoulder.

Doll and Drithon stared at the boy with amazement and concern. Klindyn crossed his arms and faced away from them.

He peeked back to discover they were still looking at him. "I don't want anyone looking at me!"

He hid his face in his hands.

Doll and Drithon began puttering about to avoid looking at the boy.

Taelmai approached Klindyn, gently embracing and comforting him.

"Who were you looking for this time?" he asked, frowning and still tearful.

Taelmai explained what had happened since they'd last met. Klindyn listened intently and asked pertinent questions, which clearly surprised Doll and Drithon. Now calm and in his adult state of mind, Klindyn introduced himself to them.

"My name is Klindyn. I live with my fourteenth-generation granddaughter, disguised as her son. Her oldest daughter is seven years old and will take her mother's place as my guardian when she comes of age. I've been a family heirloom for these many years. I also have a ring like Trem's and Drethene's. I feel very responsible for what happened to Trem and would like to help both of them."

"I've been negligent in my communications with the Realm," Drithon said, "or I would've known the third of the Sworn Seven had been identified and bestowed his ring."

Doll got up and headed toward the kettle.

Klindyn nodded at Drithon and said, "I've been experimenting with my ring and am able to sense Drethene. I can't see anyone through the ring, but I sensed another presence. I was shocked when a hand emerged and grabbed me, as if the rings themselves were entrances to the Passageways."

"Please tell me about these Passageways."

"That's how I met Trem and Taelmai, and how I discovered the other Dale. I thought it was a safe place, full of beauty and the stuff of dreams. I suspect the sap in the Passageway has something to do with my youthful appearance, and sometimes, I think, childlike disposition."

Taelmai and her friends exchanged careful glances.

"Unfortunately," Klindyn continued, seeming not to notice, "evil infiltrates that world as easily as it does this one. Are those biscuits?"

"I thought this conversation might go long, so I decided to fix a proper tea," Doll said, wearing her shop smile.

Klindyn was next to her, attempting to grab a biscuit from the plate before she could place it down. Doll swatted his hand away. She didn't tolerate rude behavior from little boys ... or old men.

Taelmai could tell Drithon was not prepared for more than one visitor at a time, as mismatched chairs and a stool were placed around his tiny tea table. Drithon found cheese and apples to go with the biscuits.

"I think I know where Drethene is," Klindyn said, his mouth full of cheese. "Each time I concentrate on her through the ring, no matter where I am, I smell the ocean. My home is near the sea. We're the only village in Unemond with a working prison."

"The sea is quite a distance from here," Doll said. "Is there a Passageway to get you home?"

"The Passageways are quicker than land travel. But what Taelmai just did is even faster."

"Flows, or Passageways as you call them, are tricky," Drithon said. "These rings are powerful and most useful, but we know little about them."

"I'd be willing to perform an experiment," Klindyn said, his face and hands sticky from an apple. "If Taelmai can get a good view of Drethene through Trem's ring, she could push me through the ring to Drethene."

"We have no way to know if Taelmai has the power to push you to another ring's location," Drithon said.

"I don't want to hurt or lose you," Taelmai said to Klindyn.

"Do we have any other options?" Klindyn demanded.

# tranquility

"I don't like this combination of naïve child and stubborn old man," Doll said, squinting at Klindyn. "This plan sounds dangerous, but something tells me you're going to try."

Pros and cons, fruit and cheese, and various ideas were all passed around the table. Doll's prediction was correct.

"Let me watch Drethene a while longer before we try anything," Taelmai said. "I don't want to waste time, but she needs to be alone for us to pop in on her."

"Wise counsel," Drithon said. "Let's be patient for success, instead of hasty for failure."

Lightning and thunder struck simultaneously underscored by the sound of crashing waves. In the darkness of the cell, the cacophony was frightening, and Drethene trembled in the corner furthest from the eerie gray-green glow of the one tiny window. Over time, the sight of the lightning and the sound of the thunder separated from one another. The lightning bid ever-fainter farewells in a reluctant adieu answered by more distant groans and bellows.

Drethene approached the window to drink in the last bits of daylight. The low storm clouds were purple. Half the sun sat above the horizon, enlivening wispy clouds a brilliant gold. The golden color seeped from the clouds and lay upon the leaves of the trees, which when seen against the gray sky, took on a vivid luminescence. The sun sank farther, and the sky turned violet above the fiery red horizon.

Drethene returned to the floor of her cell and wrapped her arms around her knees. Nights spent away from home were still new, wakeful, and melancholy.

She took a moment in the waning daylight to appreciate the beauty of her ring's turquoise stone. She caressed the intricate details of the setting and smiled through her tears.

Klindyn's stomach growled as he watched Doll pack a satchel with cheese, fruit, biscuits, and tea.

"Give this to Drethene." Doll handed him the bag. "You're certain to startle her, but food from home will assure and strengthen her. Tell her to eat and drink, and this comes with love from Doll, Drithon, and Taelmai."

"Can I—"

"No, Klindyn, you may not. If you're ever imprisoned, I'll be certain to send you a package."

Klindyn weighed the discomfort of a cell against the deliciousness of the food as he carried the satchel to Taelmai.

She placed Trem's ring on her finger and was encircled by birds and branches. Klindyn couldn't help looking over her shoulder and was happy he could also see into the expanse of the ink-black stone. A clear image of Drethene appeared, seeming to stare at them. Her hair framed her face and hung well below her shoulders. Her long, ivory neck was exposed. Her mouth formed the word "Trem" over and over again, and he could hear the word but not from the ring. One of the birds from the ring perched on Taelmai's shoulder and spoke Drethene's words into her ear.

"She's there."

Klindyn swallowed hard, slung the satchel over his shoulder, and pushed his ring as far onto his finger as possible. He looked at Drithon, who gave him an encouraging nod. Klindyn grabbed Taelmai's hand. She gave his a squeeze and pushed him toward the stone on her other hand. Klindyn put out his hands and closed his eyes. The stone flowed around him like liquid and seemingly digested him into the ring. In a moment, he was gone.

Klindyn expected a panicked time of being stuck in the ring. Thankfully, Taelmai's strength continued to surprise him, and he tumbled out quickly, landing on top of a startled Drethene.

"Jack rabbit! Who are you?" Drethene gasped, as Klindyn was peeling himself from her belly.

"Please, don't scream," he said.

"You came out of my ring. I'm not afraid of you."

"My name is Klindyn. I live with my fourteenth-generation granddaughter, disguised as her son. Her oldest daugh—"

Klindyn's speech was interrupted by a painful pinch on his ringed finger.

He massaged his finger and began again, "My name is Klindyn. I know Trem, and I have a ring like yours."

He waved his amber ring in front of her.

"Here," he thrust the satchel at Drethene, "this comes from Doll, Drithon, and Taelmai with love."

Drethene raised an eyebrow and opened the satchel. Food was in her mouth and washed down her throat by tea before her mind had time to register the bag's contents. Klindyn watched her, and Drethene held out a chunk of cheese.

"No, thank you. Doll told me she'd send me my own package if I were ever imprisoned."

Drethene laughed. "How did you get here?"

Glancing over his shoulder several times, Klindyn completed the description of his problematic genealogy and shared how his more recent history wove into Trem's and Taelmai's.

Drethene ate and drank, and Klindyn finished with the story of Trem becoming Phovul's prisoner.

When Klindyn had finished, he didn't need to ask Drethene to tell her story. She volunteered the information in great detail. She told him about the birth of the sea creatures, Phovul and Trem stopping the cart, and her encounter with Chamlon in the woods.

"Now that I know about Trem," Drethene said, "what happened in the Honor Room and in the cart makes more sense. How could I have been drawn to someone so evil? How will we find Trem without his ring?"

They heard footsteps in the hall.

"I'll come back," Klindyn whispered. "I promise."

He waited nervously with his unadorned hand outstretched next to the one wearing his ring.

The footsteps outside of Drethene's cell grew louder, and the sound of keys began to accompany the steady rhythm. A key was inserted into the lock of the fortunately windowless door as Klindyn was pulled through his ring once again.

# CHAPTER SEVENTEEN

Crouglan Bonhyn stared out his window at the bustling street. The sun was setting, and folks were moving quickly to accomplish their errands before nightfall. He felt abandoned, forgotten. He rubbed his palm where he could see the chain link beneath his skin. Why would his master be displeased? Why would he remain distant? If Phovul simply gave him a command, Crouglan would do whatever he wanted.

Crouglan had captured Drethene. Young Perthin, the only resistance he'd found amidst the turmoil of the Honor Room, was in bondage. As for the meddling magician of a librarian, he was an academic and well liked. If he disappeared, people would care.

Crouglan continued his study of the street outside. He always hoped to catch a glimpse of Phovul heading his way, knowing well enough his master never traveled by foot like average people. Crouglan worked hard to instill the importance of equality in his people, all the while believing in his own superiority. Phovul had proven the leader's elevated caliber by selecting him above everyone else.

Crouglan could feel Phovul's power through their connection but out of his grasp. The time or two he'd reached toward it, he'd received a jolt of pain and learned his lesson. He did not want the power for himself. He'd simply hoped to be closer to Phovul through their bond. Rejection hurt more than punishment. Phovul's ability to perceive his intentions only increased Crouglan's sense of awe.

Perhaps Crouglan needed to accomplish something exceptional, something to please his master without the need of his command. A gift would bring his master into his presence and provide Crouglan the praise he craved.

"Now this is interesting," Crouglan said to himself as he caught sight of new activity in the street.

# tranquility

Walking into the library were Juznyn Bidalind and his neighbor, escorting a hooded figure. Not long before, Doll had entered the same way with the rarely seen Taelmai, daughter of Juznyn's same neighbor.

"I won't be hasty. Let them meet and get comfortable. I'll visit in the morning."

He shut his window.

A knock at Drithon's door caused Taelmai to jump and lose her concentration. The speaking bird left her shoulder in fear, and the birds circling her wobbled in their pattern.

As Klindyn toppled into her, she said, "We need to practice, or else one of us is going to get hurt."

Another knock startled everyone, and Klindyn began to cry. Taelmai comforted him and watched Drithon shake his head at their unsettled nerves while approaching the door.

"Who's calling?" Drithon asked through the door.

"Your brother and two friends," said Juznyn.

Drithon sighed with relief and unlocked the door. Juznyn, Taelmai's father, and a hooded man entered the room. Drithon quickly closed and locked the door behind them.

"After all these years," Drithon said to Juznyn, "you've finally used that key I gave you. I had a feeling unusual circumstances would be necessary for you to let yourself into my home. Next time, you can also use the key to open my chamber door and save us a good deal of anxiety."

Juznyn shook his head and offered the key to his brother. "Do you truly believe nerves would have remained calm to the sound of a key unlocking your safe haven?"

Drithon smiled and refused the offer.

Taelmai's father stared open-mouthed at her and the small boy in her arms. Taelmai desperately wanted to explain, but the stranger removed his hood, and all eyes went to him.

"Perthin," Drithon said, "I never expected to find you entering my chamber in the company of my brother and his neighbor. These days hold surprises for us all."

Upon seeing the young man's inexpertly bandaged hands, Doll began rifling through Drithon's jars and tins of tea.

Almost everyone began speaking at once, either to themselves, or to someone else in the room.

Taelmai comforted Klindyn and watched Doll blend and brew her tea.

Klindyn grew brave and left Taelmai to meet Perthin.

When she was done, Doll rang Drithon's bell.

The last voices heard trailing off were Klindyn's reciting, "I've been a family heirloom for these many years," and Taelmai's father muttering "methinks."

"Emotions are running hot amongst a people trained to quell their every feeling and reaction," Doll said. "It's no coincidence we are in this room at the same time. Let's speak in turn and do well with what we hear."

No one was willing to be the first to follow Doll's words.

This allowed Taelmai to hear a low humming or chanting. She looked for the source and spotted Drithon bowed before Perthin. Clearly, the young man was uncomfortable, sitting very stiffly, his hand held by Drithon.

Perthin gasped, and everyone turned toward him. He held his hands in front of his face. He wiggled his fingers and made tight fists over and over again.

Drithon rose from his seat, clapped Perthin on the shoulder and said, "Where I come from, a few words, a simple melody, and, let's call it 'confidence in what you know,' come together to do what the One People consider impossible."

"You've got quite a knack for healing, Drithon," Taelmai's father said. "You should be the village doctor."

Taelmai felt a surge of comfort knowing she was in the company of a talented healer.

"You could've warned me, D.D.," Doll said, true perturbation in her voice. "I wouldn't have wasted these good herbs on a now useless poultice."

"My purpose isn't to heal all the woes of Dale, Tomus," Drithon said. "Still, when needed, I can fix a few things."

Drithon faced Doll.

"I'm sorry. I'll find a jar for the poultice. Something tells me we'll be needing it."

"I often wondered how my childhood bumps and scrapes disappeared overnight," Juznyn said, looking slyly at his brother.

"You were, and continue to be, a devoted brother," Drithon said. "We lived in the same room, and you kept my oddities to yourself. The least I could do was to make your life a bit less sore."

The mood had lifted, the room was quiet, so Taelmai stood up and began her story. As she spoke, she could see tears filling the eyes of Drethene's and her father, who held tight to each other's shoulders, clinging to the strength of their friendship while hearing the tribulations of their children.

"I have had an epiphany," said the quiet, dangerous voice. "Being burdened with you as my slave is the true, underhanded punishment for my crimes in the Realm. Eternal, solitary imprisonment in this hole is seeming pleasant compared to wasting my energy on a hopeless fool!"

Phovul trembled in the face of the reeking breath spitting anger in his blinded eyes.

"Did the fog burn your delicate skin? Feel this!"

Phovul screamed as his master's claws dug into the tender, pink flesh of his still-healing arm. The new skin sliced easily, like tender meat. The pain sent Phovul to the floor. He was nearly unconscious. His blood puddled next to him.

The voice, calmed by the violent act, whispered in his ear with mock patience, "The girl has the protection of the Realm as long as she wears the ring. To equal her power, you need to first find your pet's ring. Leave the girl alone until you have the strength to overcome her. Do you understand now?"

Phovul nodded.

"The Realm is powerful. Powerful enough to keep me captive. But do not underestimate me, slave. I may only have strength enough to control you, but my power is absolute. Your release into Unemond is a revocable privilege bestowed by me. You can, and will, enslave those I need to ensure my revenge. On that day of retribution, you will not regret being on my side."

Phovul felt rock hard, icy lips against his forehead. He shuddered with repulsion and retreated from consciousness to the distant lullaby of evil laughter.

# CHAPTER EIGHTEEN

They'd shared their stories, surprisingly slept a good part of the night, made a breakfast from what remained in Drithon's cupboards, and drank enough tea to feel energized. All but Klindyn, who dozed peacefully with his head on Taelmai's lap.

"This is a fine beginning," Drithon said. "Let's review. This morning, we'll all be leaving here at different times in different ways. Those who leave by foot must stagger their departures. Doll?"

"I'll leave first to go to my shop and gather food and medicines. I'll close my shop early and walk to Trem's bog."

"Perthin and I will meet you there," Drithon said. "Taelmai?"

"Klindyn and I will practice using the rings for transport and will meet you in Trem's bog—with Drethene."

"Good," Drithon said. "Juznyn?"

"Tomus and I will leave after Doll to stop home for horses and supplies. We'll walk to Trem's bog."

"Very well," Drithon said. "Perthin?"

"I'll use Drithon's secret ways through the Academy to reach my friends." Perthin looked around the room at all the eyes avoiding his. "I know you question the allegiance of the Academy students, but I have the utmost trust in these particular young men."

"Very well," Drithon said. "We have a plan. Now, to implement it."

The rap at the door was barely audible above the hubbub of voices in Drithon's chambers as everyone bade each other good-bye. Young Perthin, his nerves having been incurably on edge since returning to the Academy, was the only one to hear the first knock. Drithon sensed Perthin's discomfort and tried to quiet the companions.

The second, louder knock silenced everyone.

Drithon walked to the far end of the room and faced away from the door.

He covered his mouth with both hands and shouted, "One moment, please."

"Please realize the urgency," said Crouglan's familiar voice, "for me to be coming to you."

The friends moved quickly and quietly.

Taelmai, who'd roused Klindyn several minutes before, led him through the ring just as she had the last time, but now she held fast to his hand and was pulled through as well. The stone engulfed them both, swallowed its ring, and disappeared altogether. The sight made the mad scramble in the room slow down—just for a moment.

Then everyone got back to work. Drithon rolled a rug up from in front of his hearth. He lay on the floor, his ear against the cool rock, and rapped lightly in a circular pattern. He slid a large stone beneath its neighbors and motioned to Perthin to approach.

"Move quietly but with speed," Drithon whispered, "and keep your wits and sense of direction. In an hour, I'll meet you beneath the west hall of the sleep chambers. Meet with your friends quickly and find a way to be near the entrance to the tunnels without bringing attention to yourself."

Drithon handed Perthin a large silver key.

"This will open both doors to get you into the Academy. I'll have the key to get you back into the tunnels. Don't forget to knock and remain hidden while you wait for me."

Perthin nodded, gave a wave, and descended through the opening in the floor. Drithon replaced the stone and the rug.

Drithon looked at those who remained. Doll, Juznyn, and Tomus stared back.

"Allow me to speak first," Drithon whispered. "If you must add to what I say, don't be extravagant. All will be well. But first, be seated, and look as comfortable as possible."

Drithon unlocked the door and welcomed their leader into his chambers.

Before Crouglan could get the upper hand, Drithon began, "My apologies, Grand Leader, for the delay. I was deep in my storage room, searching for teas needed by Doll to treat Taelmai's recent illness. Juznyn and Tomus met her here to help. When I heard your voice, I asked them to avoid improper etiquette and allow me to answer the door."

"Speaking of impropriety, your bell is missing," Crouglan said. "It's a good thing I had this."

He displayed his key as a reminder of his power and proximity.

"How interesting you should mention Taelmai's name," he continued, "as I'm certain I saw you walking with her toward the library yesterday, Doll."

"This is true, Grand Leader," Doll responded. "She is desperate for relief and came into town seeking help. Taelmai's worried mother came here with Juznyn and Tomus searching for her. Her mother took Taelmai home, and the rest of us remain, hoping to find what Taelmai needs."

Drithon hoped Doll's quick thinking quelled any suspicions Crouglan might have had in case he had also witnessed the neighbors entering the Academy with the hooded Perthin.

"It's taken you quite some time. Have you found the appropriate tea to heal the girl?" Crouglan asked.

Did he believe them? Was he testing them?

"Not yet, sir," Drithon said. "I am, of course, at your service before I continue my search."

"I'm looking to find—" Crouglan began but was interrupted by another knock on Drithon's normally silent door.

Drithon bowed his way past Crouglan, and opened the door to find a nervous, middle-aged man, wearing the ancient chain, lock, and key crest of a prison guard. He was the Keeper of the Academy's small hold, the only prison-like facility in Dale.

"I've been informed," the Keeper said, "that Grand Leader Crouglan was seen approaching your chambers. I apologize for disturbing you, but the bell was missing, and the gate was left un—"

The Keeper's voice caught in his throat when he looked beyond Drithon and saw Crouglan staring at him.

"Grand Leader," he began with a bow, made more grand than necessary to avoid eye contact all the longer. "An impossible occurrence has taken place—well, what was once thought to be impossible." He took a deep breath, "The one prisoner in our hold has disappeared."

Crouglan's natural frown became a fearful scowl.

"How's this possible? I sent several men to escort Perthin and ordered them to remain until he was securely imprisoned."

"Unfortunately, Grand Leader, he was never thusly imprisoned. Those men and I fastened the prisoner's chains to the bars of a cell while we all worked to open the underused, rusted door of his hold. Incredibly, he somehow slipped from his chains and escaped. We opened the cell door to imprison him, but he was gone."

"This happened days ago, as I myself watched you lead him toward the prison?"

"Yes, Grand Leader. We began to search immediately, hoping to find him. We were thorough in our method and now know he's most assuredly escaped."

The poor excuse for a guard fell to his knees. His solely theoretical experience left him ill-equipped for prison security. Everyone in the room pitied him, except the one who held the man's fate in his hands.

Crouglan lifted the groveling man by his neck. The Keeper hung limp from his grasp. Crouglan placed him on his feet again and released him. The guard looked shocked at his inability to breathe. He stared at Crouglan, a tight chain encircling his neck. As the guard reached toward his own throat, Crouglan grabbed both of his wrists and made a downward pulling motion. Two short chains appeared, connecting a thick ring around the man's hips to a ring around each wrist. The chains pulled taut, his hands no higher than the center of his rib cage, making him unable to reach his neck.

"You'll die anyway," Crouglan growled, "but I am more pleased to watch you struggle in your futile attempt to survive."

The four friends watched in helpless horror.

Drithon regretted hesitating, but he was uncertain what power held Crouglan. The anger, the evil, were revolting and foreign. If the power were Phovul's alone, he could help this man. If it were Malgriffe's, he might succeed only in increasing the rage and costing more lives.

"Your inadequacy," Crouglan told the dying man, "has cost me much more than the worth of your life. My master's lack of attention is a thousand times more painful than your simple death. Think of this as a gift, as opposed to the torture I endure, now prolonged by your blunder."

The guard collapsed. Crouglan faced the friends, his chin dripping with saliva. His eyes were wild. He clasped his hands like an excited child.

"What power I have been given! My master mustn't be displeased with me."

"I am more than pleased," said a voice from the dark hall outside Drithon's door. "I am impressed by your unscrupulous desire to serve me."

Crouglan fell to his knees. At first, Drithon saw only a hand reaching from the darkness to pet Crouglan's head. He leaned into the attention like a loyal dog, hungry for his owner's affection.

Drithon interrupted the disturbing scene and said, "Friends, don't look this stranger in the eyes."

"Not even an attempted whisper?" Phovul said, as he revealed himself in the full light of the room.

"Oh, my boy, I refuse to be rude." Drithon looked straight at Phovul. "I'll say what's necessary to ensure my friends don't become your next pets."

"You can ensure nothing against me." Phovul's tone confessed his annoyance, punctuated by his pushing Crouglan aside. "My power has grown and will stretch throughout Unemond as I increase my command. I can smell my success like the first autumn breeze, foretelling the destruction of summer's futile attempt to sustain life."

Drithon met Phovul's stare without fear.

Phovul closed his eyes. A shiver surged through his body, and his skin turned paler. He clasped his hands in front of him, pulled them into his middle, and crouched down to the floor. The shapes of chains appeared on his skin, the physical reminders of his master's control. His head snapped up, his eyes wide, as he released the energy at the stones underfoot.

The floor began to tremble, while rocks cracked and ruptured, as Phovul began to create one of his stone rooms to imprison and eventually gain control over all those present. Drithon bowed his head, raising his hands to his silent yet working lips, and the quivering stopped. His floor was smooth once again.

Phovul stood up. Crouglan joined him and imitated his stance.

"You have been studying more than *Tranquility* within these library walls," Phovul said. "Why didn't you stop me in the Honor Room?"

"I have my reasons."

"Death and destruction you could have stopped." Phovul clicked his tongue.

"You can't unnerve me."

"And you won't attack me."

The two were locked in a stare-down again. Drithon's lack of response was agitating Phovul just enough.

"I will do what I must to gain what I need," Phovul hissed.

"Such dedication, my boy. Your commitment used to impress me."

Phovul struggled under the weight of the power he embraced.

Crouglan slunk behind him.

Drithon was thankful when he felt the strong hands of his brother grasp his shoulders. He looked behind him to see Juznyn's bowed head and closed eyes.

Phovul attempted his construction again but couldn't manage even a tremor. He looked at the brothers with anger and frustration, lashing out at them. He held his palms facing them, and transparent images of chains spun toward Juznyn and Drithon. The shimmering links sailed around them and boomeranged back at Phovul, knocking him through the doorway and against the wall of the corridor. Crouglan was caught up in the force of the impact and struggled to raise himself into a sitting position beside Phovul.

Phovul's weakness was not physical. His frustration never failed to undo him. He sat stunned, staring at Drithon and Juznyn in disbelief.

"You are not strong enough to quell my creation and reverse my own power against me. And that mortal has no Realm-born skill at all! What have you done?"

"My brother needs no access to the powers of the Realm to strengthen me. His love and faith are sufficient to increase what I'm able to accomplish alone."

Phovul searched the room for an answer to this dilemma.

Crouglan grinned and whispered, "Choose her."

Phovul looked at Doll and smiled as natural and friendly a grin as he could muster.

"Don't look at him, Doll," Drithon warned.

Doll looked as if she were struggling with Drithon's instructions. Then she turned her back on Phovul who did something so quick and simple Drithon had no chance to act. Something clinked in a glass-enclosed cabinet. Doll looked up. She caught Phovul's reflected smile in the glass and faced him.

Doll didn't have a ring. No fog appeared to guard her.

Phovul tilted his head to the side, and Doll took a step toward him.

Drithon's stomach sank. He hoped there might be enough of her natural sense still intact to hear him. "Doll, don't believe unfamiliar emotions. They're artificial and formed from evil."

"He'll rescue me from all uncertainty." Doll's voice was flat, stripped of its usual musicality. "There are too many unanswered questions. Our world crumbles. With him, I'll be safe."

Doll took slow steps toward Phovul, who appeared to do nothing more than maintain eye contact. Crouglan smiled, yet he showed uncertainty about this seemingly affectionate connection between his master and Doll.

Drithon began to move toward Doll, but his brother's grip tightened on his shoulders enough to stop him. Drithon couldn't end what evil had begun. He'd only harm himself and create an inability to go forward in helping Drethene, whose work would create the way to allow all wrongs to be undone.

Doll arrived at Phovul's side. She reached out and touched his face. He pulled her close. She laughed. He touched her face, ran his fingers down her throat, and gently placed his hand over the hollow between her collarbones. She threw back her head as if in ecstasy, and a chain link appeared under her skin like the submerged charm of a necklace. She raised her head, looked at Phovul, laughed silently, and placed her head on his shoulder.

He removed the clip from her hair. Her locks flowed as long and straight as Phovul's. She tried to speak, but her words failed her. Phovul gently closed her lips with his fingers. She touched his face tenderly and again put her head on his shoulder.

"Doll is known for her words, no?" Phovul looked at Drithon. "I often control my servants through their strength, but this one I will keep quiet. I will enjoy her silent beauty."

Drithon started toward Phovul, but Juznyn held firm with his head bowed. He was providing a very different kind of strength for Drithon. Wisdom and patience were oftentimes more difficult to sustain than otherworldly powers.

"With my new pet and my faithful one, I must return to my very first," Phovul said. "Trem may wake soon from that bump on his head."

Tomus looked at Phovul. Juznyn stepped away from his brother to stand directly in front of his neighbor. Drithon appreciated his brother's intuition and bravery in protecting Tomus from looking too long at his son's master and joining Trem in slavery.

Phovul laughed. Crouglan sneered. Doll smiled. And Drithon wept.

# CHAPTER NINETEEN

Juznyn and Tomus walked in silence. The horrific murder, Doll's disturbing abduction, the demented state of their leader—these were all shocking. Yet, what kept Juznyn speechless was they'd walked out of the library, through the village gate, and down the lane in peace. Evil had no continuity but randomly chose who'd suffer and who'd go free. At last, they were home.

"Do you want to go in alone?" Juznyn asked.

"No," Tomus said. "I feel numb. I need you to help me explain this to Thleana. I'm afraid if she begins to argue the impossibility of what I say, I'll agree and believe I fabricated everything."

The door opened.

"Are you coming in?" Thleana asked. "Or are you going to stand on the threshold all day, leaving me alone inside, sick with worry?"

"My love," Tomus said. "I don't know if what we have to tell you is going to make you feel any better."

They entered the house and shut the door.

Thleana's reaction to their stories about her children, her friends, her leader, and the dismantling of all she believed, sent her into a screaming rage. She struck her husband and Juznyn, shattered cups and plates, set her apron on fire reaching for *Tranquility* on the mantle, tore the pages from the binding, and shed countless tears.

When Thleana's fit had ended, Tomus said, "My dear, I don't want to leave you here alone. Come with us."

"Our children must come home," Thleana said. "And I must be here when they do."

Tomus looked as close to tears as Juznyn had ever seen him.

"We must go."

# tranquility

Thleana refused to look up from her work. She sat on the floor attempting to mend her beloved book. She didn't ask where they were going. For her safety, they wouldn't have told her if she had.

Tomus bent down and kissed her sweating brow and tear-streaked cheeks.

"I promise," Tomus said, "I'm doing this to help Trem and Taelmai."

In the warm noon sun, Juznyn and Tomus packed blankets and provisions. The horses were loaded, fed, and watered. Juznyn walked through his house and barn, locking doors and freeing livestock. The animals didn't wander past their favorite grazing spots. Juznyn reluctantly began opening the gates of his fields.

"Don't bother, Juznyn," Thleana said as she approached the two men, "without a family here, I'll need something to care for. I'll watch over your animals until you return."

She held a covered basket, steam escaping from the folds of the cloth.

Juznyn gave a nod of thanks and locked the gates again.

"I baked these yams in the coals from last night's dinner. I couldn't eat. They may still be somewhat warm for your lunch. I packed bacon, boiled eggs, and the last of the apple pie too."

She gave the basket to her husband, placing her hand on his.

"No discarding the yam skins," she said. "You won't have the excuse of hungry pigs to feed. You'll need every morsel of food to keep up your own strength."

Tomus took the basket and gave his wife a long kiss. She hugged him and buried her face in his neck. She removed the jug slung over her shoulder and placed it over his.

"Here is some buttermilk too. You might as well begin your journey strong and well-fed."

The couple embraced.

Thleana looked up at her husband and said, "Bring me back my babies."

She looked at Juznyn. A teary scowl returned to her face. She shook her head, silently yet clearly blaming Drethene.

"Oh, Thleana," Tomus said. "Juznyn, she's just—"

Juznyn put his hand out to stop Tomus's words, closed his eyes and breathed deeply.

Juznyn faced Thleana. "You have the key to my house. Help yourself to whatever staples remain."

Thleana's face relaxed, and she took her own deep breath.

"I'll take good care of your home. I won't let anything go to waste."

Juznyn looked at the lone cow standing near the fence skirting their property. She was still as a statue, looking in the direction of the village.

"Will you take special care—" His voice cracked before he was interrupted by Thleana.

"Yes, Juznyn. I know she pines for Drethene. I'll be careful with her. I'll build a barn over her if necessary. She'll be well fed and relaxed by the time you return. If all goes well, she might have a calf of her own to care for."

Juznyn smiled and nodded.

Thleana looked at her husband one more time and walked back to the house.

Before they'd left Drithon's chambers, Tomus had said he was not going to wait in a swamp for everyone to gather. Drithon had originally insisted they must, but between his own mourning and his sympathy for Juznyn and his neighbor, he had bidden them farewell with his blessing.

Juznyn and Tomus consulted their compass and headed east toward the ocean town of Praniah to find their daughters.

# PART THREE

# CHAPTER TWENTY

Drithon walked through the dark, damp halls under the Academy. His single-candle lantern emitted just enough light to help him avoid tripping or colliding with a wall at one of the passageway's many bends. He did his best to cease his self-degradation and put his thoughts to better use. Doll's situation was not his doing. He focused his momentum on making things right.

He came to a sharp turn. The stones making up the walls and floor were suddenly different. He was under the dormitory.

Drithon counted seventeen doors and opened the next, which led to a dark staircase. He placed his lantern at the foot of the steps and listened closely.

In moments, he heard the rhythmic knock composed by Perthin during their planning meeting in his chambers. Drithon ascended the spiral stairs to a small landing in front of another door and put his eye to the large keyhole. He shook his head when he saw Perthin's disguise. The young man was covered completely in the shapeless gray-brown frock of a cleaning woman. Such clothing was created to cover every feature and to blend into the stone walls of the Academy. The women who wore them were instructed to stand straight against the wall with their chins tucked into their chests when passed by any male in the sleep chambers.

Drithon unlocked the door, and Perthin joined him, pulling the door tight. They quickly descended the stairs and returned to the cool, damp underground tunnel. Perthin released a long breath. Drithon had taken much longer than expected.

"A creative disguise," Drithon said.

"It allowed me to wander the hall for a ridiculously long time without much notice." Perthin glared at Drithon. "That corridor has never been so clean."

Drithon grinned for the first time since Doll's capture.

"Let's walk. I'll explain the delay," Drithon handed Perthin one of the two satchels he carried. "You must be the tallest maid the Academy has ever seen."

Perthin smiled and shook his head as he removed the dress covering his clothes and followed Drithon.

"My friends didn't let me down. Our meeting went well, and they thought up my disguise. While I waited for you, they continually walked the halls, causing me to back into the wall and other students to ignore me. When the hall was clear of everyone but them, we were able to talk enough to firm up our plans."

Drithon looked forward to learning those plans, but Perthin needed to know what had happened after Crouglan arrived at his door.

"My delay was due to some sad news."

As they walked, he explained what happened in his chambers after Perthin had left. The young scholar swallowed hard after the description of his Imprisonment instructor's gruesome final moments.

"Poor man," Perthin said. "He was one of the kindest and least presumptuous faculty members."

Following Drithon's emotionally charged telling of what had happened to Doll, Perthin stopped to face him and placed his bent arm across Drithon's chest so his hand lay firmly on the librarian's shoulder. Drithon placed his hands on Perthin's arm and bowed his head in acceptance of the long-unpracticed ritual of sympathy and understanding between men. Drithon was touched by Perthin's sincerity.

"Much has changed since we parted ways in my chambers. We should be thoughtful about our plans for leaving Dale."

"We need to hide for a while, don't we?"

"You and I may be the two most hunted men the One People have ever known. The Watchmen are not to be underestimated. They will be looking everywhere, but I think even they have forgotten these underground halls or assume them to be impassable. They will be expecting us to run. I'm hoping they give our friends safe passage out of the walls to try to lure us out. They don't realize I am much older than the oldest trick in the book."

"That wasn't so bad," Taelmai said, straightening her skirt, wrinkled by her first journey through a Flow.

"Really?" said Drethene and Klindyn in ensemble.

"I felt like I was suffocating my first time," Drethene said.

"I cried for an hour after my first trip," said Klindyn.

"Well," Taelmai said, "I worried the experience into something so close to torturous death that reality had a difficult time living up to my expectations."

Drethene and Klindyn nodded thoughtfully, then smiled at their shared reaction.

"Drethene," Taelmai said, "I'm sorry about your mom. She was always patient with me and kind, especially when I had exhausted my parents."

"Thank you, Taelmai. My mom had a lot of practice being patient at home."

Taelmai smiled at her friend. Drethene's spirit had always inspired her.

"It's good to have company again," Drethene said. "Any ideas about what we do now?"

"We've never had more than two rings in one place," Klindyn said. "Let's put them together and see what happens."

"That doesn't sound exactly safe." Fear of the unknown smothered Taelmai's will to emulate Drethene's fortitude. "Perhaps we should just try yours with Drethene's first. Or maybe—"

"Don't think too much," Drethene said. "It's difficult to put your faith in something you don't understand, but we must. If we stay here, we'll be discovered. I've been put here to be stopped and controlled, and maybe, if Crouglan continues to bend the rules, worse. So far, these rings have protected and helped us. I have faith that the more stones we have in one place, the better our circumstances."

Taelmai closed her eyes and took a shuddering breath.

"I guess I can't help my brother if I'm in prison."

"That's the spirit," Klindyn said, punching Taelmai in the arm too hard.

Taelmai winced while rubbing her arm, doing her best to transform her pained expression into a smile.

They each offered their right hand. The beauty of the stones was entrancing. Taelmai had never heard sounds as beautiful as those singing from Drethene's ring. Her brother's ring gathered the tones and painted them in light and color on the walls, floor, ceiling, and in the midst of the air, illuminating the cell. Klindyn's ring took these sights and sounds and gave them shape and life.

# tranquility

The ever-shifting images—a tree, a bird, a horse, a ring—full of color and sound, traveled throughout the cell in search of something. Tendrils extended, examining items of potential interest. The washstand, basin, and pitcher trembled as they were passed by. The half-eaten tray of food near the door shook but was otherwise left undisturbed. The bars covering the window wavered as if molten, giving Taelmai hope they'd disappear to provide their escape. The bars, too, returned to their original state.

The singing, shape-changing, shimmering energy found a satisfying corner of the room where it began to spin into a sphere. The music quickened, the colors flared, the spinning intensified, and then it was gone. Taelmai and her friends dropped their hands to their sides and stared into the darkness. Taelmai heard the sound of stone rubbing stone. Drethene touched Taelmai's shoulder, and almost instinctively, Taelmai lifted her hand so Trem's ring could light the corner. A single rock slid forward from where the wall and floor met. Once the stone fully emerged, a row of tiny folk was revealed, pushing with all their might. After they cleared the wall, the little ones brushed off their hands and congratulated one another with hugs. They danced in the gentle light of Trem's ring.

"Taelmai," Drethene said, "allow me to introduce you to your faithful family."

Drethene placed her hand on the floor, and the tiny ones climbed into her palm.

Their faces were sad as they hugged her fingers and said:

"Our brother is troubled,
Your burdens are doubled,
We must free you from the cell,
So our brother may be well."

Drethene placed them back on the floor, and they scurried to the stone they'd moved. Four sat atop the rock, and one stood in front and said:

"The stone will be freedom from more than a jail,
The key to intention one never can fail,
The spark setting fire to bright diamond flames,
The palace where goodness returns and remains."

The speaker motioned for Drethene to take the stone. The little ones hopped off and ran to Taelmai who squatted down for a better look at them. They touched her ring.

Taelmai heard their voices repeatedly chanting:

"Sister, be grounded and wield your good sword,
Your purpose is great, do not fear what's endured."

Taelmai committed the words to memory and thanked her Groundling family with gentle caresses of their heads. They giggled, each grabbing one of her fingers and giving their tiny hugs.

Drethene was struggling with the large, heavy stone.

"What should I do with this? I can't possibly carry it."

The Groundlings answered:

"The Stone and the Words will be one and the same,
Place them together and call them by name,
When the time has arrived for the two things to part,
You will see what to do, illustrated in art."

The wee folk retreated through the opening in the wall created by the absent stone and gestured for the friends to follow. Clearly the three couldn't fit, but their hands could. They placed their right hands on top of each other, stacking the rings.

Taelmai felt stretched, united, and peaceful as their bodies spiraled together like wool on a spinning wheel until they could fit through the small space. Once through, she could see only the swirling colors of Trem's ring as they moved at an incredible speed. The music from Drethene's ring was percussive and syncopated, yet still somehow soothing. They slowed down, and Klindyn's ring took on the task of molding the swirling mass back into the natural shapes of the three friends.

They landed on moss-covered earth—each soul reunited with its bruised and breathless body. Night had fallen wherever they were. The friends peered into the darkness. Near them was a melon-sized black ball illustrating through its inkiness how much light there was even in the darkest night. Moths and mosquitoes spun around the ebony globe in various orbits, creating mesmerizing patterns.

"That looks like the Flow gate in the bog Trem described," Drethene said. "He had some tricky issues with time when he met up with one of these. It's suddenly night. Who knows what day it is or where we are? Let's just be careful."

Klindyn, of course, reached toward this now enticingly unpredictable object. Suddenly, the red petals of a sizable flower surrounded and swallowed the ball into its center, creating what appeared be an immense poppy. The ball disappeared. The petals returned to their normal size.

"I saw similar flowers in the Realm," Drethene said. "The Groundlings appeared from one of them there. They can travel by flower farther than I expected."

The flower's stem retracted into the earth, taking its bloom with it. All traces of the Realm were gone.

Taelmai saw flashes of light in the distance, just bright enough to reveal the trees towering above them.

"What was that?" she asked.

"We need to get out of this forest," Drethene said.

She removed a book from her satchel, placed the stone on top, and said, "*Sacred Writ* and stone."

The stone disintegrated, sowing dust atop the ancient book. The pages of the book rustled as if someone were quickly thumbing through it, and the dust settled amidst the words. There was no time or need for discussion. The tiny folk had foretold perfectly.

"We're no longer imprisoned, but we haven't traveled far," Drethene said as she placed the book in her satchel. "We're in the forest outside of Praniah."

"Praniah!" Klindyn shouted, clapping his hands. "I knew it! This is my hometown." His mood quickly changed. "We shouldn't be in these woods. They're dangerous."

"I know," Drethene said. "I also want to avoid the impending search. Keep close together, move quickly, and be watchful. Those flying beasts have a nasty sting."

Drethene began to walk as soon as she stopped speaking.

Klindyn stood still, frozen in fear. Taelmai tried to move him, but he pulled back landing himself on the ground. His strength was impressive.

"Klindyn, I don't like the sound of these beasts either, but the only way we can avoid them is to stick together and get out of these woods."

"I've always been told to avoid the forest because of the wood wasps. I'm terrified of monsters. Stinging beasts sound scary."

"Yes, they do. Please, get up. Let's catch up to Drethene and avoid meeting any of the scary beasts."

As Klindyn slowly rose from the ground, there was a bright light accompanied by a loud buzz. The outline of a large body with many legs flew above them, embracing what appeared to be a limp horse.

Klindyn fell back but was caught up by arms in the darkness before he touched the ground. Taelmai tried to scream, but a hand over her mouth stopped the sound.

A whispering voice said, "Stay silent, or the demons of these woods will find an easy meal."

# CHAPTER TWENTY~ONE

Drithon's lantern emphasized the darkness as its light was swallowed just a few feet ahead of where they walked. He and Perthin had carefully counted the hours. They hoped three days of hiding in these dark, dank halls would discourage any pursuers and still allow them to catch up with their companions. They had kept their talking to a minimum to keep their focus on the exact passage of time. Provisions and patience were running low.

As the hall curved, they were often surprised by walls but never by a creature of darkness as might be expected in such a forgotten place. The passageways were apparently kept secret even from beasts.

Now they were moving, and Drithon was happy to begin a conversation.

"You think your friends will be able to help you?"

"They're a crafty lot for students of *Tranquility*. They're curious and habitual note-takers. Recently, we were supposed to be studying ancient texts as examples of past heresy, but we weren't convinced they were blasphemous. We're natural Questioners."

Drithon smiled, which felt good.

"We wrote in our own secret code," Perthin added with a boyish sense of pride.

Drithon studied the young man. Just like Drethene, Perthin was serious and showed surprising bravery beyond his years. But then the truth of his age would shine through in a simple statement. They were so young. The fulfillment of prophecy was unstoppable, but they were so very young.

Drithon recited:

> *The students meant to be future leaders,*
> *Will truly become the most useful readers,*
> *Of texts and scriptures thought heretic,*
> *Their knowing and sharing is prophetic.*

"A quote, I assume," Perthin said, "but like nothing I've ever read."

"I'm glad you shared your affinity for ancient texts. This prophecy's fulfillment couldn't have been better timed. I'm encouraged. Please tell me the plans you've made with your friends."

"We've agreed they'll be most helpful as informants from the Academy. We've been eager to try our experimental communication network but haven't traveled far enough from Dale to do so. If our theory is correct, to stay in touch all we need are healthy forests and feathered friends."

"I hope you have an alternative plan. You do realize we dwell in Unemond, not in the Realm?"

"Yes, I do. Likewise, you told me about powers of enchantment displayed in your chambers. Unless I'm mistaken, you live in Unemond too."

"True. Yet these powers were wielded by folks or tools of the Realm. I would be surprised to discover you and all of your friends have such a connection."

"As far as I can tell, none of us do. Instead, we hope to earn the trust and help of the birds and trees. If I've researched correctly, they reflect many, if not all of the attributes of their cousins in the Realm."

"Touché." Drithon was not disappointed to have been bested by a younger theorist. "Yes, some life in Unemond hasn't allowed the choices of mortals to change its purpose and still retains powers of the Realm. You've researched well. Tell me more."

They'd reached the door to the outside and stopped to finish their conversation. Academics in the midst of hypotheses should not enter potential danger.

"During our botany studies, my friends and I stumbled across interesting battle descriptions from war-time manuscripts. They took place almost exclusively in open areas. Whenever an army was cornered against a forest, it might as well have been up against an immense fortification wall. The soldiers never entered the woods for cover. Instead, they met their doom at the outskirts of the forest. Not daring to approach our instructors regarding the details of battle, we asked one another, 'Why?'"

Drithon leaned against the wall, folded his arms, and awaited Perthin's rhetorical explanation.

"Knowing the armies were headed toward the forest, the forest must have made itself impassable, refusing to allow injury to trees and inhabitants because of the follies of man. But, how? We knew better than to look for the answer on the Academy's bookshelves."

The librarian nodded his agreement.

"A few of us attended the only class with any focus on the Realm, 'Tales and Lies of an Era Gone By.'"

Drithon shuddered at the insulting title.

"I know," Perthin said, "but this was the only class using texts of the Realm. Every day, the instructor emphasized the reading of these books was necessary for future leaders, only to answer the questions of children. He said, 'The very young still hear stories based on the magic of the Realm. You must be prepared to help them separate the real from the imaginary.' Instead, we discovered the connections remaining between Unemond and the Realm, no matter how hard the Academy works to ignore them. If only they would stop squelching the innate wisdom of children, a class with such a scathing title wouldn't need to exist."

Drithon's confidence in Perthin and his friends grew.

"We approached the children's stories as historical documentation. We read of the trees' ability to share information through their root systems. When the trees were far from one another, birds carried information from tree to tree and forest to forest. We learned of tree personalities. The long-windedness of flowering trees and the brevity of the pines. We've created a way to tap this network using birds we've talked to for two years now. They're our ambassadors, translating our intentions and our messages to the trees. Once the trees understand our purpose, we have faith they'll assist us."

"Your plan is well researched. I'm glad you shared the details, since I can help you succeed where your assumptions will surely fail."

Perthin looked disappointed.

"The trees won't trust you," Drithon said. "Your words will hold no merit. They're trees. They've been here a long time and have experienced the history of men. You mentioned the trees' innocence, which is true, and their connection to the Realm, which is strong. I can help. Their intelligence is undeniable, and their trust in the Realm is absolute. They'll help once the connection between your actions and the fulfillment of the Realm's prophecy is made clear."

Perthin nodded his thanks, his face was grim.

"We were interested in the trees. I thought we'd be using what we found to help the One People have a better connection to their surroundings. We dreamed of being known for our ingenious research. I never imagined I'd be on the run, using our findings to be in touch with my spies."

"Young Perthin, you're using your research to help the One People. You're just doing so in an unexpected way."

"Thank you." Perthin looked less disappointed. "When will you share more of these prophecies?"

"I wish there were time now. As prophecy is fulfilled, changes are taking place in Unemond and the Realm, altering their relationship to one another. What we've known as safe, secret, and undeniable may no longer be so. We must work quickly and remain wary."

"Okay." Perthin fidgeted with his satchel strap. "Perhaps it's time for us to leave this place."

"You're right." Drithon clapped Perthin's shoulder. "May there be a day when you and I surround ourselves with books, tea, and endless discussion. For now, well, this is a fine beginning."

Perthin looked dubious but nodded, and the scholarly friends entered an unspoken pact of silence.

Drithon found the correct key, unlocked the door and extinguished his lantern. They both put their weight against the rock and metal barrier. Drithon signaled to move slowly. They could not avoid the long, loud sound of stone scraping stone. Fresh, cool air rushed in the slightly opened door. Thankfully, they were under the cover of ghostly twilight.

They exited directly through the wall of Dale as they'd hoped. Not even the Watchmen knew of this door, but the two peered in every direction to be certain they were unseen.

They stepped out into the fresh air, which was quickly pushed from their lungs as they both landed on the ground under the weight of a mighty force.

Klindyn lay frozen with fear, eyes shut tight, in the arms of Juznyn, who waited for the boy to realize that he was safe. Taelmai watched them as she embraced her father. She drew back from him and caressed the welt on his face, placed there by her own hand before she knew who had grabbed her.

"Papa, I don't know how you got here so quickly, but I'm glad to see you."

"Me too, love. But we traveled for three days to get here."

"That's impossible, we were only in Drethene's cell … Wait, we traveled through a Flow. Drethene said they mess up time."

"We'll need to figure this out later. Now, we need to get out of this forest or risk a doom I think surpasses even your imagination."

Taelmai searched her mind for the most horrific fate she could conjure.

"Please, Taelmai, I'm not challenging your creativity. If you promise to just keep moving, I'll tell you what we've seen."

Klindyn grabbed her hand. Taelmai looked at Juznyn and saw the hopeful expression on his face.

"Drethene was with us until a few minutes ago. Klindyn and I were following her. We were distracted, and she continued on. We lost sight of her, and then you found us."

"We should imitate her drive to escape," her father said. "We left home with two horses but are now forced to walk. Trust me, we do not want to be reunited with our steeds."

A loud buzzing of wings caused Juznyn and her father to tackle Taelmai and Klindyn. Their lives were saved by the scrubby brush just high enough to block the stings of the deadly creatures. Unfortunately, the four companions were full of thistles when they arose. They had no time to remove the prickly barbs.

"This way!" Klindyn called out as they began to run. "I think I know a way out."

"Are those giant bugs?" Taelmai asked.

Buzzing wings were heard again, and Juznyn was almost hit in the head by a falling hoof.

"They're trying to bring us down with our own horse parts," Juznyn growled. "These things are starting to make me mad."

"Never mind anger, unless it'll make you run faster," Klindyn said, moving quickly for such a little one. "They won't leave the cover of the trees, and I see light up ahead. We're almost out of the forest."

Taelmai tripped over a root and fell hard on the ground. Her father stopped to help her and bade the others continue. Her ankle was hurt. Klindyn and Juznyn stayed at her side as well. They tried to lift her, but the approach of buzzing wings sent them to the forest floor.

The men threw themselves over both children. Taelmai lay facing up and saw the underbellies of the hideous creatures. They were dark green, almost black. Their stingers were c-shaped, not only poisoning their victims, but slicing them as the beasts moved over their prey. Huge eyes set above eerie, permanently smiling mouths looked at her. This took her fear of insects to a whole new level.

"No!" Drethene's voice was carried to them on her silent forest-nimble feet. Taelmai saw her running with her hand stretched before her.

The closest beast screamed and flew off.

Drethene kept her hand pointed in the direction of the huge bugs and slid down next to her pile of companions.

"Grab my hand!" Drethene yelled.

Taelmai and Klindyn knew the command was for them and obeyed with their ring-bearing hands. The vibration of the rings shook through Drethene, Taelmai, and Klindyn's arms. Strong branches grew from the rings, encasing the five companions.

The beasts landed next to their intended victims but were unable to break through the protective structure. For a frightening few moments, the wasps thrust their stingers in any opening they could find. Thin legs with jagged edges attempted to pull at the branches, to no avail. Yet the creatures wouldn't abandon what they saw as such a perfect meal.

"We're safe for the moment, but how determined are these wood wasps?" Juznyn asked.

"Not as determined as we are," Drethene said. She avoided looking at her father, thus missing his immense pride. "We need to break the rings free from the branches."

"You're kidding, right?" Taelmai said. "What if the branches collapse, or disappear, or—"

"Have faith, Taelmai," Drethene said. "On the count of three, pull as hard as you can. Then we need to place our hands on top of one another again. One, two, three."

Drethene, Taelmai, and Klindyn pulled the rings away from the branches. *Snap, snap, snap.* They immediately rejoined their hands.

The rocky, root-filled forest floor upon which they sat began to soften. The silty soil sank under the weight of the five captives. They descended, slowly at first, as if on a platform sliding down a chute. Taelmai looked up to see the large eyes of the confused creatures bouncing from crack to crack between the branches to watch as their enticing meal slipped away.

Although the five were soon moving at an incredible speed, they all kept their wits. There were surprised exhalations when their course suddenly bent to the right, but no one panicked. Suddenly, one by one, they erupted from a hole in the earth. They each landed on top of the other ... or so they thought.

Crouglan sat at his desk, staring straight ahead between the chairs holding the stone-still Trem and Doll. Phovul stood behind him, regarding the stationary scene, becoming bored. Having three pets was proving more challenging than he'd expected.

His boredom soon turned to a bad temper. He had them in this puppet state, because he was unable to control them simultaneously. His master had been right about Trem. The boy was strong and pulled away from Phovul whenever possible. He had to keep Trem subdued until he could manage him better. Crouglan was easy. Phovul could give him full autonomy, and he wouldn't stray from his grasp. Doll presented a different challenge. Phovul wanted her fully aware and alive.

He had found a place to practice wielding his mortal weapons. Crouglan's office was out from under his master's nose and was a place never entered uninvited by the One People.

Trem was looking at Phovul. One corner of Trem's mouth held a small smirk. Phovul's temper grew from foul to furious. He leapt at Trem, sailing over Crouglan and the desk. Phovul stood tall and fierce in front of Trem. He yanked the boy's head back by his hair, knowing from experience the pain he inflicted.

"Fool," Trem whispered, and struck Phovul in the face.

Too infuriated to fathom how Trem was able to act of his own accord, Phovul closed his eyes. In the darkness behind his lids, he saw an endless landscape of chains. These connected him to Malgriffe somewhere in the blackness in the far distance of the dreadful scene. In his mind's eye, he looked down at himself, and he was but one huge chain link. From him dangled three small chains, confirming all of his pets, even Trem, remained bound to him. Phovul could feel the power seductively vibrating from the distant blackness beyond the sea of chains. He prepared to reach for the evil, to welcome and embrace the nausea. Trem hadn't been wasting time as Phovul's prisoner. As soon as the energy was called up from darkness, Phovul saw one of those three small chains stretching to steal the power before he gained possession. He knew it was Trem. The chain held the energy, but the weight and the evil must have been too much for Trem to bear. The subconscious images shattered.

Phovul was too shocked to reach for the power himself once Trem dropped it. He let the seductive energy fall away. Trem lay half conscious on the floor, retching.

The boy had actually stolen his strength from him. Phovul's anger subsided. He was strangely impressed by Trem's will. He put admiration aside and focused instead on never letting Trem get close to overcoming him again. Doll and Crouglan were also on the floor, knocked there by the shockwaves of Trem's attempt. With Trem semiconscious, Phovul found controlling the other two to be simple and had them sit themselves upright once again.

Phovul laughed. By trying to break free and attack Phovul with his own power, the fool boy had helped him discover how to control his three pets. The weight of his master's power was too much for a mortal. He could use the energy as a paperweight to keep one of his captives fully subdued. He would then have just two to control, and *that* he could do. A temporary solution, but a decent one.

Phovul was certain his powers would increase and allow him more control over his captives. Until then, Phovul was pleased with his plan. Trem wouldn't be able to cause any more trouble, Crouglan would continue Phovul's bidding at the Academy, and Doll would be Phovul's constant companion.

Phovul smiled, then winced. He touched his cheek. Trem had drawn blood and caused bruising to his face, something even his master had avoided doing. He thought this boy might be more troublesome than helpful. His master saw power in numbers. All three of his pets would remain—for now.

# CHAPTER TWENTY~TWO

Darkness. But not as dark as inside the Flow. They were outside in the breezy openness and not in the forest. Klindyn was lying face-up, rubbing his eyes and whimpering. Tomus sat up from his place next to him, startling Klindyn and causing him to roll down the heap of squirming bodies to the ground.

"Methinks three rings just saved us from giant killer wasps!" Tomus said, hoping the articulation of the ridiculousness he just experienced would wake him up from what certainly must be the strangest dream. It didn't work.

Tomus leaned over to find where Klindyn had landed and found himself nose-to-nose with Drithon, whose spectacles were nearly vertical on his face. Tomus burst into such a laugh he spat directly into the librarian's unprotected eyes, causing Drithon's head to lurch back square into Taelmai's chin. She bit her tongue, hard, and rolled over to Klindyn, joining him in a good cry.

Tomus helped Drithon to the ground and leaned against a nearby wall to see who else would emerge from this strange pile of people.

Drethene and her father each reached out and patted Taelmai's back. Their hands met, and they both suddenly sat upright. Drethene averted her gaze. Her father lifted her chin and kissed her on the cheek. They embraced, then walked away to find a comfortable place to talk.

This revealed Perthin at the bottom of the jumble. Tomus rose and walked over to offer him his hand. Perthin gladly accepted the kindness, stood up, and the two men found a place to sit against the wall, which belonged, unmistakably, to Dale.

Tomus kept looking up the height of the wall.

"No worries, my friend," Perthin said. "The Watchmen don't believe Flows exist. As far as they're concerned, the only way to get this close to the wall is to walk across the fields. I've never seen a Watchman look straight down the wall."

"Regardless, I'd like to move along."

"Drithon's waving for us to join him. I'm sure he has a plan."

They began to walk, and Tomus saw Juznyn farther along the wall with Drethene curled up against him. Next to her sat Klindyn, looking displaced. Taelmai was not far away, but she was clearly nursing her bitten tongue. By her labored breaths, her mind had grown her injury into a swelling, breath-defeating, choking hazard.

Klindyn looked even lonelier as he watched Drethene melt into the warmth of her father's embrace. Tomus stopped walking as she unleashed unbridled tears and passionate wails of mourning.

"Daughter, the last time your mother left our home, she did so with the intention of giving all she had to support you and your purpose. She knew what you'd be up against, and she followed you without fear."

Drethene choked back her tears. "How's her death helped at all, Pa?"

Juznyn held his daughter close.

"I don't have the answer, Drethene. The *Sacred Writ* says to 'continue boldly forward, without question, knowing what happens is right as long as we walk in the light no matter how dark our path.'"

Drethene's tears slowed, and she sniffed as she worked to catch her breath.

"You read and remembered."

"I've been reading that book every day."

"Ma said you were searching for *Tranquility* the day we went to the Honor Room."

"To burn it."

Juznyn's face was peaceful. Drethene smiled.

Tomus struggled with his friend's intent. He decided to move closer to his daughter to comfort her. Perthin continued walking toward Drithon.

"I miss her," Drethene said, and paused, taking a deep breath, "but I know we can do this."

"That's my girl. We can do this."

Klindyn inched closer to Drethene.

"This group was gathered at least in part by what happened in the Honor Room," Juznyn said. "Your ma might have helped us already, Drethene. Now she's in blissful peace for eternity in Valndana."

He held his daughter's face in his hands and kissed her forehead.

"I have a very wise brother," Juznyn said, making Drethene's smile broader. "He'd spoken to me of Valndana many times before you did, but I'm a stubborn man, and I chose to stick with what was familiar. He yammered enough for me to retain sufficient details to help us both when we're missing your ma, like we are now."

Drethene laughed. Her father released her cheeks from his grasp and tucked a lock of her wayward hair behind her ear.

Klindyn moved toward Drethene until he was touching her. She put her arm around him, and he snuggled into her side.

"Entering Valndana is a homecoming," Juznyn said. "You know the warmth you feel when offered a pot of tea and biscuits upon entering a loved one's home? Valndana is a million times better. Ma is at an endless tea party, and she'll pour us our first cup when we join her."

Klindyn sniffled. Drethene stroked his hair and looked at her father.

"I love you, Pa."

"I love you, Drethene. We're destined for a perfect place. However, this world is still worth fixing. Let's get to work."

The three stood and walked toward Drithon, who was talking with Perthin.

"Pa, isn't that the Questioner?" Drethene asked.

Perthin half-smiled and waved at Drethene.

"I'll explain later," Juznyn said.

Tomus helped Taelmai over to the group.

Drithon embraced Drethene, "This is a fine beginning, my nieceling, a fine beginning indeed."

A subdued but heartfelt cheer went up from the group.

Drithon released his niece from his arms but held her hand as he said, "Let's plan quickly. We've been brought together for a reason and need a safer haven to decide what we do next. These rings are incredibly powerful, and I wonder if Unemond can bear them. Ancient powers are being reborn into new manifestations eliciting excitement but warranting prudence."

"Where'th Doll?" Taelmai asked, holding the tip of her tongue in the handkerchief Tomus had given her.

Tomus shook his head but felt strangely comforted by the normalcy of his daughter's worrying ways.

Klindyn ran to her and held her free hand.

"Uncle, is she still inside the village?" Drethene asked. "She could be in danger. We could probably create a Flow—"

Drethene was stopped short by her uncle's raised palm and sorrowful eyes.

"Hers is a sad tale, young ones," Drithon said, "but sharing now will only delay us. She's alive, as far as we know."

Taelmai hugged Klindyn, but the comfort was insufficient, so she embraced Tomus. She seemed to melt out of his arms and fell to the ground, sobbing.

"Taelmai," Drithon said, "I want nothing more than to join you in your sorrow, but if we want to avoid the same fate as Doll and Trem, we need to work together—immediately. We do have the herbs Doll brought to your house. I can find an elixir to calm you."

Taelmai raised her tear-streaked face. "While we were at my house, I asked Doll not to give me any remedies. She honored my request. I'll stay true to my own words."

She swallowed hard, seeming pleased she could do so.

"I'll find and help my brother with full awareness, even if that means an occasional setback on my part."

Drethene was clearly sad about Doll, but she and Juznyn smiled at Taelmai, who was now standing tall and firm, even though her breathing was labored as she struggled against the hyperventilation she often suffered following bouts of sobbing.

"I'm proud of you, Taelmai," Tomus said.

He knelt before her, holding both of her hands.

"Your mother wants nothing more than for you and Trem to return to her. I know you're going to bring joy to your ma. You're growing brave and strong. I'll be here with you. If ever you're not feeling courageous, Pa is here."

Tomus stood up, and Taelmai embraced him with great relief.

Klindyn grabbed her hand as soon as she released her father, and she smiled warmly at him.

Drithon seemed relieved to put the subject of Doll's situation aside. He gestured toward the small black globe nestled in the scrubby bush next to the wall of Dale.

"This Flow is strange to me. But right now, we need a safe place and good counsel. The Realm provides both, and here we stand before a Flow gate. Okay. Once we're inside, I hope to be able to guide us to the Realm. Everyone stay close."

Drithon walked toward the orb. His words didn't evoke great confidence, but everyone followed him.

In the distance, the sound of a rooster crowing and cow bells jingling announced the beginning of a new day. Drithon approached the Flow gate, touched it, and disappeared. Drethene and Juznyn followed quickly, as did Perthin.

Although a Flow had saved Tomus from the wood wasps, falling into one unknowingly was quite different from entering one of his own volition. The responsibility of emboldening her father was just what Taelmai needed.

She took Tomus by the hand and brought him to the Flow with an encouraging smile. Klindyn followed close behind, awkwardly patting Tomus's arm. They heard the cry from across Hushed Pond, and Klindyn became unsettled by the haunting call. Taelmai and Tomus both reached out to reassure Klindyn, and the three of them entered the Flow with unexpected ease.

Entering the Flow was surprisingly uneventful for everyone. Once all seven companions were accounted for, Drethene focused on following her Uncle Drithon, who kept a quick, steady pace.

"Uncle, why don't we stop for a while?"

"I feel a blackness in the Flow, Drethene. Not the absence of light but a lack of good intent. I fear evil things have found their way into our sacred Flows."

Taelmai drew in her breath, which resounded loudly. The thought of what frightening creatures might dwell in this cavernous darkness was unwholesome nourishment for her keen imagination.

Uncle Drithon walked with his jar of luminescence held in front of him. Like moths attracted to the light, the group followed close behind. He discovered a wall, causing minor collisions amongst his followers.

"This is made of dirt and root. It's natural, not the stone walls of the ancient Flows. This creation is raw and new."

Drethene left her uncle to talk to himself, and by following the whimpers, quickly found her way to Taelmai.

"Don't fret, Taelmai, we won't be here long. I remember seeing shadows when Trem and I were in a Flow. We spent a long time there, and nothing happened. If the shadows were anything more than figments of my imagination, they were afraid of us. They seemed to scatter in the face of Trem's ring."

Without realizing, Drethene had prompted her friend to action.

"It's not working," Taelmai said.

"What's not working?"

"The ring isn't giving out its light."

"Taelmai, I don't think that's a good idea any—" Unwittingly, Drethene grabbed Taelmai's adorned hand, touching her ring to Trem's.

Her uncle heard Drethene's ring singing before Trem's could emit enough light to cut through the darkness.

"What's this mischief?"

The light exploded from Taelmai's ring, along with flowers and birds. Hundreds of pale eyes appeared throughout the Flow and then quickly extinguished as their lids closed to block the brightness. Loud scurrying and slithering were heard all around as mysterious creatures found their way to darker places.

"Enough!" Uncle Drithon grabbed the two girls, each by a shoulder.

The music and light were extinguished. The group stood in darkness, listening to the disturbing yips and hisses of the startled, retreating beasts.

"That little display will be discussed in a safer place," Uncle Drithon scolded. "Now that you've shouted our presence from the top of a mountain, finding our way to the Realm has become more urgent."

Drethene was thankful for the return to darkness. She detested being treated like a child. Nonetheless, she'd been careless. How could she be a leader if she was a troublesome follower?

"Your judgment was far keener in the midst of the Honor Room," said a voice close to Drethene's ear.

Her clarity of thought was fogged with self-loathing and guilt. She jumped to the worst possible conclusion about the vaguely familiar voice, spun around in a wild panic, and kicked with all of her might. She heard a deep groan and the thump of someone falling to his knees.

"What now?" Uncle Drithon exclaimed.

He found Drethene and pushed his jar against her nose.

"I got him with one kick." Drethene pointed downward.

Her uncle lowered the light to reveal Perthin, writhing in pain. Uncle Drithon, her father, and Tomus all moved in, and Drethene watched them help him. She realized her mistake but was still wondering why the Questioner was with them.

"You're on a roll, Drethene," her uncle said. "You kicked the poor boy's barely healed hand."

When Perthin's watering eyes met hers, she wanted to look away but bit her lip instead.

Perthin managed a smile through his gritted teeth and said, "I should've begun with hello."

Drethene shrugged, feeling unsure and uncomfortable. She watched her uncle, father, and neighbor continue to care for him, and she trusted their genuine concern. He was not their prisoner. He was a comrade. Honestly, she hadn't disliked him, even in the Honor Room.

"You're a friend," she said to Perthin.

He looked at her and nodded during the painful examination of his reinjured hand.

Drethene's thoughts returned to that horrid day in the Honor Room. Memories of her mother's death made her bury her face in her hands. She remembered Trem approaching her and being warned not to trust him. Then there was the quilt, followed by exhaustion.

"'The friend may be foe, and those feared become friends,'" she said, remembering the prophecy her uncle recited before they entered the Honor Room.

She looked up at Perthin with sudden realization.

"You carried me."

"I barely lifted you, really. I tried to help you. I failed."

Reminiscence and emotion spun in Drethene's head. Perthin had put himself in harm's way to attempt her rescue. He must have abandoned a lofty position in the Academy to join her now. She'd read about such drastic, poignant changes in allegiance in her history books. Then she remembered another passage from the *History and Prophecies of the Realm*.

*Through the years, souls are called hither and nigh,*
*Paths as well numbered as stars in the sky,*
*There is one way that is perfect and true,*
*Age after age it retains just a few.*
*All other choices appear to be right,*
*Convincing their people, they're worth a good fight,*

# tranquility

*One will appear to guide those who have scattered,*
*Rich and bejeweled, and those ragged and tattered,*
*Once there was certainty, fervor, and pride,*
*Now truth breaks through and provides a new guide.*

She wanted to question the Questioner for more details but allowed wisdom to silence her.

"Thank you," she said, "and I'm sorry. Clearly, my choices have big consequences, and they're only going to get bigger."

"I think everyone here has made tough decisions lately," Perthin said. "But we've all chosen to be here with you. Let's continue on—together."

Drethene held Perthin's uninjured hand. They spoke quietly while the other was rebandaged.

"Thankfully, we have Doll's poultice, which will keep the pain and swelling at bay until I can focus on healing again. We must move on," her uncle announced.

He picked up his jar and began to walk. Everyone followed. Uncle Drithon knocked the walls with his fist as he walked.

"What I want to know," he said, "is how you exited your Flow at the exact spot where Perthin and I escaped the village, and how we all arrived there within moments of one another. All Flows are timeless, but this one might be equipped with other traits."

"Does anything evil know how to access the Flows?" Klindyn asked.

Uncle Drithon stopped and performed an about-face, followed by successions of deep inhalations and frustrated exhalations as he struggled to find his words. Drethene didn't know the answer, but based on his reaction, was glad she wasn't the one who'd asked the question. Klindyn hid behind her.

"Not one of you knows against whom we stand, do you?" Uncle Drithon asked.

His question was rhetorical, but disgraced heads hung low.

"Most of you don't even know his name," he continued, the pitch of his voice rising. "Do you even realize one dark power wields the evil in both of our worlds?"

Drethene wanted to stand strong for their world but didn't even know their enemy or where he was. Klindyn seemed the wisest and bravest amongst them for asking a question important enough to astonish her uncle.

"Forgive me, my friends," Uncle Drithon said, his smile tinged with embarrassment. "By now I should've told you more about Malgriffe, who controls the evil against which we fight."

Drethene joined in the collective sigh of relief as the friends realized they weren't being blamed for their ignorance.

"To answer your question, Klindyn," Uncle Drithon said, "Malgriffe has been banned from the Realm. All Flows, even this new one, are made from elements of the Realm. Malgriffe can't enter here, but his servants can. We're as safe—or vulnerable—here as anywhere in Unemond."

He placed his jar down and sat.

"Malgriffe is immortal, born in the Realm. Until his birth, evil in the Realm was kept at bay by overwhelming goodness and resulted in relatively harmless manifestations such as an imp's impulse to hide things not belonging to her.

"When it came to marriage, the ancient folk of the Realm preferred their own kind. Sometimes a sprite and an imp might marry, but no great surprise came of their union. There appeared to be no need to control bonds between folks with varied vexing qualities. A complicated, almost impossible family tree would be necessary to result in pure evil. Unfortunately, the almost impossible is still possible."

"So, a group of gentle, peace-loving people need to overcome heinous immortal evil." Tomus rubbed his forehead. "Saying that out loud wasn't any better than hearing it in my mind."

"You'll be well equipped to stand against this evil, and stand you must, for Unemond and for the Realm. You see, the place in the Realm where Malgriffe was born and where he committed his first evil deeds remains unable to support life. As Malgriffe gains strength, this dead part of the Realm grows. Unemond's in danger of losing its people to Malgriffe's evil. The Realm's in danger of being physically destroyed by it."

No one offered a decent response to the grave news. Uncle Drithon rose and walked away from the group.

Drethene's thoughts returned to a gnawing question. She got up and followed her uncle.

"Uncle?" She broke his concentration and sent him tripping over his robes to land on the sandy floor of the Flow.

His jar thudded at Drethene's feet. "Yes, my nieceling?"

She picked up the jar and sat beside him.

"Um, never mind. I think you just answered my question. I thought I had lost my clumsy, disorganized uncle. I'm strangely relieved you just fell."

"So am I! That tumble was the best step I've taken in this Flow. You came to Dale from Praniah by the sea. All the Flows I've known are as hard as stone, but the floor of this one is covered in sand."

He let sand run through his fingers.

"You opened yourselves to the power of the rings seeking safety beyond your own ability and reunion with us. The Flows created by the rings aren't a part of the network connecting Unemond to the Realm. Well, at least this one isn't. This Flow was created with a purpose now fulfilled. Why the passage still remains is another question."

An uncertain silence was in the air.

"So," Taelmai said, "do you have any idea how to get us to the Realm, hopefully before this Flow begins to tumble in on itself?"

"We shouldn't fear this Flow's sudden destruction. Flows, even those not leading to the Realm, are of the Realm. They're helpful to us, and in our own sentimental ways, we might consider them comrades. At the same time, Flows aren't alive and have neither the ability to hesitate nor to plot against us. This Flow remains intact and won't disappear until its purpose has been fulfilled. Still, just to be on the safe side, when we do exit the Flow, we'll have Drethene, Taelmai, and Klindyn be the last ones out."

They exchanged less than confident glances, and the group seemed to shrink as everyone drew closer together. Except for Uncle Drithon, who continued to gaze thoughtfully farther into the Flow.

"Their rings have already proven themselves full of surprises. I'm confident there's much more to be discovered. Everyone, lay your hands on someone with a ring. Even if you've never been there, fill your minds with thoughts of the Realm, and let's see what can be done."

# PART FOUR

# CHAPTER TWENTY~THREE

The ticking of the large clock in the corner was the only sound in the classroom. The Academy students sat with their history books closed on their desks. Clean quills stood at the ready, with ink jars still tightly closed. On this beautiful, breezy morning, the windows were locked tight. Bearlon sat in the front row wrinkling his nose at the smell of dusty books hanging heavy in the stuffy room.

The thick wood door scraped against the stone floor as Professor Magones entered. Nostrils flared as students breathed in the cool air accompanying him from the hallway. The door creaked shut. The rhythm of the clock was a portent of the two hours yet to be endured in the stale classroom.

Professor Magones was tall and thin, his head covered in thick white wavy hair. He was already wearing winter robes, although the autumn days were in their post-frost warm period. He complained the heat seeped from his bones more quickly each year.

Thankfully, he'd not begun his tradition of keeping a roaring fire in the large hearth taking up most of the interior wall. There was barely enough oxygen for the room's stifled occupants, and Bearlon wasn't ready for the fire to take its share.

The heavy smell of pipe smoke surrounded the professor. His face was a map of wrinkled pathways, and unless he was surprised or passionate about a subject, his eyes hid behind heavy, squinting lids. Bearlon wasn't overly curious about the color of Magones's eyes, as they were certain to be some shade of brown.

He took a book from a shelf and walked toward the students, dangling the text from his fingertips as if it were a weapon with which he was familiar and deft. Using his other hand with surprising strength, he picked up and spun a student desk around to face them. The desk hit the floor with a bang, and a rattle threatening its stability. He sat down right in front of Bearlon, their knees nearly touching.

Tucked into the squat student desk, Professor Magones looked even more elongated. His wiry legs bent to one side, he leaned over the book he'd placed in front of him.

"Good morning," the professor intoned, sounding bored by his own impending lesson. "We'll continue our examination of the barbaric rituals of pre-*Tranquility* peoples and how they promulgated violent activities leading to war and death. Open to page 947 in your books and prepare your quills." Clicking ink caps and rustling paper punctuated the shifting sounds of restless bodies searching in vain for comfortable positions.

Professor Magones opened his book in one turn to the correct page, leaned close, and began reading aloud. Occasionally, he'd lean back and continue speaking in the same slow, monotone tempo. He may have been elaborating or inserting an ancient passage edited out years ago. He was often referred to as a walking history book—dusty and dry, yet impressively knowledgeable.

Bearlon felt pressured to act engaged in today's lesson. Nine days had passed since the Honor Room tragedy. He'd been up late with his friends, working on their latest attempt at passing messages through a network of trees. Their work needed to take place under the cover of darkness, so morning classes, especially lectures, were difficult to endure.

He and his friends were stumped by unanticipated challenges. He scribbled simple statements to be used as test messages. These samples needed to be thoughtful enough to engage the trees' cooperation, yet contain no information that if intercepted, could lead to him or his cohorts.

They'd created an official study group. When Perthin had failed to return from that fateful Honor Room meeting, Bearlon and another friend had approached their science professor with their proposed group and purpose.

The study of science was deemed negligible in the upholding of *Tranquility*. Consequently, this professor was also Department Chair, albeit a department of one, and had the authority to approve the creation of study groups. Any interest shown by students in further exploring science pleased him, therefore Bearlon and his friends' application had been approved forthwith.

The friends' quick thinking proved fortuitous. Following their meeting with Perthin in the halls of the dormitory, his disappearance was made public. Bearlon and his friends found themselves under scrutiny. Their science professor vouched for their sincere interest in, and the academic integrity of, their proposed area of study. He'd recorded the date and time of their application. The submission occurred while Perthin was in captivity, which had never been announced, and no proof of their involvement in his disappearance could be found.

After the students were cleared of any wrongdoing, Academy officials were busy rebuilding the Honor Room and creating propaganda blaming every problem at the Academy on Drethene. They could find no harm in a group of history students who wanted to study the stars through tree canopies to "further explore ancient constellation interpretation by forest dwelling nomadic warriors and how this affected their participation in the Great War."

When Perthin had visited the dormitory, Bearlon and his friends had made him an honorary and anonymous member of the Dendrologist Astronomists. While voting him in, they'd brainstormed how to keep Perthin hidden from suspicious eyes until Drithon arrived. They'd come up with two equally dependable ideas. The one landing Perthin in a woman's frock was selected by unanimous vote—it was simply more entertaining. They never shared with him their less embarrassing alternative.

Bearlon and his friends were quite pleased with themselves—their group name, their mission, and the permission given them to leave the village walls after dark to enter the forest.

They'd stopped patting each other on the back since they were having less success than they'd hoped. They'd read a great deal about how various trees communicated. If they gave a juniper a complicated message such as, "Run through the oak forest, around the west side of the pond, up the hill to the end of the pine trees and send a return message when you've reached the clearing," the recipient received the message, "Hurry." A message such as "Eat fruit," sent through a group of young apple trees, returned as, "The trees awake, the rains begin, the flowers bloom, the leaves dost grow, we feel the light, the insects act, our young are born. Reap and spread our seed for future generations."

Through experimentation with the more cooperative members of the forest, they'd discovered messages were sent with more clarity from tree to tree. As a result, they were working on the best combination of trees through which to send a message in order for the recipient to receive a true translation of the original.

The birds, with whom the Dedrologist Astronomists had learned to communicate, were taking the messages to and from the trees. Bearlon and his friends were pleased to have the birds' cooperation and commitment. The young men could simply speak their messages to the birds, but a complicated code of vocalizations, head movements, pecks, and scratches was needed for the birds to pass a message back to them. As for the trees, thus far they were willing to play this game with the birds, but the students had yet to see how messages of importance would be received.

Bearlon bounced his knee to avoid falling asleep. He kept his quill scribbling simple sentences and his mind running through normal progressions of trees in a forest. He hoped they'd add up to a good mixture of personalities.

"Stop that!"

Bearlon jumped, toppling his ink jar and sending his quill flying into the next row of seats. Professor Magones had firmly placed a long-fingered hand on Bearlon's now motionless knee. The tips of his fingers dug into Bearlon's robes. His thick nails were clipped short, but the ancient skin on his fingertips was hard and dry. Bearlon was sure his leg would show red marks for days. For the first time, he saw the professor's eyes—no surprise, they were brown. Evidently, fury opened them wide as well.

"I ... I'm sorry."

Professor Magones nodded and leaned back in his chair. His eyes relaxed into their slits, and he resumed his lecture.

Bearlon sighed and looked around the room. The rest of the class was sitting upright, wide-eyed, clearly woken from their own stupors. He smiled apologetically and faced their professor. He could hear the rest of the students slowly slumping back into their history class slouch. A tap on his arm almost sent his newly recapped ink jar tumbling again. A classmate was returning his quill. He smiled gratefully over his shoulder.

Bearlon crossed his legs and thought about the trees. *If we begin with deciduous trees, the message might be plenty exaggerated by the time it reaches the pines. They'll filter, hopefully to the basic essence of the information. If a small fruit tree grove is on the other side, the message might be close to the original meaning by the time it gets to the recipient.*

He was distracted by a drumming sound on the other side of the classroom. Was another student so amused by Magones's outburst he was trying out a new annoyance? Bearlon scanned the room until he heard the sound again. There was a woodpecker on the window ledge, looking straight at him! The bird began swaying its head back and forth either for joy of being seen by him or in an attempt to communicate urgency. Either way, he couldn't get up and go to the window to talk to a bird. Other students were now pointing at the window and gesturing to one another, happy with the diversion. Professor Magones droned on.

Bearlon needed to get outside before someone realized this bird was trying to communicate with him.

He raised his hand, but Magones rarely looked at his students during class. After a few moments, Bearlon put his hand down. *Tap—tap—t—t—t—t—t—tap*. Bearlon glanced over. The bird, perched on the thin metal frame surrounding the glass of the window, began flipping upside down and right side up repeatedly. A strong gust of wind threw him off of his perch momentarily. His quick return, with ruffled feathers and an earnest gaze made him even more a center of attention. Students looked at each other in amazement and began glancing around the room.

Bearlon needed to think. Quick. *Got it!*

Bearlon began bouncing his leg again. Professor Magones went from his reclined position to his stooping angle over the book and saw the bouncing leg. His words slowed, his eyelids parted, and he looked up. This time, Bearlon made eye contact with him before the professor stopped his lecture, which ceaselessly drooled from his lips even when he was distracted. Bearlon displayed his most desperate face and nodded toward the door, bouncing both legs and holding his belly.

A look of understanding melted Magones's agitated expression. He nodded and gestured toward the door, never fully stopping his lecture.

Bearlon scooped his belongings into his satchel and ran for the door.

Everyone looked his way, as any movement in class ignited curiosity. When the door closed behind him, he peeked through the high window. Those who had been watching the woodpecker returned their attention outside. They were disappointed to find the bird had disappeared. They returned to their slouches.

# tranquility

Bearlon ran down the hall toward the main entrance of the Academy. He then realized the windows of his history class faced the street in front of the Academy. He was about to meet the bird in a busy public area.

Bearlon skidded to a stop. The bird had found him in his classroom and would find him again. He needed to use stealth. A woodpecker landing on his shoulder in the middle of town in broad daylight was not a covert act.

He headed toward the kitchens. They were closer to the wall and had their own entrance. Kitchen staff would be abundant, but they would not voice suspicion.

He grabbed an apple from the ubiquitous snack trays and began eating as he headed for the door.

The dinner vegetable delivery was being unloaded, workers were sweeping up, and lunch was cooking in the huge pots hanging in the multiple hearths lining the long wall of the kitchen.

Bearlon walked outside into the bustling courtyard under a gray, breezy sky. He was halfway across when he saw the woodpecker heading straight for him.

He pointed toward the direction of the wall and said, "Forest."

The bird flew toward the woods. Bearlon continued walking in the same direction.

"That's it, young sir," said an older man working in a line passing crates of cabbages into the kitchens, "Tell'm where to go. Those birds are always looking for a handout."

Bearlon smiled and nodded in agreement, tipping his apple to the man.

The man grinned broadly and said, "You'll make a fine leader some day, young sir. You've a nice way and maybe a talent with the animals."

Some workers paused to witness this little exchange. Kitchen staff and students usually bowed and nodded to one another. A friendly interaction was refreshing to behold.

Bearlon stopped. "Thank you for the encouragement. I hope to succeed in my studies. As for what talents I may have, they'll need to be kept secret."

Immediately, the smiles were gone, the brooms were sweeping, the wheelbarrows were rolling, and everyone was busy. Workers bustled around Bearlon, leaving him sufficient space to proceed in whatever direction he chose. The man with whom Bearlon had spoken moved mechanically as he grabbed crate after crate.

Bearlon was pleased to have quelled any interest in his apparent power over a bird, but he regretted wielding influence to stifle a cheerful conversation with a nice person due to fear of suspicion. He nodded and resumed his walk toward the gate. Secrets held no intrigue or romance to an Academy employee. Workers avoided overhearing conversations between faculty or students knowing even the accidental sharing of secrets outside of the Academy resulted in a date in the Honor Room.

By the time Bearlon was leaving the village, classes were being dismissed, filling the streets with students. There were no rules against students leaving the confines of the village as long as their travels didn't affect their class attendance or performance. Bearlon passed through the gates.

He walked, scanning the skies for the woodpecker. Now that he was outside the walls, the threat of rain was more apparent. The sky grew darker, and the wind blew stronger. As he neared the trees, more birds flitted about, but not his little messenger.

The forest birds had chosen the woodpeckers as the communicators between bird and man. The trees had no desire to talk with drilling birds. So, more wood-friendly birds exchanged information with the trees.

Bearlon studied the woods and saw a splotch of red moving up and down the trunk of a dying maple tree. He heard the familiar drumming. As he approached the edge of the forest, the bird saw him and began dancing horizontally on the tree, flipping upside down and vice versa with impressive agility.

Whereas the trees were very sensitive to the meaning of the messages they passed along, the birds were pleased to act merely as translators, never questioning the content of what they expressed to fellow bird, tree, or man.

Bearlon passed the woodpecker and walked into the cover of the forest. The bird flew past him to rest on a tree in a well-hidden grove. Bearlon reached out his hand and the woodpecker flew to him. He stroked the bird, who appeared pleased with his own success.

"You have a message?" Bearlon asked.

# CHAPTER TWENTY~FOUR

Drithon had told them to lay their hands on someone with a ring. As soon as the rings began their work, those hands were no longer lying but clutching and grasping. Those same hands—and the rest of their bodies—were now sprawled on the ground of the Realm. Drithon helped the friends up from where they lay. They all had to work at shaking dead ferret-sized creatures from their legs, arms, and the occasional buttock.

"Ew—what are they?" Taelmai shrieked as the corpses piled around the group.

"I shouldn't have been so quick to dismiss that darkness in the Flow," Drithon said. "These are Sneaking Spinnats. Evil little spies of darkness. I haven't seen one in ages. They're fast, and most people dismiss them as rodents when they catch a glimpse of them scurrying away."

"The little bugger bit into my ankle as soon as I touched Taelmai," Tomus said.

"They were watching us and listening," Drithon said. "Thankfully, these will never report to their master. But there's no guarantee more cowardly sneakers didn't slink back to tell what they could."

"What killed them?" asked Perthin, looking at his bandaged hand from which a Sneaking Spinnat dangled by its teeth.

"They're bred for one purpose—to serve their master. Their minds are constantly filled with thoughts of him, and hence, of evil. If you attempt to Flow to the Realm with thoughts of evil, well," Drithon gestured at the dead creatures, "you don't succeed. Just one of the many protections put in place to defend the Realm from invasion."

"So, if one of us were having dark thoughts during our trip," said Taelmai, "we could've ended up like them?"

She gestured at the Spinnats without removing her terrified gaze from Drithon.

"Well, it depends on how you define 'dark,' Taelmai."

# tranquility

Drithon was about to begin a dissertation on the difference between true evil and dark moods when he realized everyone was looking at him with various, but unmistakable, levels of incredulous shock.

"I'll be clearer in the future. For now, do your best to concentrate on what I tell you to do, when the time comes for us to travel in, um, unconventional ways."

Everyone finally began to look at their surroundings beyond the Sneaking Spinnats and Drithon. All eyes fell on Drethene, who hadn't been listening to this conversation. Neither had she noticed the creatures, including the one still attached to her boot.

She was turning in a slow, steady circle, looking up and down and pointing silently in various directions. Her mouth clearly formed the words "jack rabbit" a few times, but she had no breath to push out the sound. By her look of awe, which increased every time she pointed, she seemed to be in the midst of a fit of visions.

Klindyn sat near Drethene with a peaceful smile on his face, staring out into nothingness and giggling occasionally. A Spinnat was splayed out behind him, its teeth sunk, fortunately for Klindyn, into his belt.

Drithon faced the confused companions.

"Welcome to the Realm, my friends. Drethene's first impression of this place was similar to what I assume yours is now. A bright yet empty space. A clean slate to be painted with the true beauties held within once you're prepared to see them. Drethene and Klindyn are now experiencing the true Realm. I hope this makes you look forward to the time when you'll be able to share what we experience here."

Drithon sat next to Klindyn, put his arm around him and looked in the same direction. They both broke out in laughter simultaneously. Startled out of her stupor by their guffawing, Drethene walked toward them, dragging her Spinnat with her. She sat down and joined in with the next outbreak of hilarity.

Drithon patted his niece's shoulder and joined Tomus, Taelmai, and Perthin.

"Why can't I see?" Juznyn asked, tears choking his voice. "I believe everything Drethene's shared with me. Why do I remain unfit?"

"*Tranquility* and its enforcers have built solid walls in the hearts of the One People," Drithon said. "You're stronger than those walls, brother, but it takes work to break through brick and mortar. These barriers are enforced by habits and life practices as strong as metal. Razing such a fortification takes time."

"Your philosophical talk has never made sense to me. After all these years, don't you know I'm more of a black and white type of person than you are? Speak plainly to me, Drithon, and maybe I'll finally understand you."

Drithon grabbed Juznyn's shoulders and waited for his brother's eyes to look into his. "When thoughts of Zivasa's death enter your heart, greet them with forgiveness. When you feel fear, counter with trust. When you feel pain, ask for strength. When you're confused, seek wisdom. Don't hide emotion, as *Tranquility* prescribes for the sake of Peace. Instead, confront your feelings. You need to stop trying to control the uncontrollable and to hide the conspicuous. Your heart must openly give and receive for you to gain sight in this place."

Juznyn nodded, his eyes still indicating this would be difficult.

"How can Klindyn see?" Juznyn asked. "He's never been introduced to the *Sacred Writ*."

"Ah, you always were good at searching out the apparent exception to the rule." Drithon gave Juznyn's shoulder a small punch.

Juznyn grabbed his shoulder and produced a silent "oof." Everyone laughed, and the brothers realized their entire party had been reunited, and all ears were on their conversation.

Klindyn took advantage of the pause and said, "Well, you see, I live with my fourteenth generation—"

"We know!" resounded his friends.

"I think we can agree," finished Drithon, "Klindyn's often child-like innocence keeps his heart open and allows him to see the Realm."

Klindyn smiled shyly and noticed everyone was looking at him rather adoringly. Embarrassed by the attention, he pouted and spun on his heel with a harrumph. Everyone fought back laughter, especially since the Spinnat still swung from his belt, but they looked at Drithon to allow Klindyn privacy.

The sound of fluttering wings turned everyone's attention to the pond. The Lady had arrived, floating gracefully in the water, surrounded by an entourage of flitting fairies.

"This is a fine beginning," Drithon said.

"Indeed," called the voice of the Lady. "Your numbers have increased. This is good."

The Lady's breast hit the shore, and Drethene immediately ran to her. The Lady warmly wrapped her arms and long wings around the tearful girl.

"You all require rest, and some of you need healing as well." The Lady preened Drethene's long black hair.

Her voice carried more of a trill as she said, "I welcome you to the Realm and promise you rejuvenation. There is plenty for you to eat and drink, as well."

On her cue, sprites appeared with plates overflowing with fruit, bread, and cheese. Some carried jugs sloshing with a rainbow of nectars they poured into goblets.

Drithon happily sipped the drink handed to him as he watched a pair of raccoons lead Perthin to the pond's edge. They each held one of his forearms, careful not to touch his bandaged hand, and walked on hind legs to lead him. Once they were at the water's edge, the raccoons motioned for him to kneel. They gingerly removed the bandages from his hand. They washed their own hands, beckoning him to place his in the water. He closed his eyes and followed their direction. When he opened his eyes, he looked from side to side, clearly able to see more than he could moments ago. The raccoons bade him remove his hands from the water and led him to the Lady. He bowed before her.

Drethene removed herself from the Lady's embrace to take Perthin's arm and lead him closer to her.

"Greetings, Perthin," the Lady said, once again in her nobler register. "You have shown great bravery and loyalty. Give me your hand."

Perthin held his injured hand up in front of her. Laying her wings over the hand, the Lady closed her eyes, and her feathers trembled, rustling like the wind through dry leaves. Perthin winced and closed his eyes as well. The Lady's wings stopped shaking, and she gently tucked them behind her. Perthin opened his eyes to find his reinjured hand healed once again. He clenched his hands into fists, relaxed them, and smiled.

He looked at the Lady, surrounded by tiny fairies swarming around her in celebration of his healing. In pairs, they grabbed one another by the arms and swung around until one let go and the other went tumbling into the water. Others flew high and dived into the pond. One bounced off the

Lady's back. She made no reaction but looked pleasantly at Perthin as he watched the fairies' hijinks.

"Thank you," he said, bowing once again.

She bowed back, and Perthin wisely bowed one more time.

The Lady said, "I do have information regarding your friends at the Academy, but there is much to discuss first."

She looked at Drethene, who stood expectantly at Perthin's side.

"My dearling," she spoke in a tone a mother might use before she's about to disappoint her child. "Perthin has been, and will continue to be, an important part of this clutch. However, no ring exists for him."

Drethene kept her chin up, clearly embarrassed her desire was transparent.

"Perthin, Drethene has many ways to protect herself. Of course, even the strongest have times of weakness. Your journey to this place began with your abandonment of all you'd been taught, to follow the one who showed you what was truly right. Have you discovered what you are called to do?"

Perthin stood behind Drethene, placing his now strong hands on her shoulders. "No one will wrestle her from me again. I will keep her safe."

Drethene lifted her eyes to gaze up at her tall champion. He continued to look into the Lady's blazing red eyes, emphasizing his commitment. The Lady nodded. He smiled, and Drethene did too.

The Lady tilted her head to one side and emitted a tremolo making the companions smile. The similarity to Drethene's laughter was uncanny.

Drithon was thankful for the confirmation his friends could, at least, hear the Realm.

Sprites descended toward the Lady, carrying a rope of flowers. They dived into the water and appeared on the other side of her, flying straight up into the tree from which they'd come. The Lady slowly rose while small birds and sprites placed buds in her feathers then flew to Taelmai and adorned her hair with flowers. The Lady beckoned Taelmai toward her as she continued to rise.

"Tell me what you see, youngling."

Taelmai hesitated. "I see you and the birds and the flowers, but not much else. Ooh—what a beautiful butterfly!"

"You have a lovely imagination wasted on worry. Open your mind and heart beyond your fears, and you will see much more. The more you see of the Realm, the more peace you will receive. The more peace you have, the more room there will be in your heart for strength. A strong resolve and proper focus will allow you to accomplish your task."

The Lady's eyes went to Taelmai's waist where the unicorn horn lay hidden. Taelmai's hand went to the hilt, and she bowed to the Lady.

The Lady's swing stopped rising, and she addressed the group, "Please, refresh yourselves."

The companions turned to the forgotten feast. Plates and goblets were set upon silken blankets on the ground. They sat and ate and drank heartily, talking amongst themselves as if at a celebration. Drithon smiled at how even those who could see the Realm ignored the presence of the Lady and her host of fascinating creatures. The Lady swung a bit, clearly enjoying their exuberance as sprites brought her plates of fishes and fruits.

"I've thought a lot about how I was able to strengthen your uncle during the attack on Doll," Juznyn said to Drethene, refilling his goblet with a rose-colored juice smelling of lilac. "I've come up with an analogy."

"An analogy from my black and white brother," Drithon chimed in. "Please continue."

"Now, how else could I define love, but by example." Juznyn's voice was loud with annoyance.

"I'd say such a comparison is more brown and tan than black and white, but if that's what you've got, please proceed."

"Unlike you, I refuse to give some supercilious, incomprehensible explanation—"

"Ooh, and I thought I was the one who worked in a library!"

"Boys!" Drethene said, jumping to her knees.

Drithon was taken aback by how much she sounded like her mother, who'd spent a good many family dinners breaking up sophomoric arguments between her husband and brother-in-law. Drethene looked at each of them, a glimmer of a smile on her lips.

Juznyn took another bite of pungent pink cheese and a sip of nectar. "If I may continue my conversation with my daughter without interruption."

Drithon smiled into his goblet.

Juznyn cleared his throat. "Drethene, I've never tried to explain anything without first referring to *Tranquility*. I had to resort to the 'Children's Index' frequently, having you as my daughter. I know other parents who didn't even know the resource existed."

Drethene smiled and settled comfortably, eagerly awaiting her father's words.

"When the air is full of moisture on a hot day, the day feels hotter."

Juznyn's eyes shot to Drithon, who purposely remained expressionless, nibbling on his bread.

Juznyn took a deep breath. "When the air is full of moisture on a cold day, it drives that cold into your bones."

Drithon nodded.

"A breeze can bring delightful relief to a sultry afternoon, but that same wind on a freezing winter's day can be unbearably frigid. My point is invisible, natural forces everywhere, not just in the Realm, can cause dramatic changes when they make themselves known."

Drithon was staring hard at a small half-eaten purple fruit in his hand, listening intently.

"My love, made apparent to my brother by a simple touch, strengthened his powers and took the edge from Phovul's attack on him, just as moisture and wind enhance or weaken the effect of the temperatures surrounding us. We've learned to harness the wind to mill wheat. Imagine what we'll be able to do when we explore the power of love."

Drithon looked at his brother with an impressed smile. He swallowed the barely chewed piece of fruit and began a fit of coughing Drethene tried to alleviate with whacks on his back, never taking her eyes from her father's face.

"I love you, Pa." She relied on others to refill Drithon's goblet and instead, hugged her father.

The embrace was long. Drithon caught his brother's eye. He made an *X* over his chest with his arms, signifying his love. Drithon was thankful for the fit of coughing so he could get his point across without saying the words often difficult to speak between brothers.

Juznyn nodded his mutual feelings for Drithon and buried his face in his daughter's hair.

# CHAPTER TWENTY~FIVE

Bearlon's speculation on the reason for the woodpecker rendezvous had put a knot in his stomach. The bird found him in his class instead of waiting for nightfall. This was big. He feared the trees or the birds had had enough of this communication experiment.

The woodpecker flew to the tree and remained still, as if waiting for Bearlon to do something.

"Oh! Right." Bearlon scanned the ground for a fallen branch.

The Dendrologist Astronomists had learned how painful a woodpecker's message could be. The trees had complained too. Dead branches didn't fuss.

The bird flew to the stick Bearlon held and began pecking in-between shrill calls and expressive movements.

Relief swept over Bearlon as he grasped the meaning in the bird's behavior. "Perthin and Drithon are in the Realm."

The bird did some happy flips, but there was more to the message, and the bird wanted to hear the translation in Bearlon's words. He waited with obvious anticipation, as excited as a player of charades.

"The trees are pleased to hear from Drithon. They speak of him with compliments and respect. They're now committed to our cause."

The woodpecker took off, flying jagged sinking and rising circles around him. Bearlon realized tonight the Dendrologist Astronomists would send their first message of legitimate importance through the network.

"Ow!"

The woodpecker had landed on the branch and given a solid peck on Bearlon's hand.

"Oh. Sorry. Thank you, little friend, you did a fine job."

Bearlon offered the woodpecker his half-eaten apple, and the bird happily nibbled away.

"Will you thank the trees for me, and tell them we'll send a message to Drithon tonight?"

# tranquility

The woodpecker looked up and nodded, a piece of apple skin hanging from his beak. Bearlon always smiled at seeing a bird nod. "Yes" was the simplest word and correlated movement to teach them—also the most human and amusing.

The forest was filling with the sounds of creaking branches and rustling leaves. The winds were increasing, and Bearlon was eager to share the news with his friends.

"I must return to the Academy now."

He gingerly placed the branch with the perched bird on the ground and set the apple next to the woodpecker.

"I appreciate your coming to get me today, but unless there is an emergency, please keep your messages until we come to the forest at night. And if you do come during the day, try to find one of us outside."

The bird looked abashed.

"Not everyone at the Academy is a friend. For many, birds talking with people is suspicious."

The bird turned his back on Bearlon.

Bearlon sighed and walked around the branch to face the woodpecker. He lay on the ground to look into the bird's eyes.

"Make yourself plain to us. We're your friends. We'll be looking for you. Don't attract the attention of enemies. We want you to stay safe."

The bird nodded, a bit less downtrodden. Small birds understood avoiding the attention of larger birds.

Bearlon smiled and patted the little messenger on his head. He'd grown to love their forest friends and considered kissing the little creature to express his pleasure with their successful communication and the innocent commitment of the birds. But before he could show his affection, the woodpecker had his fill of the apple and flew off with a squeak of a goodbye to deliver Bearlon's message.

Bearlon rose from the forest floor and walked toward the edge of the woods. The sound of rain drops grew louder, punctuating the creaking and rustling of the trees.

In fact, as he drew nearer to the clearing between the forest and the village, he expected to see sheets of rain falling. He was surprised to find steady but light precipitation. He could see the village clearly. Then he wished he couldn't.

The sound he'd heard was not the rain, but the gates grinding closed. They were nearly sealed shut. None of his friends knew he'd left the village. No one would know where to look for him.

Something serious must be happening. Bearlon began to panic. What would happen when he was discovered missing? His professor would tell of his bathroom emergency. What then?

His friends would certainly cover for him once his disappearance was discovered. They were quick thinkers and would link his absence to Dendrologist Astronomist research. They'd protect him. Certainly. Somehow.

Bearlon returned to the cover of the forest and stared through foliage at the now-sealed gates. He walked back into the woods. He'd told the woodpecker they'd return tonight. He'd wait until then and include the closing of the gates in the list of significant happenings at the Academy. Would someone from the Realm help him?

He suddenly realized Perthin was in the Realm! The place was not just the setting of children's tales. Bearlon was not closed-minded, yet he almost felt the crumbling of brick walls surrounding the edges of his imagination. What other realities were hiding in children's books? Unicorns and fairies? Bearlon laughed to himself. Should the Academy texts be hidden on the rearmost dusty shelves of the library and anthologies of fairy tales be placed in easy reach?

Bearlon began to relax as he walked past the place where he'd met with the woodpecker. Maybe his being outside the gates was good. The Watchmen were sure to be on high alert and the villagers on edge, making man-to-bird communication even more risky.

He felt safe amidst the trees. Mostly cherry and sassafras surrounded him. He continued to walk deeper into the forest. Majestic oaks now towered overhead. The air became perfectly still and cool. The fragrance of the forest changed from the earthy smell of fallen leaves to the heady scent of pine needles. Enveloped by evergreens, he felt as protected as he was inside the Academy halls.

The trees rooted, literally, into family groups had no choice but to live together with those like them and next to clusters of various species. The forest was full of harmony. If only the One People could unite without forced cross-pollination.

Bearlon's thoughts were interrupted by voices behind him. He rounded a tree of impressive girth and looked from whence he came. He tried to find the path he'd walked, but there were only dense forest thickets and brambles.

"No one could penetrate this section without leaving a path," said a deep voice.

"You walk that way, and I'll go this way to see if we have any better luck," said another voice, less deep, but equally gruff.

Watchmen! Bearlon tried not to panic. He might not be the only student outside of the walls. There was no rule against his being where he was. They might just be rounding everyone up to give them safe passage back inside the village. Bearlon wished he weren't alone so someone could give him the unconvinced eye roll he deserved. He'd just been walking down a clear path now nowhere to be found. Bearlon felt lost. He looked all around him. He was in a small clearing encircling a huge pine. The clearing was surrounded by other, smaller pines. The spaces between the trees were thick with ferns, and beyond them the density of vegetation appeared impermeable. But how? The trees! They knew he was a friend who required protection not even he knew he needed. That made him feel much better.

"Thank you." He hoped the trees understood his sincere appreciation for what they just did, without the need of an avian interpreter.

A woodpecker flitted down from high within the needles of the tree under which Bearlon now sat. The bird alighted on his knee, spread its wings, and bowed a "you're welcome." Bearlon didn't move until he remembered birds require a "thank you" for being welcomed. He bowed. The bird bowed once more then stood straight and folded his wings. Birds were highly ritualistic. A mournful cry normally only heard near the pond sang through the forest. Bearlon was certainly nowhere near the pond. The wail repeated, this time even closer. He looked in the direction of the sound through the trees and could clearly see he was less than fifty paces from the pond's edge. Seemingly, he and his little dell had moved a mile or more through the forest.

"Am I dead?" He did not expect an answer from the woodpecker but looked to his only companion for direction.

The bird trilled and shook his head. He flew from Bearlon's knee to a nearby tree trunk. He looked at Bearlon, beckoning him to come. Bearlon got up and followed him. The bird flew from tree to tree until he landed on one at the water's edge.

The haunting wail sounded again, quite loudly, convincing Bearlon to stay put. His knees felt weak, so he sat against the tree. The woodpecker landed once again on his knee, reinforcing remaining still was the right choice.

He looked over the water. The rain continued, light and steady, speckling the pond. A black shape floated in the middle of the water, barely visible, then disappeared. Bearlon listened to the rain. The woodpecker stood still as a statue on his knee. Soundlessly, the black head appeared above the surface of the water, very near the edge. The woodpecker flew from Bearlon's knee and landed directly behind the head, apparently on the water. Bearlon moved closer and could see the little bird stood on the almost submerged back of a water-loving cousin. The bird was dappled black and white, difficult to discern from the rain-kissed waters. She craned her neck to face the woodpecker, with whom she seemed to be engaged in important conversation. Bearlon peered into her fabulous red eye looking at him with a piercing intensity.

After a few long moments, the woodpecker returned to Bearlon's knee, then flew to a nearby tree and stared at him. The loon remained still and watched him as well. Bearlon realized they were waiting for him to do something. He stood up clumsily and began searching for a fallen branch, eager to find out what the birds had to tell him.

The woodpecker leapt to the stick, and Bearlon spoke what he understood of the bird's frantic dance, "Our brother and sister trees have exhausted themselves to save you and bring you here. The anger of evil has ignited in the village of men. You must return there soon. First, you must learn why. Trust my sister of the water."

The woodpecker stopped moving, folded its wings, and looked up at Bearlon's expression of mixed expectation and confusion.

"What in *Tranquility's* name are—"

Both birds twitched at the mention of the book.

"Sorry, bad habit, this is just all so—"

Bearlon stopped short again and bowed his apology, and the birds bowed their forgiveness. Much like "you're welcome," the birds held their stance until Bearlon bowed his thankfulness for their pardon.

The birds stared at him. Bearlon inhaled thoughtfully. "What do I need to do?"

The loon swam a few feet into the pond. She looked back at him. Bearlon looked at her, waiting for clarification. The woodpecker flew to his shoulder and nipped his ear.

"Ow!"

He took a step forward.

The loon swam a foot farther and looked back again.

"You really want me to—Ow!"

Another nip brought him to the water's edge.

The loon moved forward a bit more.

The woodpecker flitted to the ground to relay another message.

"You want me to remove my robes? This is all just too—"

The woodpecker snapped his beak loudly. The threat of another ear nip transformed Bearlon's argument into indiscernible mumbling as he undressed.

The birds looked at each other, exchanging unmistakable lipless smiles.

In the steady rain, the wind had ceased, but there was a sudden stir to the leaves of the trees. Might they be laughing at him too?

He stood at the water's edge in long underwear. The birds looked at each other again. The loon hooted, and the woodpecker gave a shrill call.

Bearlon suspected mockery. "Fine, I may be the next Professor Magones someday. It's not exactly warm out, and I tend to be chilly, okay?"

The loon paddled farther into the pond and stuck a black leg out of the water. Bearlon's eyes were slits as he looked at the woodpecker, who gave a tiny, soundless snap of his beak. Bearlon sighed.

His feet touched the water, and he shivered. The loon moved forward again and extended her foot back toward him. He gathered his resolve, marched in, and took hold of the thin leg above her webbed foot. She moved forward slowly, having lost a paddle to Bearlon. Once they were over deeper waters, she yanked her foot away and faced Bearlon, who treaded water to stay afloat. Her red eyes penetrated his. She touched her beak to each of his nostrils. Bearlon quickly grabbed her reextended leg and disappeared with her under the water.

# CHAPTER TWENTY~SIX

The feasting eventually slowed. Drethene watched the Lady's swing gently lower her into a nest of glittering leaves and sparkling flowers. When she landed, hundreds of butterflies flew away in every direction like a ring of rainbow-colored smoke. Birds and fairies continued their finishing touches until she was comfortable.

Everyone abandoned what was left of the feast and stood before the Lady.

"Please, sit."

Drethene prepared to sit down and was delighted to find a free-standing tree stump covered in the softest moss awaiting her. Each of her friends found a similar seat.

A family of wood elves surrounded Klindyn's stool. Standing about waist-high on Klindyn, they were each significantly larger than the fairies attending the Lady. They were wingless and thin, with long arms and legs. Their skin was dark brown and lined with deep crevices like the bark of an oak. Their fingers were long and nimble, a great advantage for wood carving and weaving. Their hair, in hues of gold, orange, and red was clipped short and resembled rustling leaves whenever they moved. They smelled of maple syrup. Their eyes were deep and dark, like the knots of a tree.

One particularly wizened elf gestured for Klindyn and his companions to sit. They did, and each looked delighted as they discovered how comfortable the seats were. The elves looked pleased. Klindyn was the last to sit. He took time to pick up and inspect the little stool.

Drethene was curious. She stood and lifted her stool. Immensely detailed images covered its sides. The longer she examined the stool, the more she believed she was not looking at carved images, but a window into a distant reality. Surely, she was looking at the sky itself, turned to wood, full of constellations, planets, and shooting stars. As she turned the seat, the wooden sky brightened slowly, and she could see the stuff of dreams shaped in the billowing clouds lit by a brilliant sun.

"I see now my own work is child's play," Klindyn said.

The elves congratulated one another on the fine compliment. Drethene remembered reading about these forest folks. Every project they took on was approached with the greatest care. Before even selecting the wood, they fasted and meditated in search of inspiration. Once their ideas took shape, they spent days in the woods, searching the forest floors for what was offered by the trees. They never took living wood for their work. They might adorn the trees themselves, but never would they cut, break, or pull from them. They ate only what had already fallen from their rooted brethren. This is how they referred to all plants.

"May I see the ring on your finger, brother?"

The question startled Klindyn. One of the apparently younger elves had separated herself from the elven celebration and now stood in front of Klindyn, gazing up at him with deep, dark eyes. She was immediately descended upon and reprimanded by a swarm of larger elves, their voices creaking like the branches of trees in the wind.

"Oh, I'm happy to show the ring to all of you," Klindyn said.

The wood elves quickly gathered around Klindyn's outstretched hand and began talking at once.

Through the screeching and scratching of their voices, certain phrases came through clearly enough to be heard by Drethene's unaccustomed, mortal ears.

"Shoddy crafting. This setting will hold no more than a thousand years. Mediocre quality. Someone was drinking too much sap. Needs adjustment."

Tiny tools were brought out from under shirts made of vine and leaf. Deft fingers began to make improvements to the ring.

"Come here, sons and daughters of the wood," the Lady called.

The elves quieted their arguments and walked to the Lady. Those who'd brought out their tools finished their work before answering her call. The Lady waited patiently.

"Your work is fine and strong."

The small perfectionists wrinkled their noses and shook their heads.

"You will see your brother of Unemond and the others before one thousand years have passed. You may make adjustments to increase the durability of your craft whenever you are with them."

The wood elves bowed to the Lady. Their conversations were less argumentative as they bid her farewell and walked toward the forest.

"Moody little ones, aren't they," Taelmai said, smiling wryly at Klindyn.

"Passion comes with being an inspired artist." Klindyn did his best to act his adult age. Drethene could tell he wanted to pout and stomp off.

"Juznyn, by the look on your face, you are already seeing more than when first you arrived," said the Lady, who'd taken a moment to survey the seated companions while most watched the wood elves disappear amidst the trees.

Drethene saw her father was in a similar state of awe as she'd found herself in not long ago.

"Your pondering of love opened your heart a great deal," continued the Lady. "Reading the *Sacred Writ,* sharing with others, and living what you learn will continue your growth."

There was a rippling in the lake behind her.

"I am caretaker of all you do and do not see of the Realm. Faith requires acceptance of the reality of the unseen. Keep this in your hearts."

Drethene saw three creatures swimming toward them, close to the surface of the water.

Uncle Drithon stood up and faced his friends. "Every one of you was brought here by invisible, yet strong, forces—love, persuasion, hope, commitment. I doubt my brother has an analogy to make each of these plain to us."

Drethene saw her pa shake his head.

Drithon smiled. "Here we sit before the Lady of the Realm after eating a feast prepared for us by fairy folk. Open your hearts, and we'll be prepared to come together as an unstoppable force to bring about what's right."

He exchanged bows with the Lady.

She turned toward the lake. "Come, friends of the water. Make yourselves known to our guests."

Three beautiful beings lifted their heads from the water. Iridescent blue and green feathers covered their heads and cascaded down their necks. The creatures slowly rose from the water. Shimmering feathers covered the upper parts of their bodies and thinned at their waists, where fish scales of the same colors began. Their arms were stretched in front of them, with their webbed fingers spread in a sign of welcome. Simultaneously, the three unfurled their wings with an impressive whoosh and a spray of water.

Flapping their wings raised them out of the water a few more feet and showed the remainder of their aquatic bodies. They leaped gracefully into the air displaying large shark-like tails and dived into the water to emerge very near the edge of the lake once more.

The fairies surrounding the Lady chittered, applauded, and performed their own acrobatics in admiration of the sea folk display. The Lady nodded to them and Uncle Drithon shook his head at the grandiose performance.

The Lady gestured toward the mermaid in the middle. "This is Mubahgy, my seer."

Mubahgy came forward, and the other two followed closely behind. Their faces looked like porcelain, almost doll-like, but directly under their transparent skin swam opal-like brilliant yellows, greens, blues, and pinks. Their noses and mouths were reminiscent of the fairies'—small and pretty. The eyes of the two seafolk flanking Mubahgy were like black pearls. Mubahgy's eyes were covered with golden scallop shells. Most of those gathered looked at her shells, avoiding the lidless, bulging eyes of her companions.

"I find honor in meeting friends from Unemond." Mubahgy's voice was shrill and bubbly.

"I've seen your folk in Unemond," Drethene said, full of wonder and abandoning propriety.

Mubahgy turned toward her, as did her companions. Drethene felt very small.

"My children did well." A note of pride mixed with yearning in Mubahgy's voice. "I was called to sacrifice my eggs to your world to renew a long-neglected union."

"I witnessed their birth. They brought me hope."

"They have indeed done well."

"Will they," Drethene hesitated, wondering if her question would be too personal, "be okay?"

Mubahgy laughed. "They are in no danger from the mortals of Unemond. For ages past, we lived in their oceans. Fishermen were our sport. We enjoyed flights in the night air that, when glimpsed by mortals, became part of tall tales."

Mubahgy's explanation was interrupted as the merfolk suddenly disappeared under the water. She shook her head but remained silent. There was a sudden explosion from the water, giving Drethene and her friends quite a start but not affecting the serenity of the Lady or Mubahgy. The Lady's fairy attendants squealed and whirled with delight once again as Mubahgy's companions rocketed into the sky. They were lean and strong, but one was clearly male and the other female, simply by their length and the more muscular and broader build of the merman. When they reached the apex of their ascension, they spread their wings simultaneously and flew grand circles over the heads of the gathering. After five rounds, they tucked their wings behind them and plummeted into the water with nary a splash. The Lady's tiny fey helpers soared out over the water, some of them attempting to imitate the sea folk, resulting in larger splashes than those of their more graceful, watery cousins.

When Mubahgy's escorts returned to their places at her side, she continued, "Of course, there were accidents leaving remains of our kin on land, and others perished by beasts of the ocean. All bodies of our folk are under an enchantment of the Realm. Should we die, our bones take on a new shape as they burrow into their death bed in the ocean or forest floor, mountain rock, or desert dust. Each skeleton is as varied from any other as snowflakes differ from their brethren. In ages past, our mourning over the loss of our kin was tempered by our knowing future mortals would find the bones and likely attribute them to the discovery of some long-lost species. Mortals were bent on discovering an earthly origin of life. The bones of our lost ones provided endless fodder for the impossible puzzle they attempted to solve."

She giggled, which made Drethene smile and like Mubahgy even more.

"Endless, inconclusive research kept them busy and out of worse trouble." Mubahgy turned toward the rest of the group. "Now that same worse trouble rules their lives, there is no need for us to provide creative answers to questions they no longer ask."

Mubahgy's face was once again serene. and there was greater strength in her high voice. "The father of Phovul's second captive is in our midst. I have words for him."

Uncle Drithon nodded at Tomus, who, being the only member of the group known to have a captive child, had been looking for some sign he should be the one to respond.

Taelmai led her father to the water. Tomus's finger was bleeding where he'd touched the tip of the unicorn horn he still held in his other hand. Taelmai had given him the dagger in an attempt to help her father toward acceptance of what was real and true. Mubahgy gestured to Taelmai to lead her father into the lake.

"Do you see the water, Pa?"

"No, Taelmai, I told you I see nothing but you and our friends."

"But you can hear other voices besides those of our friends?"

"I'm hearing lots of voices. I'm just hoping they're the same ones you're hearing."

"We're walking into the water, just about waist deep."

Drethene watched Tomus allow himself to be led, clearly brimming with frustration and anger at his inability to see anything. His daughter's coddling was not helping.

Once he stood firmly in front of Mubahgy, she said to Taelmai, "He'll be fine now. You need not stay in the water."

Taelmai looked slightly offended but patted her father on his shoulder, kissed him on his forehead, and rejoined Drethene and their friends.

Tomus shook his head. Mubahgy took Tomus's face in her webbed hands. He shivered at her cold touch. "Yours is a long, winding path, Tomus. Although your heart wants to lead you in the right way, the strength of your resolve fights hard and desires more convincing." She took her hands from Tomus's face and placed them on the shells covering her eyes. She slid the shells down her face and held them out behind her. Her companions each took one shell in their cupped hands.

Mubahgy returned her hands to Tomus's face, which she positioned to align his eyes with hers. The light gray lids covering her eyes shot open, and a brilliant white light beamed from beneath them, penetrating Tomus's eyes. He gasped, his hands went limp, and he almost dropped the unicorn dagger. Tears fell from his eyes. Mubahgy released Tomus, severing him from the assisted view of his surroundings. She closed her gray lids, reached out for her shells, and covered her eyes with them once again.

Tomus wept. Mubahgy nodded at the anxious Taelmai, who ran into the water to lead her father back to the shore.

Mubahgy turned toward the Lady. They exchanged bows.

Drethene embraced Taelmai. Uncle Drithon put his arm around the sobbing Tomus and said, "This is a fine beginning, truly, a fine beginning."

Tomus burst out, "I hope my heart talks to the rest of my body since Moo-bah-gee, or whatever her name is, seems confident it knows so much. I just witnessed beauty and joy I could never have imagined. I again see nothing, and now all I hear in my head is 'it was a trick—a moving painting placed in front of me to fool my mind.' All I want is my son back. I want to go back to my farm with my family and find peace."

"Mubahgy knows hearts, Tomus," the Lady said, unfazed by his outburst. "You will need to conquer your stubborness before you can know your own heart as well as she does."

"My stubbornness? My stubbornness!" Even Drethene had to nod in agreement with the Lady's words.

Tomus sighed and looked down at his now profusely bleeding finger, which had spent too much time tapping the edge of the unicorn horn in frustration.

"Can anyone here fix this?" He raised his finger above his head, the blood trickling down his hand and dripping on his forehead caused him to blink.

"'Moo-bah-gee will help you," said Mubahgy from the water.

Tomus returned to the water, his eyes downcast and his finger pointing in front of him. The mermaid grasped his hand before he could walk into her. He stopped suddenly and mumbled an apology. She smiled, murmured her acceptance, and cupped his outstretched hand in hers. She released him, and he examined his healed finger.

"Thank you."

"You are welcome."

Tomus still stared at his finger. "I want to see the Realm again."

"You will, Tomus. But without my help. You will."

Tomus sighed.

"Please give the dagger back to your daughter."

Tomus walked back toward Taelmai. Drethene stopped him and reached into her satchel. As Taelmai appeared at her side, Drethene handed Tomus the *Sacred Writ*. He sighed again, handed the unicorn horn back to his daughter and took the book. He walked a few steps, sat on his stump and began to read.

"My lady," Mubahgy said.

The Lady nodded.

"The one whom Drithon has named my mortal sister in sight has had a quiet, dark mind in recent days."

The Lady turned to Uncle Drithon with a look of concern and impatience.

"Phovul captured Doll before we could flee from Dale. He's forged a similar connection to her as he has with Trem."

"Tell me what happened."

Uncle Drithon explained what had passed in his chambers, struggling with the details of Doll's abduction. The others who'd been there quickly assisted him.

The Lady listened attentively until all were done with the tale. She addressed the group, "I assume you all know something of Malgriffe."

Everyone nodded fervently. Drethene was relieved their ignorance had been cured by Uncle Drithon.

Apparently satisfied, she continued, "Malgriffe gains strength from the One People's growing complacency. Evil festers in some of these empty souls, apathy in others. Malgriffe has released Phovul upon Unemond to reap this disheartening harvest. Crouglan's hunger for power darkened his heart and made him easy prey. He is leading Phovul to still more ideal captives."

Taelmai stepped forward, her hand resting on the hilt of the dagger nestled safely in its sheath. Drethene suspected she was gathering some sort of unusual fortitude from the weapon. Taelmai's eyes were filled with anger instead of angst. Her breathing was erratic, not from panic, but like a child who had been insulted by a cruel companion. Her voice was loud and demanding. "How can Phovul, who controls Crouglan because of his dark heart, just as easily overpower my good brother?"

The Lady drew herself up and spread her wings. Fairies, birds, and butterflies scattered. She was about to throw back her head when Uncle Drithon prostrated himself before her. She sighed, settled down, and bowed in acknowledgment of his apology on Taelmai's behalf.

"She's a child," Uncle Drithon said to the Lady. "A mortal child, we must remember, whose life has been upended, and who's taken on great responsibility. This has changed her. Clearly, questioning is something new to her."

"Drithon," the Lady said, her tone not thoroughly calmed, "please respond to the fledgling's display."

He approached Taelmai. "Youngling, asking questions isn't prohibited in the Realm, as it is in the Land of the One People. Your questions are impressively relevant, but please, they must be posed with respect. Wait for the Lady to acknowledge she's finished speaking before asking what's in your heart. She may very well answer your questions before you voice them."

He turned back to the Lady. "Please, my lady, have patience with Taelmai's—and everyone's—inexperience and edginess."

Uncle Drithon bowed again.

Taelmai sat down.

"Trem remains strong, Taelmai." Uncle Drithon knelt before her and held her hands. "I doubt very much that he allowed Phovul to gain control over him without a fight. I know he continues to resist. Although slight and fleeting, I saw Trem's concern for Drethene and Zivasa in the Honor Room. His mind and heart are still his, at least at times."

"He helped me too," Drethene added, slapping her hands on her head, wondering how she'd nearly forgotten what had happened in the cart of the Horse Force. "The fog that burned Phovul did nothing to Trem. First, he told me to always wear my ring, and then told Phovul I wasn't in the cart. He lied to him! He *is* fighting him."

"My dear nieceling," Uncle Drithon said, "just hours before he was captured, Doll said to Trem, 'You will protect her, I know it! You must help her, even in darkness, so she may light the way for others.' Neither he nor I could have guessed what her words would come to mean. Let us find hope in what we are sharing, not frustration in our lack of immediate understanding."

The Lady's attendants surrounded her once again, placing flowers in her feathers to replace those shaken loose when her anger had flared.

"Phovul will break his bond with his second captive," Mubahgy's shrill voice suddenly carried over the din of hushed conversations.

Everyone looked at her. She held her hands over the shells covering her eyes, and her attendants supported her on either side. She was quickly regaining her breath and composure. She looked at the Lady, whose red eyes studied her intently.

"Thank you, Mubahgy, for sharing your gift."

"What did she say?" Tomus asked.

He'd been reading fervently since Drethene had given him the *Sacred Writ*. Not even the Lady's angry tremolo had interrupted his study. However, Mubahgy's voice had a way of piercing the conscience.

"She said," responded Klindyn in his more eloquent adult voice, "'Phovul will break his bond with his second captive.'"

227

Tomus looked at Uncle Drithon.

"Mubahgy's words are always true, Tomus, but they are rarely as distinct as we think necessary, especially when they tell us of a loved one."

Tomus stood up from his stool. "If Phovul's going to break his bond with Trem, is there any reason to put both of my children in danger? I'll wait at the ready for as long as it takes."

"Let's make our plans and keep Mubahgy's words repeating in our hearts." Drithon placed his hand on Tomus's shoulder. "Allow them to guide but not stop us."

Five dragonflies flitted across the water toward the Lady and alighted on her back. She twisted her graceful neck and nodded to them. They flew in front of her and landed in a neat row facing her. They flapped their wings in turn. The Lady fixed her gaze upon whichever one was in motion. When they all remained motionless, she nodded.

"More helpful information is coming," the Lady said, staring out over the pond.

Drethene was pleased to see a loon approaching, proud and graceful. She was surprised to see what appeared to be a man following her. He was a decent swimmer by Unemond standards, but compared with the sea folk, he was easily identified as a splashing, gasping mortal. The bird let out the familiar wail Drethene recognized from Hushed Pond. The Lady answered, causing the friends to cover their ears.

The loon swam near the Lady, and the man pulled himself to shore. Once his head reached the soft earth, he stopped and collapsed, the bottom of his body still submerged in the pond.

"Bearlon!" Perthin yelled, running to his friend.

"A woodpecker ... gate closed ... trees ... under the pond ..." Bearlon looked at Perthin as if he expected him to understand. The weight of his head became too much, and he landed face down in the mud.

Juznyn came to Perthin's aid. They dragged Bearlon onto the grass and lay him on his side.

The Lady and the loon were deep in conversation.

Uncle Drithon was standing in the water talking to Mubahgy, who handed him what looked like seaweed. They exchanged bows, and he walked to Bearlon.

Uncle Drithon knelt beside him and instructed Perthin and Juznyn to rip the young man's clothing to allow the weeds to be placed on his chest.

The remaining plants went under his nose. Bearlon coughed up a puddle of water.

He began to breathe easier and started speaking with each exhale, "I ... need to ... talk to ... Perthin."

Perthin returned to his side, convincing his friend there was time for him to regain his strength before talking.

The loon was now enjoying a floating plate of fishes brought to her by the Lady's attendants.

"Dark times have fallen on the Village of Dale," the Lady announced. "We now know where Phovul may be found."

# CHAPTER TWENTY~SEVEN

Phovul squatted, trembling, before the twisted roots of an ancient tree. The roots dived under and emerged from the soil like petrified serpents. His master described the entryway as, "the tree bent to my will." The roots were unmistakable, plunging in and escaping out of the earth in every direction, in a futile attempt to escape Malgriffe's filth and fury. Instead, they succeeded only in stitching the tree to the ground and sealing its fate as Malgriffe's front door.

Phovul searched the base of the trunk for the Flow gate. His master had lodged the black sphere in a knot, the scar of an amputated root. Phovul nearly turned away, aborting his plan. He was supposed to come here only to answer Malgriffe's summons. This visit was of his own volition. Within the walls of the Academy, he'd felt confident. He'd just closed the village gates. Power was shifting to him. Now, less than an hour later, he was filled with disbelief at his own impudence.

Phovul fell backwards as the snarling head of a small fur-covered wild-eyed creature popped out of the Flow.

"Rotten stinking Sneaking Spinnat vermin," Phovul mumbled as he recovered from his fall and brought himself to his knees.

The creature stared hungrily at Phovul, bared its teeth, and hissed. The hiss continued as the unmistakable voice of Malgriffe spoke through the beast.

"How rude to loiter at someone's door, Phovul. Please announce yourself or return to your work."

"Master, I—"

"Silence! Since you are still here, I assume you have something of magnitude to share. My messenger shall depart, and you will reach your hand through my doorway."

The Sneaking Spinnat disappeared, and Phovul did as he was told. He screamed as his fingers were each bitten by what could only have been an ambush of his master's rodent servants. They yanked him in. He yelped again in pain and thrust himself through the Flow gate, hoping to avoid any further "assistance" from the creatures.

He landed on a cold, hard floor and shook his hand free of beasts. They skittered away into the darkness. Their sharp claws clicked on the stone as they bumped into each other making sniveling, laughing sounds.

"You come to me unbidden."

The voice was distant as massive chains snaked their way around Phovul. Cold fingers caressed the bruise and scar on Phovul's face.

"You have allowed the beauty I spared to be marred. Do you come to me for help?" Malgriffe's voice was suddenly hot and loud in Phovul's ear.

"I come to you with an offering, if it is pleasing to you." Phovul bowed his head, the only unchained part of his body. Sweat dripped from his brow.

"A gift!" Malgriffe's voice was filled with mock delight. "But you arrived empty-handed. Oh, the shame."

"What I have for you is mortal, and you do not allow me to bring—"

"Do not pronounce my rules to me!" Malgriffe's breath filled Phovul's nose as claws raised his head, almost piercing his skin. "I hope you thought to lock up your pets before you left your new den." Malgriffe's voice was fainter, less angry. "Someone might steal the pretty one."

Phovul's eyes, now blinded by chains, glared in the direction of the voice.

"Oh, you like her. Isn't that sweet! I hope your relationship blossoms."

Phovul growled and fought against the chains. Suddenly, raw, icy air was forced into his lungs, filling them. He could neither inhale nor exhale.

"You are moments from death." Malgriffe's voice was calm and echoing in Phovul's other ear now. "You do not have full control over your second capture. He has left his mark on your face. He is no gift to me. I am not your papa who will gladly receive the gift of a toy you are too small to use."

The cold air was released from Phovul's lungs.

"He is strong." Phovul gasped. "He could serve you well."

The chill air was pushed again into Phovul's lungs.

"I choose my slaves, filth. I also invite my guests. You don't knock on my door bestowing your burdens as offerings."

Phovul struggled and began to lose consciousness. The frozen air again escaped him. He drank the life-sustaining air. He needed to think and act quickly. Another few moments with the Breath of Death, and he might never breathe again.

"I take no pleasure in sharing your favor with another. This offer is to increase my master's power, at my own great expense."

Phovul did his best to bow.

His breath remained his own. He kept his head lowered. His chains shook with his fear.

"Your words are not sincere, but neither are they empty. Your work is not fruitless."

Malgriffe held Phovul's face in his frigid hands.

"I will not heal your wounds. They will remain a reminder to you of your incapacity. I will not add to them, either."

"Thank you, Master."

"Remember this, servant. Never come to me without my invitation. I will ponder your gift and will bring you here with it, if I so choose."

"Thank you, Master."

"I see what you do in the village, Phovul. This has the potential to gather the numbers we need. Do not disappoint me."

"As you say, Master."

"Leave my presence."

Malgriffe pushed Phovul, who rolled, locked in his chains, through what felt like a stone tunnel. The chains fell away, and he landed on his back in Crouglan's chambers, at the feet of his three captives. He saw a glimmer of a smile on Trem's face and hoped Malgriffe would call for the boy soon.

Phovul stood, trying his best to appear unfazed, but he was unable to regain breath. Still struggling, he looked down and saw, instead of chains covering his torso, he was locked into a solid-metal, lung-constricting bodice.

Laughter rang in his ears, followed by Malgriffe's voice, "I am unable to leave the confines of my dwelling place. For now, I am reliant on your successes in Unemond to increase my power. Your limitations are my burden. Weakness, not loyalty, keeps you from seeking power beyond what I command. Even in my imprisonment, I remain more adept and powerful than you. Perhaps decreasing your physical ability will force you to make better use of the powers I give you. Impress me ... now!"

Phovul wanted to roar with rage, but his attempt only landed him on the floor, his head spinning from the lack of air. He panted, pulling himself to his hands and knees.

He looked up at Trem and without any physical motion, sent him hurtling against the wall. Trem slumped in an unconscious heap.

A distant "That's more like it!" followed by fading laughter filled Phovul's head.

He summoned Doll to his side and permitted her adequate strength to lift him to his feet and support him. She smiled up at him. A look of concern crossed her face as she caressed his bruised, scratched cheek.

"My queen."

She smiled.

"Crouglan," Phovul croaked.

Crouglan woke from his stupor and came before him.

"The Academy is ours." Phovul choked from stringing together so many words.

His ribs felt as if they were breaking with every breath. Doll stood proudly at his side, embracing him.

He was forced to speak to Crouglan through his thoughts.

"Use your cunning to bring me those who will be useful and loyal to our cause. Begin the training of those who obey. Imprison the rest. I will deal with them."

Crouglan understood and walked toward the door.

"They'll begin arriving at this door within the hour," Crouglan said. "You may let them wait until I return, or you may entertain them if you desire, Master."

Phovul hated that Malgriffe's latest punishment was indeed increasing his power. If only he could use this new strength for his own purpose, instead of benefiting the one who held tight to his yoke.

As he walked, Crouglan looked out the windows lining the second-floor hallway of the Academy's main building. The streets were empty, as the townsfolk were gathered in the Hall, and the students had been sent to the dormitories.

Crouglan approached the head secretary's desk. She was crowded by a room full of faculty looking for answers regarding the sudden, unannounced closing of the gates.

Upon Crouglan's appearance, the room became quiet. He addressed the gathering.

"Recent events have revealed a threat to the sanctity of our lives of *Tranquility*. I've taken the extraordinary measure of closing the gates of Dale to stop the influx of evil pervading our society. The Academy is the soul of *Tranquility* and must be protected. A committee must gather to create additional Defining Actions to more clearly explain the proper application of *Tranquility's* teachings to the lives of the One People. Who better to make up this committee than those who spend their lives teaching future leaders? I hope every one of you will submit your name for consideration. I ask you to form groups and visit each section of the student dormitories. Please inform the students classes will be postponed until the Defining Actions Committee has completed its work. Until classes resume, students are to remain in their dormitories. They may leave those premises only to eat in the dining room or to study in the library. Every one of you, please make an appearance in my chambers within the next three hours to let me know if you do, or do not, plan to enter your name for possible appointment."

Crouglan left the room without hesitation. He knew they were shocked by his abruptness and wished to ask questions. His intensity would undoubtedly convince them to do what he asked. His master would be pleased.

Crouglan left the building and headed for the Hall. The cool air and bright sunlight were wasted on him. He entered the Hall, walking under the Arch of Remembrance, the images of the Great Council frowning down upon him. He strode quickly down the aisle. The noise of the citizens bustling to seat themselves as he passed their rows filled the Hall. He faced the gathered One People. He was just about to speak when the congregation roared, "Keep the Peace!"

He hesitated for a moment, pressing his lips together. Those words had meant something to him. "Keep the Peace." He questioned what he was about to do.

The doubt was gone in an instant.

Crouglan raised his arms. "Dale has been secured to stop the influx of evil permeating our home. As you know, our village is more than our dwelling place. This is the seat of *Tranquility*. Extreme measures must be enforced to protect the sanctity of our Peace. Drethene Bidalind has escaped from prison."

Shocked and frightened gasps filled the Hall.

"I fear she'll attempt to return to Dale and destroy *Tranquility*. Its teachings and our Peaceful ways are what she despises. *Tranquility* will protect us from her wicked ways. If you're here and reside outside of the walls, you'll need to remain in the village until we're prepared to reveal the location of the Doors of Necessity and have them opened."

Crouglan was pleased to see the One People nodding their heads at one another in fervent agreement. There was not one doubtful look or whispered question. Their trust in him was absolute.

No one in the Hall had ever seen the Doors of Necessity. Most considered them akin to the fairies and magic passageways they'd heard of in bedtime tales. Crouglan speaking of these doors as a reality caused the people to simply accept their existence. Crouglan knew if any did stumble on their road to acceptance, they swallowed hard on the desire to display distracting emotion or to ask a question. Crouglan was pleased with the ensuing quiet.

"Return now to your homes, and welcome those from outside the walls as your honored guests. Come to the Hall for the next Gathering when I shall provide more instruction for how you'll take part in Keeping the Peace."

"Keep the Peace!" echoed once again, and Crouglan walked up the aisle, the bows greeting him deeper and more enthusiastic than most days. He continued through the archway and straight outside.

He was startled by a small blow to his head. He rubbed his hand over his hairless scalp and discovered a large deposit of bird droppings. He shook his fist in the air, searching unsuccessfully for the culprit in the blinding sunlight.

Crouglan wiped his hand and head with a cloth kept in his pocket and walked to the main Academy entrance. He knew his sudden exit from the Hall would be seen as an act of his dedication to resuming his work in protecting them from "that girl," as they called Drethene, and any trouble accompanying her.

Every entrance to the Academy was inlaid with marble and had soaring ceilings to exemplify the vastness of the Academy's purpose. Upon entering the main and grandest entryway, Crouglan looked up at the ceiling's sparkling mosaic tiles echoing the seven colorful teardrop shapes on the library's floor. A golden likeness of *Tranquility* hung from the center, a constant reminder of its singularity in curing the One People of their ancient division.

Crouglan never slowed his pace. He marched through the entrance, two hallways, and down many flights of steps. The Watchman guarding the door to the Council's Honor Room entrance stepped aside to allow Crouglan to enter.

"Ah, Leader Crouglan has arrived," the rickety voice of one of the elder members of the Grand Council croaked. "Now we await only the arrival of the one to be Questioned."

"The cart approaches the walls of Dale," gasped a young messenger, clearly just returning from a visit to the Watchmen on the wall. He was one of the few students allowed to remain outside of the dormitories to serve the Grand Council.

"Excellent," said Crouglan, taking his seat. "Go back to the wall and tell the Watchmen to open the Doors of Necessity and to allow only the one being questioned entrance to the village. Quickly. Run if you must."

"It will be my great honor."

The young man pivoted and walked swiftly from the room. His feet could be heard running through the hall outside the great doors.

# CHAPTER TWENTY~EIGHT

A breeze blew through the crudely sewn patchwork quilt acting as one side of a tent. The edges were unfinished, and a length of frayed cloth tickled Drethene's neck. How did she get here? She had been in the Realm by the lake where the loon had just delivered Perthin's friend. She had no memory of entering a tent. She was just suddenly here, as in a dream. *A dream, this must be a ...*

"Imagine one huge land we all can call our own," said a woman with one arm in a sling fashioned from rags. This stranger was clearly mortal. She had a strange accent, and although her clothing was dirty and ragged, it was still more colorful than anything the One People would dare to wear.

She sat on a blanket and waved her other arm over a huge map resembling a colorless version of the pinwheel-shaped mosaic on the floor of the Academy's library.

"That would take more imagination than I have," said a man. His voice, carrying a different but equally foreign accent, was too deep for his gaunt body.

"Well, think about this," said another woman, a trickle of blood seeping from beneath her eye patch. "You would never have to worry about my armies laying siege to your fortress again."

She limped over to the skinny man and pinched what little skin she could find on his cheek. He swatted her hand away. Laughter echoed around the tent. These people were clearly all war-torn, but the similarity between them ended there.

"Jack Rabbit!" Drethene slapped both hands over her mouth. No one noticed her outburst. She was in the company of the Great Council! The Academy's books and tributes to this group always presented them as noble, serene leaders passionately but politely discussing the details of *Tranquility*. Drethene had read enough of her uncle's books to recognize this group of kings and queens—callous unarmed warriors stuck in a tent with their enemies until they found a way to quit battling. The process had not always been peaceful or polite.

The insulted king reached for a sword no longer laying in its sheath. The laughter grew louder as he stormed away to the far side of the tent where a group of people stood attentively observing the discussion of the map. A woman placed her hand on his shoulder and spoke softly to him.

These men and women looked less battle fatigued than the royal warriors surrounding the map. Their clothing, though simple, was untarnished. They wore long robes, each of a different color. Drethene remembered reading of the countries' religious leaders standing by their kings and queens for counsel and spiritual support during the wars.

Drethene thought she heard distant music. Those around the map continued their discussion, but a couple of the robed folk peered out of an opening cut in the cloth wall. The rhythm was growing louder and soon sounded like someone repeating a simple pattern on a low-pitched pan pipe.

All eyes were now on the entrance of the tent. The two people who stood nearest the draped entryway pulled back the cloths, welcoming daylight and the repetitive song.

The two musicians walked through the entryway. They were black, turkey-sized birds, proud and tall with their wings folded neatly on their backs. The first bird continually repeated one half of their short, rhythmic song. He was answered faithfully by the second, slightly smaller bird. They used matching red throat pouches to create their call. Puffy red skin surrounded their light-colored, black-pupiled eyes. With their long, thick eyelashes, their gaze seemed eerily human. The larger bird carried a rolled parchment in its very long, prominent bill. The other carried a smooth stone the size of an apricot. They walked and called until they stood in the center of the map on the floor. The larger bird dropped the scroll and waited. Birds and people were silent.

One of the women who'd been seated on the floor approached the scroll and bowed to the birds. They bowed back to her. She bowed again and bent to retrieve the parchment. As she lifted it, the smaller bird approached the larger one and dropped the stone in front of him. He snatched up the rock in his large bill and held it high. He eyed the men and women who watched this exchange and turned his profile to each of them to display the treasure of which he was apparently quite proud. The woman who held the scroll nodded to him again, clearly amused by his boast. She untied the strips of strong leaves binding the parchment and broke the seal of beeswax. She unrolled the message and read aloud.

> Greetings from the Lady of the Realm,
>
> I find great joy in knowing the fighting over the Valley of Hrithto has ceased. My condolences for the losses your people have suffered. I hope you will welcome the Realm's participation in the discussions of how to proceed peacefully. A rift has grown between Unemond and the Realm during these long years of war, and I hope this may be healed, along with your battle wounds. Three Realm folk approach. Two are my delegates, and one is a fledgling who shows great passion for this process. He will be in attendance solely to observe and do small tasks as might seem fit. I hope you see the value in the presence of youth, as the young will be trusted to uphold what is determined today.

The letter ended with no closing, as was the way of the Realm. They found greetings appropriate but felt their sincerity should ring throughout their words and need not be emphasized again once they'd ended.

Drethene scanned the room to see if she could catch any reactions before those gathered had a chance to force their faces back into the expressionless masks of wartime negotiations. All remained stoic, but she gasped when she met the eyes of a robed woman who stood against the far wall. She looked directly into Drethene's eyes, gave a small smile, and nodded. Drethene returned the nod, and the tall gray-haired woman dressed in turquoise resumed her focus on the reader, who allowed the scroll to reroll itself.

Drethene's eyes were wide with disbelief. Was this religious leader the only one aware of her presence? She must be. A room full of military heroes would notice an intruder. The woman clearly had no problem with her being there, and Drethene had no idea where else to go. Drethene took a deep breath and trusted she was there to observe—so, she did.

Both birds bowed to those gathered, and everyone returned the gesture. The birds bowed once more and walked out of the tent, over the hill, and out of sight.

# tranquility

Before conversation could resume, three shapes appeared on the horizon. As they approached, Drethene could see they were from the Realm. One was tall with long black hair hanging down her back in what appeared to be a solid silken sheet. Anyone who looked at her was instantly captivated. Her eyes were violet, as were her lips. The skin on her face was white with swirling pastels swimming below its surface. She was like a living opal. Her arms and legs were long and slender. They resembled delicate porcelain. She was draped in gossamer, which added to her shimmering beauty, but the material looked reluctantly and carelessly thrown over her. There was no question that in the Realm, she lived unadorned.

The features of the one who walked next to her were made more striking by comparison. Although considerably shorter, he appeared to be quite strong. He had shaggy hair, actually, short, dense, unkempt feathers in differing shades of brown. Each feather had a dark circle surrounded by a lighter one. From the disarray of these eye-like feathers upon his head, he seemed to watch everyone at once. His true eyes were golden and piercing, handsome and kind. His nose was prominent, and his face wise. The rest of his body appeared very mortal, although only his head, neck, and arms remained uncovered by his brown robes.

The final companion followed closely behind them and was clearly their son. He had his mother's long silken black hair, her height, her beauty, and her skin color without the opalescence. His eyes were definitely his father's, and although young, he looked as if he'd grow to resemble his father's strong build within his mother's slender frame. He wore long black sleeveless robes matching his hair and magnifying the fairness of his skin. He kept rearranging the robes as he walked, implying, like his mother, he was unaccustomed to being covered in cloth.

They walked to the tent and were ushered inside. Everyone's eyes fixed on the beauty of the party's tallest member. As she walked in, the perfume of spring flowers filled the tent. She beamed, meeting everyone's eyes in turn. Each person smiled back, blushing under her gaze. They were filled with such sweet emotions their minds were swept from the business at hand. She opened her mouth to give a greeting, but her husband raised his hands quickly to quiet her. She smiled at him, understanding the need for her silence. The unblinking eyes adorning the rustling feathers upon his head woke everyone from their stupor with their relentless gaze. The mortals shook off the enchantment, blushing with embarrassment.

Drethene relaxed a bit, realizing she was unnoticed by these visitors.

The feathered one said, "Thank you for your warm welcome." He smiled kindly and turned slowly to look at everyone with his true eyes. "Do not be sheepish. Even those of the Realm struggle to resist my wife's beauty. Excuse my rudeness, dear wife and gathered friends, for my interruption of her greeting. She is descended from the sirens, and if she had spoken to you, I might have needed days to get you all back on task. She will not remain silent for long. You will just need time to become accustomed to her presence. I speak from experience, mind you. I am married to her. The friends we make together do, eventually, look at me too."

Everyone in the tent laughed freely, happy the joke was not pointed at one of them.

"You have read the Lady's letter. Please know we share her sentiments. We are honored to be a part of this parley. Our hope is we can work together to create a peaceable union in which we can all flourish."

His wife looked at him. Indeed, even he seemed unable to ignore her gaze for long.

He met her eyes and understood. "Forgive me, friends. I have not even introduced myself, or my family. My wife would have begun with greetings, but I do not share her social graces. As you know, we of the Realm are unaccustomed to naming ourselves and often struggle with finding one satisfying word to do the job. We are doing our best to implement this tradition, as you do, at the celebration of the birth of our young ones. This may seem a meager attempt at making us more accessible to you, but please do not underestimate the effort needed to effect such a change to the customs of the Realm. This is a fine beginning."

Drethene jumped at hearing this final phrase. She'd been listening intently while attempting, along with everyone else, to look at the speaker, not his wife. Drethene had decided to look instead at their son, feeling she shared something in common with his youth. She was having difficulty wrenching her eyes away from him, until these last words startled her. She knew the voice and the manner of speaking had seemed familiar. After searching his face, she knew she was in the presence of her Uncle Drithon in some Realmified form.

His wife still stared at him.

He looked at her. "All right. I know, I use too many words."

He looked at those gathered around them. "Please, call me Owl-Eyes and my wife, Lilac. We are pleased to have been one of the first sets of parents in the Realm to add a naming when we welcomed our son into our lives."

He walked toward his son and led him with beaming pride to stand in full view of those gathered in the tent.

"This is Phovul."

END

# ABOUT THE AUTHOR

Christa Conklin is the author of several articles, and two short stories: "Moontail" and "Kat, the Jailer, and Jack." *Tranquility* is her debut novel for which she received the 2016 Cascade Award for Unpublished Speculative Fiction. Fantasy is her favorite genre to read and write. She spent her childhood *wrinkling time* in Narnia, Prydain, and Middle Earth. Adulthood found her old enough to read fairy tales again and to create new worlds to better understand ours.

When she's not fashioning creatures and developing nations, Christa teaches piano and woodwinds at a music school in her small New Jersey town. She and her family hike mountains, paddle lakes, stroll city streets, and pick their own everything at local farms and from their own gardens. Prior to parenthood, she studied in France, earned a couple of degrees, worked in Manhattan for the New York Philharmonic, in Princeton for Young Audiences New Jersey, and once took first place in a women's solo kayak river race.

She loves to travel and returns often to the Adirondack Mountains from which she drew inspiration for the creation of *Tranquility*. She and her meteorologist husband homeschool their children, creating a happy environment for their miniature Goldendoodle, who spends his days sleeping on laps created by learning and writing. Visit her at christaconklin. com.

CPSIA information can be obtained
at www.ICGtesting.com
Printed in the USA
LVHW081007220519
618618LV00033B/831/P